THE RESISTANCE KNITTING CLUB

JENNY O'BRIEN

Storm
PUBLISHING

Ebook ISBN: 978-1-83700-254-2
Paperback ISBN: 978-1-83700-256-6

Cover design: Eileen Carey
Cover images: Trevillion, iStock, Shutterstock

Published by Storm Publishing.
For further information, visit:
www.stormpublishing.co

'...the heart has its own memory and I have forgotten nothing'.
    Albert Camus

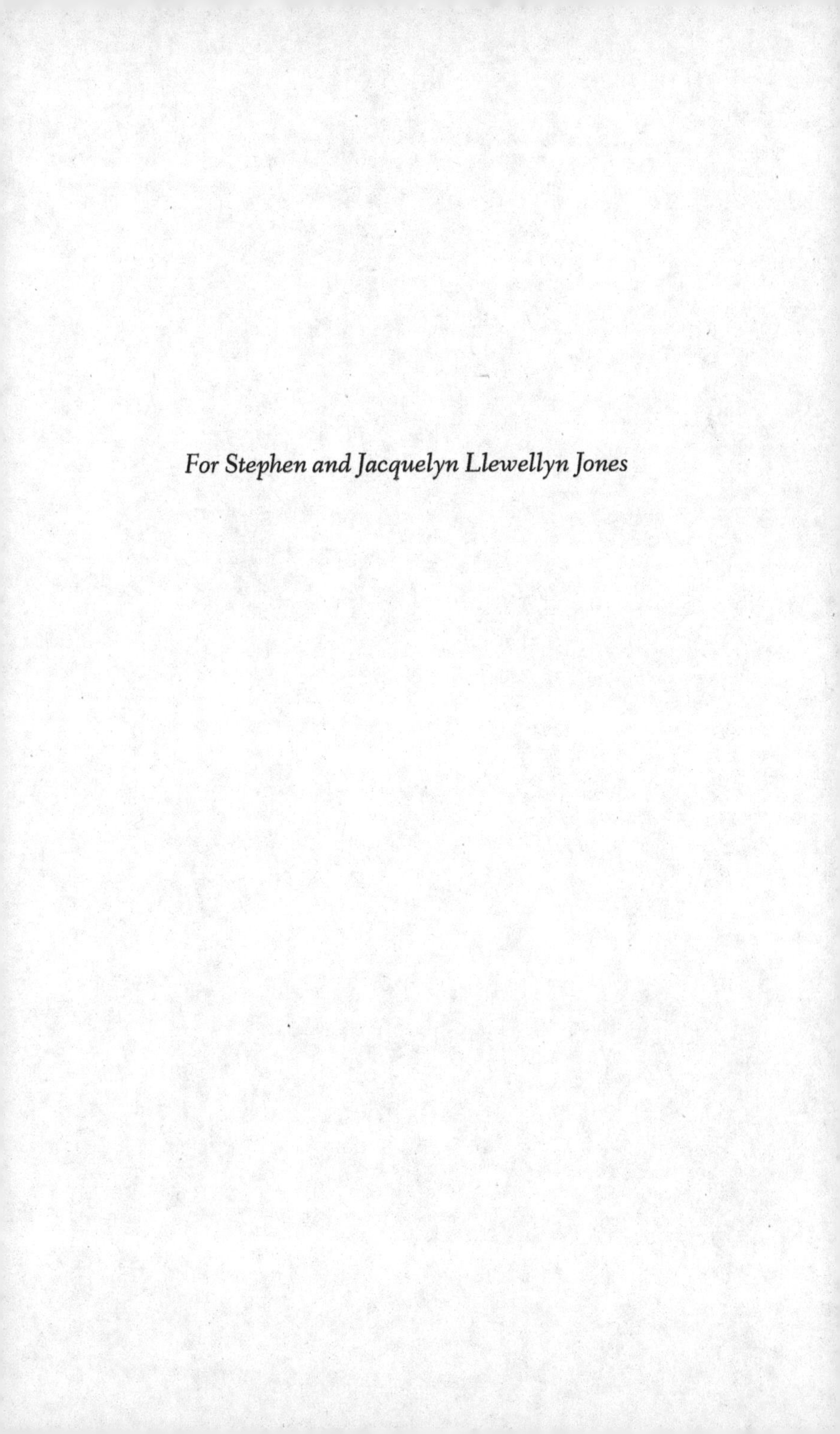

For Stephen and Jacquelyn Llewellyn Jones

PROLOGUE

Tuesday 9 March, 2010 – Guernsey 4 pm

'I think she's coming round, Anna. I'm sure I saw her blink. 'Mum. It's Liz and Anna... your granddaughter. You're in the hospital.' She raised her voice a little, leaning closer to her mother's good ear. 'Everything's fine. We're with you and it's all going to be okay.'

Anna shifted closer, her hand covering her gran's, searching her face for any sign of recognition.

A flicker of her eyelids, then those familiar blue eyes, the lower lids red rimmed. Her grandmother blinked slowly, her gaze drifting from Anna to Liz before sharpening with clarity.

'Vite. Mon pull. Les Allemands... je les entends venir.' She spoke urgently, her neck straining off the pillow, her eyes widening in panic.

The words hung in the air between them.

'Gran's speaking French,' Anna said, staring at her mother.

Liz's face drained of colour. 'Mum's never spoken French in her life.'

'Well, she is now.' Anna slipped her phone out of her pocket. 'I'm pretty sure pull means pullover and isn't Allemands what the French call Germans?' she said slowly, reading off the screen.

'Might be something like, "Quick. My jumper. The Germans are coming..." It's a long time since I studied French.'

She spotted her grandmother's favourite knitted blue jumper on the back of the chair.

'Here you go, Gran. Is this what you want?' She laid it across her lap, noticing the way her hand instinctively started smoothing over the wool, her head now resting back against the pillows in relief.

'Merci, chérie.'

'I don't understand.' Anna's voice was barely a whisper as she watched her grandmother's face settle into peaceful sleep, the blue jumper clutched protectively against her chest.

She stared down at her phone, the French translation still glowing on the screen. The words blurred as the impossible reality hit her: the woman lying in the hospital bed wasn't who they thought she was.

Her grandmother had spent her life glued to the island, refusing to step off the rock, and proud of the fact.

Why would I leave when I have everything I could ever need right here?

And as for languages? Anna's throat tightened as she remembered struggling with her homework in her grandparents' kitchen while her parents were at work. Maths, geography, history. Her grandmother had helped with them all except for the languages.

I'm sorry, darling. I never learnt and it's too late now.

It had all been lies.

The woman who had just spoken perfect French in her moment of terror had spent decades pretending she couldn't help with basic French conjugations. But why? And what did the Germans have to do with a hand-knitted jumper?

PART ONE

ONE

Monday, 10 June, 1940 – Guernsey 5 pm

Leonora wandered through the narrow, winding streets that made up the town of St Peter Port, her steps unhurried for the first time that day. The rain, which had pelted down relentlessly throughout the morning, had stopped as abruptly as it had started. In its place, the skies had cleared to reveal soft hues of blue. The cobbled streets, though wet in patches, were drying quickly under the summer sunshine.

The town was alive, people bustling home eager to get supper on the table. Lenny was in no such rush. With work finished for the day, her time was now her own. She dawdled, stopping to greet acquaintances and window shopping at the paltry displays, where make do and mend was the order of the day. Even if she had the money, which she didn't, there was very little to buy that wasn't a necessity.

The library was situated across from the busy market. Glancing up at the clock on the Town Church, she paused to watch the sellers packing up their stalls for the day. Crates of produce loaded into the back of lorries, the smell of ripe tomatoes and earthy potatoes lingering in the air. The bunches of fresh flowers, their colours vibrant against the cerulean sky. There was never any spare money for flowers, but just the sight of them lightened her mood as she crossed to the library.

Lenny had been visiting the library since she was a small child. The building was in the classical style, with high ceilings and bay windows as befitting the former Assembly Halls. The place to see and be seen in the eighteenth century. As a devoted follower of Jane Austen, she used to love imagining herself dressed to impress while handsome suitors vied for her hand during the quadrilles and country dances favoured. She'd wear a pink or peach satin Robe à la Française with a full skirt and wear matching ribbons in her elaborately styled hair. The war had ripped that side of her away, along with the remains of her childhood.

Walking into the quiet foyer, her shoes clattering against the tiled floor, she barely remembered that earlier enthusiasm or the disparity between her sensible drip-dry grey skirt and plain white blouse and the dress of her dreams. Now her day revolved around surviving and doing whatever she could to lift her brother's spirits until the dratted war came to an end.

The little slice of normal life in the form of the socks she'd posted him earlier, while she waited for his next letter. An evening spent with her knitting friends was just what she needed to keep her mind off the fact that his last letter had been over three weeks ago. The mail from London was increasingly sporadic, but three weeks... It was a long time to wait for news.

'You're early, dear.' Vivienne Gardiner, an old friend of her mother's, came to greet her, both arms extended as she pressed a gentle kiss onto her cheek.

'Not very. I decided to come straight from work.'

It was always difficult for Lenny when meeting her mother's best friend. The woman was kindness itself, but so like her mother in her manner that the pain was as sharp as it was unyielding. If her parents hadn't decided to go for a drive that Sunday afternoon, and if the tyre hadn't burst on their way down one of the steepest hills in Torteval, propelling them into the wall below... Her life was full of so many ifs that she often felt dizzy. But it was these ifs that had shaped her. As the daughter of an Austrian mother and French father, who'd come to the island in search of work following the Great War, she'd learnt resilience from a young age. She couldn't change the past, but she could try and be the type of woman her parents would have been proud of.

'Come and have some tea. I managed to get a few jam tarts from Maison Carré. There's nothing like fresh cakes, especially when I don't have to make them.' Mrs Gardiner drew her towards the small group of early arrivals, pausing slightly, her hand still on her arm. 'I had a nice letter from my dear friend Mr Ozanne during the week. He didn't mention James.' She frowned. 'Didn't say very much at all but, reading between the lines, things are starting to hot up.'

Lenny nodded and smiled, not really knowing how else to respond. Guy Ozanne was something big in the War Office, and the person James had contacted when he'd wanted to join the Navy. He'd managed to get him a job as an interpreter working in the Baker Street Coding Office in the short term, making use of the fact that he was fluent not only in French but in German too. She didn't know more than that, but the thought that her brother could be sent overseas at some point in the future was terrifying.

Within half an hour, the former ballroom was full of chatter as stories were exchanged along with tips and recipes on stretching the housekeeping now that rationing was starting to bite.

'Anyone tried the recipe for carrot jam in last week's newspaper?' Mrs Gardiner said, settling down in her chair, her glasses propped on her nose as she counted the number of stitches on her needles.

'Still using up the last of our blackberry one.' Mrs Monro let out a heartfelt sigh. 'Not sure what my Sid will do when it runs out. He can't abide carrots.'

The conversation continued on a similar theme. A little light relief to keep their minds off thoughts of husbands, sons and brothers away fighting the war.

They sat around the two large tables, teacups and saucers in front of them, a pile of scuffed knitting patterns off to one side. Nonessential items like patterns were increasingly difficult to come by, as was wool.

'What are you working on, Brenda?' Lenny asked, watching as the woman slid her knitting off her needles and started to unravel it.

'A jumper for Janice. Thought I'd best knit it in the next size the way she's shot up in the last week. Either that or someone has shrunk my wool,' she grumbled.

Lenny laughed, along with the rest of the women, feeling her worries slip a little further along her shoulders. She was the only one present who wasn't either a mother or a wife, but that didn't seem to matter. The knitting group was becoming increasingly important to her. She might only be knitting socks, but at least she was doing something for the war effort.

'Well, there's plenty of wool to go around.' Mrs Gardiner nodded at the pile in the centre. 'As long as she's not fussy about the colour. Not sure anyone would choose that hideous shade of brown though.'

Lenny knit to the end of needle, and shifted to the next, her gaze flickering from the sock to the dung-brown skeins of wool in the centre. With no wool left, she had to rely on the kindness of others to provide her with any leftovers.

'If it's going free?' She nodded at her sock. 'I'm sure the troops will be thankful for anything they can get and it's not as if they're not hidden by their boots.'

'You're such a sweetheart knitting for the troops.' Mrs Gardiner leant across and picked up two skeins. 'That should keep you out of mischief for a while.'

'Thank you.' Lenny added the wool to her bag, before smoothing out the half-finished sock to check where she was in the pattern. Each pair was unique, but not only in their unusual colour combinations. On completion, she hid little messages inside the toes: thin strips of paper, which she cut from the discarded envelopes at work. Sometimes it would be a line harvested from one of her favourite poems. Sometimes just a few words about how proud she was. She signed them with her initials.

With one eye on her knitting, Lenny glanced up at the sound of someone running in the corridor outside before bursting through the door, their face beetroot red.

She pushed to her feet, her knitting forgotten at the sight of her landlady clutching a hand to her chest, her breath coming out in short gasps.

'Mrs Church?'

'Oh my dear.' Mrs Church's colour faded back to its usual clotted cream, her apron still tied around her waist, her slippers on her feet, and no hat. Lenny felt her legs start to tremble, her gaze drawn to the crushed telegram squashed between her landlady's work-reddened hands.

The days when a telegram revealed good news had long gone.

She felt a hand on her arm pushing her back down into her chair, as Mrs Gardiner took control of the situation.

'What is it, Mrs Church?'

'A telegram. I'm so sorry, luv.' She handed her the paper before stepping back, wringing her hands in anguish. 'What a thing.'

Lenny peeled it open before placing the paper flat against the table, among the knitting projects and skeins of wool.

The room fell into silence, all knitting paused.

Dear Miss Gallienne,

It is with the deepest regret and solemn duty that we write to inform you that Navy Volunteer Reserve James Gallienne is missing in action, presumed dead following an incident on 1st June.

Please accept our deepest condolences.

Captain W. Williams.

War Office

Lenny dropped the paper, the telegram fluttering to the floor, her breath caught in her throat. A single thought flitted through her mind.

Not James. Please, not James.

The table blurred, the ache in her chest spreading to her back and her shoulders. The arms of her chair were the only thing stopping her from sliding to the floor.

There was no room for doubt or denial.

Her brother was gone.

TWO

Monday 24 June, 1940 – Weymouth 12 pm

Lenny held her suitcase between both hands as she walked down the gangplank, her gas mask banging against her hip, her Sunday hat pinned onto her unruly hair. Gasping in the thick, murky air, her stomach resisted the sudden movement as the boat shifted on its mooring. It was the first time she'd been on a steamboat, and as far as she was concerned, it would be the last.

She hesitated when she reached the harbour, glancing over her shoulder at the remainder of the passengers making their way off the overcrowded vessel, before turning her gaze back to Weymouth. Dock hands shouted to one another as they unloaded the boat. Families clustered together on the cobbled waterfront, some being met by friends and relatives, others arguing about what to do next. An official-looking man, with a sign in French, seemed determined to herd them into some sort of order. Children clutching at their mothers' skirts, wide-eyed and bewildered.

I know how they feel.

Lenny felt a kinship with her fellow travellers. They'd fled the same island and endured the same journey. Yet, she also stood apart, feeling strangely distant. She wasn't there to escape the threat of the invaders occupying her island. She was only there to find out what had happened to her brother.

The sharp cries of gulls overhead cut through the din, swooping low to snatch up discarded crusts of bread left over from the packets of sandwiches everyone seemed to have brought with them for the journey. Lenny tightened her grip on her suitcase and willed herself to move, though her legs still felt like jelly. She shuffled forward, her shoes scraping against the uneven cobblestones, the weight of the suitcase pulling at her arms. Everything she had left in the world was packed inside. Her clothes, a few keepsakes and the cherished letters from James. The rest, anything too bulky to carry, had been left in Mrs Gardiner's loft, a reminder of a life that was already fading to memory.

She bypassed the queue, instead hurrying in the opposite direction, weaving through clusters of people as she made for the nearest bench. When she finally lowered herself onto the seat, she let out a long, shaky breath. The movement of the boat still echoed, making her head swim and her stomach lurch. She rested the suitcase on the ground between her feet and wrapped her arms around herself for warmth despite the blazing sunshine overhead.

It's time to make a plan, she thought. *Work out how I'm going to get to London.*

Weymouth's stone buildings loomed in the distance, streaked with soot and grime, large chimneys belching out thick black smoke. A tram rattled past, porters hauling goods. Lenny baulked at the busyness, having to remind herself that the trip had been her choice. Mrs Gardiner had done everything in her power to stop her, but Lenny had been determined. She'd meet with James's boss to find out exactly what had happened to her brother, before joining the war effort, in whatever capacity they offered her.

'You alright, miss?'

Lenny looked up from where she'd been staring at her dusty shoes and straight into the face of someone she recognised from the boat. He'd been sitting a few feet away on the first part of the journey, she remembered. She'd noticed him seconds before she'd had to leap to her feet and run outside, just in time to deposit the contents of her stomach into the churning seas below. Lenny had decided on the wisdom of completing the remainder of the trip out on deck.

He reminded her a little of James, except for being a few years older. About the same height, his hair a pale brown instead of James's blond. His clothes, though neatly arranged, were clearly well-worn. A brown tweed jacket that had seen better days, a thin grey waistcoat underneath and a cream shirt, the collar frayed at the edge.

'You alright, Miss Gallienne?' he repeated. 'It is Miss Gallienne, isn't it? James's sister? I'm Harry Dennison. We played on the same hockey team.' He held out his hand, which she shook briefly.

She couldn't recall a Harry Dennison but that meant nothing. She'd been far too busy with her own life to take much notice of anyone outside of their immediate group.

'Yes, that's right. Leonora Gallienne, but everyone calls me Lenny, less vowels,' she confirmed, managing a faint smile. 'You evacuating, or...' She paused briefly. 'Off to war?'

He returned her smile, though his seemed easier, more natural. 'Neither. I have a job in London. Just popped back to check on the parents. How is James? I hear he's doing something in the War Office. All very hush hush.'

Lenny couldn't talk about James to him. She wouldn't lie, but she wouldn't tell the truth either. To share the news would be tantamount to accepting that she would never see him again.

With only eleven months between them, they'd always had a special bond growing up, but there'd been no sudden pang of dread. No inexplicable sense of loss. No premonition. That was the only thing that was keeping her going. The belief that she'd have known if something bad had happened to him.

'The occasional letter. You know James,' she said, annoyed that her voice held a slight wobble. 'I'll catch up with all the news when I'm in London.'

Harry nodded. 'Well, in that case, as we're going in the same direction let me escort you, if I may?' He stopped and gestured towards the tram rumbling into view. 'There, look. A tram to the train station.'

Instead of waiting for her reply, he grabbed her suitcase, his rucksack slung over his shoulder.

Lenny opened her mouth to object only to close it again.

Half an hour later found her settled in a train carriage heading for London, the repetitive thud of the wheels soothing her frayed nerves. Harry was seated opposite, but she felt too shy to strike up a conversation. Instead, she drew comfort from the view speeding past in a blur of images.

The countryside stretched out in a rolling patchwork, occasionally punctuated by clusters of cottages and the spires of distant churches, so unlike the familiarity of home. Guernsey, though not built-up, was small, with every inch of its land carefully cultivated. Fields were either dotted with greenhouses for the important tomato crop or full of lush green grazing for the island's world-renowned cows, with the sea always only a whisper away.

The horizon shifted on the approach to London, the open fields giving way to rows of identical houses and narrow streets. Chimneys lined the skyline, smoke curling into the air as the city showed its true self, grey and uninviting to Lenny's untutored gaze.

'Right. That's me.' Lenny was startled to find Harry standing in front of her, his gaze strangely intent as if there was something else he wanted to say.

'So soon?' She felt a blush burn her cheeks at her rudeness. 'I'm sorry. I...'

The train pulled to a halt, masking her words.

'Give James my best,' he said, holding out a torn sheet of paper between his gloved fingers. 'This is my number if you find you're in need of assistance.' Then, with a polite nod, he disappeared into the flow of passengers disembarking from the train.

Lenny stared after him, suddenly aware of the abruptness of his parting, and all the things she might have done to change that.

Speaking to him might have helped, instead of ignoring him for the whole journey.

Now, she'd lost the only person she knew.

She blinked, then blinked again as she realised how many of the passengers were getting off at the same station.

'Excuse me,' she asked the matronly woman sitting beside her. 'Which station is this?'

'Charing Cross, ducks. I've been caught out a fair few times meself with them removing the bleedin' signs. It's all very well making it difficult for Jerry, but what about the locals?'

Charing Cross. That was her station too. Lenny jolted upright, her heart suddenly hammering as she realised what little time she had to get off and perversely annoyed that Harry hadn't seen fit to tell her.

She grabbed at her suitcase, its weight nearly toppling her as she wrestled it down from the rack overhead.

I'll phone him and apologise as soon as I've found out what happened to James.

She scrambled towards the door, weaving through the passengers and barely squeezing out onto the platform as the whistle blew.

It wasn't until she stood amidst the bustling chaos of Charing Cross Station, clutching her suitcase, the soot-tinged air snagging the back of her throat that she realised she'd left something behind.

Harry's telephone number.

Lenny stopped at the newspaper stand outside the station to ask for directions, her second-best dress clinging to her skin, a trickle of sweat coursing down her back as the sun baked her into the pavement.

She was almost dragging her suitcase by the time she reached the War Office. In hindsight, she should have taken a taxi. There were certainly enough of the iconic black cabs about. Or even a bus. She eyed the large red double-deckers in wonder. Anything other than walking.

London was showing its shiny side this close to Whitehall. Men in black suits, wearing bowler hats and carrying briefcases. Women in jaw-dropping outfits sported hemlines a good two inches shorter than those worn in Guernsey, their hats perched jauntily on their heads. Among the pedestrians, she spotted several soldiers in an assortment of uniforms from the Army, Navy and the Air Force, their presence a stark reminder of the reason she was here.

The buildings towered above her. They were unlike anything she had seen back home, with their intricate stonework and grand columns, a testament to a history she barely understood. If she hadn't been so worried about the time stretching into the late afternoon, she would have stopped in a doorway to watch the world go by. Instead, she put on a final spurt of speed and marched up to the War Office building, her confident strides masking the nerves snaking through her stomach.

She'd barely made it through the entrance when the doorman appeared, blocking her from going further.

'Can I help you, miss?'

'Yes. I'm here to see Mr GD Ozanne.'

'And is he expecting you, miss?' The man glared down at her from under bushy brows.

'He is, yes. If you could tell him Miss Gallienne is here to see him, from Guernsey. Mrs Gardiner's friend.' She blushed at that, feeling she'd lost some ground by admitting that she didn't actually know Mr Ozanne.

'If you could wait here, miss.'

Well, at least I'm inside the lobby, or whatever it's called, she thought, taking the opportunity to sink into the nearest chair, partially hidden from the many people entering and exiting the building.

The lobby was cool, a welcome relief from the heat outside. Lenny shifted in her seat, her suitcase wedged awkwardly between her legs and the wall. She felt like an imposter sitting there with no real purpose other than finding out what had happened to James. A telegram was all very well, but it didn't begin to answer any of her questions.

Five minutes passed before the doorman returned, his expression somewhat softened. 'I'll take you up, Miss Gallienne. You can leave your suitcase here. It will be safe enough. Follow me.'

She rose quickly, her legs feeling wobbly as she followed him up the stairs to the first floor. He led her down a long corridor, finally stopping outside a door marked with a brass plaque bearing the name Mr. H Dalton. Minister of Economic Warfare.

'Mr Ozanne is unavailable, but Mr Dalton should be able to sort you out, miss. Good luck,' he said, offering her a nod before stepping back.

The room was filled with a haze of smoke, which caused her eyes to smart. Her attention focused on the overfilled ashtray before meeting the intense gaze of the man seated behind a large, cluttered desk, a telephone to one side. He wasn't old but older than her. Probably mid-twenties at a guess, with rounded cheeks and dark hair, a smattering of grey starting at the temples. He also appeared far too young for the title Minister of Economic Warfare.

'Mr Dalton, I'm...'

'No. I'm Finlay Stewart, Mr Dalton's clerk, Miss Gallienne,' he said, rushing to his feet. 'I'm afraid it's impossible for you to see him today. He's in a meeting for the rest of the afternoon.' His voice was a mixture of apology and curiosity, which shouldn't have come as a surprise, she thought, hysteria starting to build.

How many seventeen-year-olds found their way into the War Office without an invite?

'If you let me know where I can contact you, I'll see if we can fit you in next week, or the week after.'

'You don't understand, Mr Stewart. I need to see Mr Dalton, or Mr Ozanne, or anyone else who can help me. It's about my brother, James.'

He spread his hands. 'I'm not sure how you think we can help you with that, Miss Gallienne.'

'But I need to speak to someone,' she said, her voice rising despite her best efforts to stay composed. 'My brother is... missing, presumed dead, and no one has told me anything more. I *insist* on knowing. Where he was when it happened. Where he is now. I have a right to know, if only to arrange a Christian burial.'

Finlay's expression shifted. 'James Gallienne?' he clarified with a frown. 'He's with the War Office?'

Lenny nodded, lifting her hand and weaving it through the air. 'Yes. Since January. Initially in the coding department before being sent overseas on some mission or other. He didn't tell me a lot. Partially the reason I'm in such a mess.'

'He'll have signed the Official Secrets Act, Miss Gallienne. It would have been a criminal offence to—'

'You think I care about that?' she interrupted, only to stop. The room started to spin, the last couple of days catching up with her. The overnight trip on the steamboat. The hot walk in an unfamiliar city. The realisation that she hadn't eaten a crumb since the stale sandwich on the boat.

'Why don't you sit down for a moment, miss?' Finlay came from around the desk and helped her into a chair. 'Let me see what I can do.'

She sank down without protest, her hands fisting into tight balls to stop them from shaking.

What a mess. I can't even get this right without collapsing in a fit of the vapours. What on earth possessed me to come?

Consumed by self-flagellation, Lenny didn't notice the door opening at the far end of the room until the sound of a deep, unmistakable voice reverberated through the air.

'Your appointment is all but agreed then, Dalton. I'll just need to get it sanctioned by the Cabinet, but that shouldn't be a problem.'

Lenny jerked back in her seat as if stung.

She knew that voice. Everyone knew that voice, though she'd never imagined she'd hear it in person.

Winston Churchill strode through the room with an energy that defied his stocky frame. His face was flushed, his polka dot bow tie slightly askew under his pinstriped suit, a long cigar jutting confidently from his fingers.

Good to know where all that smoke is coming from. Thought we were on fire.

Lenny's irrepressible spirit bounced back at the sight of the prime minister in person, instead of on the radio or the front of the newspapers where he belonged.

Behind him, two men followed. The first a stranger but the second, lankier in stature and with a moustache that looked in need of a trim, Neville Chamberlain. The recent prime minister, she thought, a touch of hysteria returning. Or someone who bore a striking resemblance.

Part of her wanted to fade into the background but the other part, the larger part wanted to know what they were doing.

Lenny wasn't a gossip, far from it, but she was as eager to learn about the war effort as the next person. They'd been told Guernsey was safe, the British military presence confirmed that, but for how much longer? With the German army only thirty miles from their coastline every man, woman and child feared for their life. The English Channel was the only thing separating them from the madness cutting across Europe with a blade of steel.

'What the devil have I got myself into!'

Her eyes widened as all three men turned towards her, their expressions ranging from surprise to mild curiosity. Lenny had recently started talking to herself, but mostly in her head. It was with a jolt of horror, that she realised she must have spoken out loud.

Not just out loud. In French. Her mother tongue and the one she turned to in times of stress.

Winston Churchill's brows rose for the briefest of moments

before his expression shifted into something that looked alarmingly like approval. He turned to Dalton, a glint of triumph in his eye.

'That's exactly right, Dalton,' he declared, his deep, resonant voice filled with conviction. 'We need to fill Europe with an army of people like her. Did you hear the accent? Impeccable diction. Speaks it better than me. Wherever did you recruit her from?'

Dalton, who had clearly not been expecting this twist, scrambled for an answer and finding none in the immediate vicinity of Lenny's blank expression, turned to Finlay. 'Stewart, remind me where we recruited Miss er... from?'

'Miss Gallienne is from Guernsey, sir.'

'Guernsey, you say?' Churchill leant forward, peering at Lenny as though she was a specimen pinned behind a glass frame. 'That's even better. Someone who's been living under the threat of occupation and understands what's at stake.' He turned back to Dalton, jabbing his cigar in the air for emphasis, wafting a thin plume of smoke upwards. 'Sterling effort, Dalton. Bodes well for the future of our little project. We'll need more like her for my special army. A lot more.'

Lenny blinked. The idea of being part of anything Churchill deemed important was enough to make her head spin.

'Wait, I think there's been some mistake,' she finally managed.

Churchill silenced her with a raised hand and a thick grin. 'No mistake, Miss Gallienne. Welcome to the fight.'

THREE

Mr Dalton had James's open folder in front of him, his hand on top presumably in case she was able to read upside down. She felt like leaning forward and whisking it out from under his grasp, but she wouldn't get farther than the door. The place was swarming with army types keen to do their duty, and presumably that duty included preventing her from learning the truth.

The knock on the door had her sit upright in her chair as Finlay deposited a tray of tea and a plate of dainty sandwiches on the desk between them. Cucumber with the crusts cut off and presented on one of those lace doilies that Mrs Gardiner favoured.

Good to know rationing hasn't reached the War Office in the same way it has Guernsey.

That she'd nearly fainted after the prime minister had left had worked in her favour. It had also delayed her having to think up something that would make Mr Dalton help her.

'James worked at the War Office for six months, Mr Dalton, and seemed very happy here. His last letter explained that he was in transit somewhere and would be in touch. The telegram I received after in no way satisfies my curiosity as to what followed. Surely there must be something more you can tell me?'

She noted her pleading tone, but didn't care. If he wasn't careful, she'd be removing her handkerchief from her bag. All the signs were there. It was only by digging her nails into her gloved palm that she was able to stave off a deluge.

'Look, Miss Gallienne, you must know that I can't tell you much. There's the Official Secrets Act for a start. The national security of Great Britain could…'

'Well, get me a copy and I'll sign it,' she interrupted, her thoughts melding into a workable outcome that would suit them both admirably. She'd find out about James and Mr Dalton would get the assurances he seemed to need that she wasn't about to blab to some German or other. 'In fact, that's the ideal solution. Mr Churchill seems to think that I'm perfect for his scheme. Let's make that happen. Then you can tell me about my brother.' She removed her gloves carefully before plucking a sandwich from the plate.

As a suggestion it was inspired, but it was infused with more holes than a tea strainer.

A job? Where would she live? She didn't know anyone in London, no one apart from James and Harry: James was missing, and she'd gone and lost Harry's telephone number.

Hugh Dalton sighed. Lenny knew he was called Hugh because Mr Churchill had called him that as he'd departed the office, a trail of stinky smoke streaming behind him. Hugh was either exasperated or annoyed, quite possibly both. James had told her on numerous occasions that she had the power to drive a man to distraction. If only she could meet a man worthy enough of her affections, she'd be quite happy to put his observation to good use.

'I suppose there's no harm. We're always looking to recruit staff to Section D.' He pressed a button on his phone and within seconds Finlay was knocking on the door before slipping inside. 'Get me a copy of the Official Secrets Act, Finlay, and see if Miss Maxse is available for an interview. Miss Gallienne has decided to join our happy breed.' He turned back to her. 'Finish your tea while you're waiting, then we'll talk. The cucumber sandwiches are rather good.'

Lenny had lost her appetite, but managed to finish her drink before a cursory knock on the door revealed Finlay, with a sheaf of papers in his hand.

'Miss Maxse sends her apologies, but has said there's a post for a typist/messenger/Girl Friday for the right recruit. I've brought a contract as well, in case Miss Gallienne is suitable.'

Instead of leaving, Finlay hovered near the door, looking awkward.

'Yes, what is it?' Dalton asked, shuffling through the papers.

'Well.' Finlay took a step closer. 'I was thinking, sir... I imagine finding accommodation in London right now... well, it won't be easy for Miss Gallienne. My wife and I have a spare room. She's welcome to have it until she gets a place of her own.'

Hugh raised an eyebrow briefly. 'Commendable, Finlay. Though I suggest you ask Miss Gallienne directly, rather than addressing me.'

'There's no need, Mr Dalton.' Lenny intervened quickly, noting the flush racing up Finlay's cheeks. She wasn't sure she liked the way Mr Dalton spoke to his staff, but it sounded like she'd be having very little to do with him. 'That's very kind of you, and of your wife, Mr Stewart. Perhaps we could discuss it after I've spoken with Mr Dalton? I hope you understand that I want to hear about my brother first.'

'Of course.'

'Alright. Firstly, allow me to explain that James was working for another part of the War Office,' Mr Dalton started, as soon as Finlay had left the room.

'I know that,' she said, wanting to shift the conversation forward. 'Working in some staid coding office doesn't equate to missing in action, or am I wrong in thinking that?'

She watched a muscle flicker at the edge of his mouth. 'Have you heard of Dunkirk, Miss Gallienne?'

'Pardon?'

'Dunkirk, Miss Gallienne?' he pressed.

She stared at him, her mouth slightly open until she remembered to close it. The question shouldn't be all that unexpected, but it still came as a shock. Lenny had read the recent headlines about Dunkirk and wept with the knitting group, their hands working damp wool as they'd prayed for the soldiers' safe return, but this was different. This wasn't about distant soldiers.

This was personal.

'We will fight on the beaches,' she finally whispered, quoting a line from Churchill's recent speech. It was the only line she could remember.

'Yes, exactly that. Good.' He coughed briefly, taking out a pressed handkerchief and wiping his face.

Nothing was good about what had happened in Dunkirk. Yes, Operation Dynamo had saved many thousands of lives but what about the ones missing? What about the ones who didn't make it? What about James? Lenny could feel her heart thumping in her ears as the room began to spin, but she wouldn't faint. She wouldn't give this pompous man the satisfaction. Instead, she bit her bottom lip hard.

'Yes, well.' He dropped his chin in preference to holding her gaze, which she took as a bad sign. 'Interpreters were key to success, as you can imagine, given the Anglo-French nature of the operation. We asked for volunteers, and your brother was one of the first to respond.' He coughed again, his attention on the folder, his index finger marking where he was in the report. 'He was assigned to the Royal Naval destroyer, HMS *Anthony*, as interpreter and liaison officer. Things were going well. They'd managed to rescue over 3,000 soldiers from the beaches before the ship was damaged during heavy air attacks by the Luftwaffe.' He finally managed to meet her gaze. 'Are you sure you want to hear the rest?'

Lenny wasn't sure of anything anymore but, leaning forward, she realised she needed this. She needed to know what had happened to James in his last moments, if only to try and make sense of a war that, to her mind, was senseless.

'Carry on, Mr Dalton.'

'There was a direct hit. James was on deck, helping to load the wounded from another ship, when it happened. He was one of thirty men presumed to have lost their lives on the ship that day.'

'Why presumed?'

'Standard terminology for when so many are lost in one go.'

She said nothing, she couldn't. Everything had been said, except where his body was.

'What about burying him? I'd like to take him back to Guernsey for that.'

'You need to understand that there was no time, Miss Galli-enne. The ship was still under threat, barely able to stay afloat. The captain made the decision to bury the fallen at sea, with full honours, of course.'

Lenny's breath caught at that. A short, involuntary gasp that drew a compassionate glance in her direction.

'So, there's no grave,' she whispered.

There would be nowhere to visit. Nowhere to say her last goodbyes. Nowhere to grieve.

He gave a solemn nod, the folder closed, his hand resting on top. 'Just the sea. I'm sorry. That's all we have.'

She closed her eyes a moment, grief pressing in from all sides. But she'd been here before. The grief felt familiar if no less intense. Dalton hadn't told her anything new really. The damage had been done by the telegram and not here in his office.

'Indulge me for a moment,' she said, her voice trembling with something close to defiance. 'What if he wasn't killed? What if he was thrown clear and picked up by the Germans?'

'Let's be realistic, Miss Gallienne. There were eyewitnesses…'

'Please, Mr Dalton.'

'Very well. If he was picked up, then he'd be held as a prisoner of war. If that's the case, under the Geneva Convention, you might still hear from him. Letters. Parcels.' He waved an arm. 'That sort of thing. If there's any further updates about James's status then, of course, you'll hear in due course via letter.'

He was only pandering to her, in the same way he might offer a distressed child a lollypop.

Eyeing him across the desk, the surface littered with the remains of their tea, Lenny let go of the last shred of hope she'd been clinging to.

The sea would be James's burial plot, the ocean his graveyard and every time she caught sight of a wave or a ripple across the glassy surface she'd remember. She'd never forget.

Lenny straightened as she blinked back her tears before clearing her throat and putting on her most practical voice.

'Right. Thank you for telling me. It mustn't have been easy. Now, about this job. Where do I sign?'

'You don't have any questions first?' Dalton sounded shocked at the sudden change, but there was nothing she could do about that. It was talk about the job or run out of the room screaming.

'Typist, messenger, Girl Friday. Seems self-explanatory, don't you think?' she said, her voice as steady as she could make it. She opened her bag and pulled out her pen. 'I do have one question,' she said, when she realised that his continued silence meant that he was expecting it. 'What does Section D stand for?'

Number 11 Peldon Avenue was a red-bricked, semi-detached house indistinguishable from its forty or so identical neighbours and very different to the granite houses Lenny was used to. But the cul-de-sac was tree-lined, and the properties appeared to be well maintained, which told her more about her new neighbourhood than the colour of the bricks or the uniformity of the roofs.

Finlay walked towards the white gate, removing his bowler hat before gesturing for her to precede him. The journey across town had been primarily in silence, Lenny's attention on the unfamiliar view. The Tube had been packed, which had added to the difficulty in questioning him. Signing the Official Secrets Act had done the rest.

The sound of a bird warbling caught her attention and they both stopped a moment to scan the trees opposite.

'Our resident cuckoo.' He pushed open the front door. 'A pleasant country sound for somewhere so central. It's a nice enough area. You're welcome to stay as long as you need.'

They had cuckoos in Guernsey too, along with a host of wildlife and sea life, including seals and dolphins. The cuckoo's forlorn call was a sound so familiar that it brought a sudden lump to the back of her throat.

Home was only yesterday. Weymouth only this morning. Harry Dennison and the lost phone number earlier that afternoon. It felt like she'd lived a thousand lives since then. She certainly felt older, if no less wise.

Lenny examined the papered hall in passing, the carpet showing signs of wear and tear. But it was a good quality carpet, and the décor was well maintained. A nice house in a nice location. Exactly what she needed to come home to after a busy day at the War Office. Probably very different to a busy day working at the supermarket, but she had no way of knowing.

'Be honest, Finlay. What exactly have I let myself in for?'

The interview, which wasn't an interview but more of a formality, hadn't lasted long. Five minutes where Mr Dalton told her where she'd be working and who she had to report to the following day. He'd encouraged her to take tomorrow off, but she wouldn't hear of it. Sitting in her bedroom staring at four walls wasn't why she'd travelled to London. She needed to keep busy, and work was part of that.

'I'm not sure what to say.' He picked up her case and effort-lessly carried it to the stairs. 'Working in the typing pool I guess, initially. Nothing dangerous if that's what you mean.'

'At least that's something even if the D in Section D stands for Destruction.' She thought of something else. 'I take it there's Sections ABCE too? You know. A for Annihilation. B for Bedlam.

C for Carnage, E for Evisceration, or is it only the D that gets special treatment?'

He laughed at that, a laugh that changed his serious expression to something softer. A man she could like, and trust.

'That's a good one. Yes, there are more sections than I've had meatloaf dinners and certainly an A to C, but on a need-to-know basis and, as you and I don't need to know...'

'Okay.' She held up her hands, palm facing. 'So, all I need to know is that I'm assigned to Section D?'

'Sort of.' He hemmed slightly, shooing her up the stairs ahead of him, as he struggled with her case.

'Sort of? What aren't you telling me, Finlay?' she said over her shoulder.

'I thought Dalton would have explained. He should have told you. Mr Churchill and Mr Dalton have agreed to amalgamate three of the departments formed by MI6, in an attempt to coordinate civilian warfare overseas, now we're at war.'

'And this new department will be who I'm working for?'

'That's the plan but the government still has to agree, and contracts still have to be signed. There are people to be appointed into senior positions before they can start filling the junior ones. You know what it's like.'

No, she didn't. She had no idea, but she thought it best not to show her ignorance. She would find out for herself in good time.

'It doesn't even have a name as yet,' he continued. 'And no staff, other than those Dalton and the rest of them will be able to cobble together from other departments. In fact, you could say that you're the first employee, after Marjorie Maxse, that is. Section D's Chief of Staff.'

'Why doesn't that fill me with confidence?' she muttered under her breath, watching as he opened the door to his flat.

'Ellen, darling. Where are you?'

Lenny hung back in the small hall, feeling awkward as she heard footsteps hurrying across the room. Finlay had mentioned his wife on the journey over, and it was easy to tell how in love they were.

There's no rush, she thought, starting to remove her gloves and unpin her hat, her hair falling around her shoulders in a riot of brown curls as a small barrel of a woman rushed through the door, a ginger cat weaving around her ankles.

'Silly Finlay, leaving you in the hall. I'm Ellen and you're Lenny. Good to meet you.'

Lenny took her hand, unable to withhold her grin at the sight of Finlay's wife. As short as she was round, but not overweight. Pregnant and heavily so.

'And you. Finlay didn't tell me about...'

'Well, he wouldn't. Never bothers with the essentials, does my Finlay. Come in. come in,' she repeated, ushering her into the lounge and through a door at the end. 'Kitchen and bathroom on the left. Your bedroom is second on the right. Finlay has popped your case on the bed for you. Make yourself at home. Supper in thirty minutes. I hope you like hotpot. Getting good meat from the butcher's is pretty much impossible these days.'

With her hat and gloves laid neatly on the mahogany tallboy, Lenny sank onto the bed, relishing the sudden quiet. She slipped off her shoes and curled herself around the suitcase, where Finlay had left it.

She should unpack. Hang her dresses in the wardrobe, line up her tops and jumpers in the drawers. Do something ordinary.

But she didn't.

Instead, she stared at the ceiling. Until now, she'd been moving forward on instinct, one foot in front of the other, clinging to the idea of usefulness. She hadn't let herself miss Guernsey, hadn't dared. But now it crept back.

Here in London, the air was thick with smog and strangers. She didn't know the streets, didn't know who to trust. Even her new job, in a department so secret it didn't have a name or an address, felt unreal. Mr Dalton had said they'd be using a hotel as a temporary base. 'No one's booking holidays these days,' he'd said with a grim smile.

She was expected to show up tomorrow. All she had was a time and a name. Something entirely different from ordering supplies and sending out invoices for Guernsey's prime supermarket.

She hugged her pillow to her chest, as grief finally found a way around the strangeness and the pain.

The first sob was muffled by the pillow. Then the next...

FOUR

Tuesday 2 July 1940 – London 7 pm

Ellen was just what Lenny needed. They spent their evenings in the front room, their needles clacking to the background noise from the radio in the corner, while Finlay read the newspaper in the chair opposite, his slippered feet stretched out in front of him.

She'd suggested that once Lenny had settled in, she accompanied her to the weekly WI knitting club situated in a church hall only five minutes away.

It didn't take much for Lenny to agree. Over the last week or so, she'd lost her brother, and with the recent occupation of the Channel Islands, her home. A handful of women chatting over tea, with a pile of wool on their laps sounded like the ideal way to make new friends. If she found that it wasn't for her then she didn't have to attend next week.

Pushing open the door of St Matthew's Hall was like stepping across the threshold of the library, although the air felt decidedly chillier. She pulled her jumper over her shoulders and followed Ellen across the room, where a small group of women started fussing over her.

'Not long now, my dear. Only a few weeks,' cooed one of them, patting Ellen's arm with a knowing smile.

'Sit yourself down. I'll pour you a cuppa – and one for your friend.'

'This is Lenny Gallienne,' Ellen said warmly, turning to her. 'A friend from Guernsey who's decided to stay for a while.'

Lenny mustered a small smile, her hands tightening around the strap of her bag. They'd agreed on the way over that it might be best to omit that she was working at the War Office. That way neither of them would have to lie if one of the women decided to ask any awkward questions.

'Hello and welcome. I'm Mrs Veron, but do call me Mary.' Mary patted the seat beside her before rummaging in her bag and pulling out a new skein of white wool. 'We don't bother with the formalities here, do we, ladies? Ellen tells us you know your way around a pair of needles. What are you knitting?'

Lenny slipped into the chair offered, her bag on her lap as she held up the sock she was working on. 'Socks for the troops.'

'Really?' Mary popped on a pair of tortoiseshell glasses to examine the sock more closely. 'They're intricate for a pair of socks. Lucky soldier. What's the pattern called?'

Lenny glanced down at the navy socks on her lap and the twisted ribbing she'd used for the cuff in bemusement. She liked experimenting with different stitches and this particular one didn't have a name. It was quick and easy to do, as well as looking attractive. The message for the toe was already in place. Ideally she'd like to find a different way to include messages but hadn't been able to come up with a simple, workable plan yet.

'Oh, nothing really. I get bored with just knitting stocking stitch.' She shrugged, embarrassed at the way the other women had homed in on the sock. 'I'm thinking of Fair Isle next for a bit of variety.' She smiled gently as Ellen took the chair opposite. 'Might have to knit a baby cardigan or two if I can get some four-ply. How's the wool situation holding out, by the way? It's desperate straits in Guernsey. Barely a skein to be had.'

'Not so bad yet but I reckon it won't last.' Mary nodded towards the centre of the table and the pile of multi-coloured balls. 'Help yourself. There's a nice blue four-ply there, although I reckon our Ellen is having a girl.'

Lenny laughed briefly. 'What makes you say that?'

Mary only smiled. 'You wouldn't believe me if I told you, but I'm sure you can guess who this is for?' She held up a delicate, pale pink matinee jacket.

'If I do end up having a boy, there are a lot of pink jackets I'm going to have to rip back.' Ellen grinned, raising both hands. 'Six and counting.'

'And you'll need every one, my girl.' Mary picked up the skein of the dung-brown wool that Lenny had brought with her from Guernsey with a frown. 'And I'm sure our boys overseas wouldn't object to the odd pair or two of pink socks. Not if the knitting is to Lenny's standard.'

'Thank you.' Lenny cast off the sock and folded it carefully before placing it on top of its pair, the thin sliver of paper secreted in the toe rustling under her fingers. She'd decided on the idea last night and put it into action before bed.

Instead of the 'Good luck' message she'd changed it to *James Gallienne, missing in action since Dunkirk. Please contact the War Office with any news.*

Not that she held out any hope. Not really, which didn't stop her from refusing to think of him in any other terms apart from lost. Lost to her.

And despite everything Dalton had said, the lost could still be found.

FIVE

Friday 20 September, 1940 – London 7.20 am

'There you go, Finlay.' Lenny eyed the lumpy porridge with a jaundiced eye as she placed the bowl in front of him before slipping into the chair opposite. Cooking had never been her forte but, with Ellen resting in bed, she thought she'd give it a go. It was cook or starve.

There had been so many changes over the last three months that she struggled to keep up. There was no thought of returning to Guernsey. That avenue had been blocked off to her with the arrival of the Germans. A small fire curled under her breastbone at the thought. If the Germans wanted a fight on their hands, they were going the right way about it. She'd jumped at the chance of becoming Miss Maxse's personal secretary when the opportunity had arisen. Anything to get back at the enemy for murdering her beloved brother and occupying her island.

It wasn't only her work life that had changed. They now had an Anderson shelter in the back garden, a necessity with the onset of the Blitzkrieg. The small, dark and damp space filled her with dread as well as a sense of claustrophobia.

There was a kernel of happiness too in number 11 Peldon

Avenue with the early arrival of Betty Stewart. Ellen had left hospital with a beatific smile and the most perfect bundle Lenny had ever seen. Up to that point, she'd never thought of babies other than as an extension of her friends, the few who'd decided to reach out for happiness in a world that had descended into madness. Seeing Betty up close had changed that in a beat. Her heart expanded every time her gaze clashed with Betty's pure blue eyes, to the point that she wondered how the narrow space under her ribs could contain it.

Ellen had taken to having her breakfast in bed while she nursed Betty, which left Finlay and Lenny to fend for themselves. Ellen needed to rest, and Lenny was perfectly able to cater for Finlay.

She just treated him like a brother... like James. The rest came naturally.

Finlay was particularly quiet as he spooned in his porridge. He wasn't the chatty sort, but he was worried about Ellen, and Lenny couldn't blame him. She was as worried about her new friend as he was. The Blitz, the term coined by the papers for this new wave of bombings, had shaken Ellen in a way none of them had quite anticipated. The constant fear, the sleepless nights and the way her hands quivered slightly as she rocked Betty, her eyes darting to the windows at every distant rumble.

'I'm worried she'll never return to the Ellen we know.'

Lenny touched his arm briefly. 'Remember, it's not just Ellen who's worried. Everyone across London is saying an extra prayer or two this morning for being saved, and for those who weren't so lucky. It's going to be harder for Ellen with her emotions in a tangle, but she's a strong woman. She just needs a bit more time.'

'Thank you.' He stared at her a moment, a warm expression flickering in the back of his eyes. 'I don't know what we'd do without you.'

'There's no need. Whether you like it or not you're my family now.'

· · ·

'Ah, there you are.' Marjorie Maxse was in the process of packing up her briefcase when Lenny arrived at the office. She was wearing another one of her all-grey ensembles along with an air of impatience, which Lenny had quickly realised was her trademark.

Section D's Chief of Staff had a finger in all the organisation's pies and a reluctance to share the responsibility with any of her team. She also wanted *all her little jobs*, as she termed them, done with an expedience that had Lenny working late most evenings. Until recently, it was something she'd embraced as a tool to keep her mind off her own problems, but not since Betty had arrived on the scene.

There were some things more important than work.

'Morning Miss Maxse.'

'Indeed, it is.' She picked up her briefcase in one hand and her coat and hat in the other. 'We're going on a trip. Guildford. It's only in Surrey, so we should be back late afternoon.' She stopped by the door to position her hat in place. 'There's a car waiting. I'll see you outside in a moment. I've already told Gloria to hold the fort. You are pleased with her progress?'

'Yes, Miss Maxse. She seems to be fitting in well.' Gloria was their latest recruit, and Lenny had already marked her as someone deserving of quick progression up the ladder.

She didn't bother removing her hat. There was no thought that she wouldn't accompany her. As far as Marjorie was concerned, Lenny's life was at her disposal during her working hours, and a fair few of her leisure ones. She just had time to put a call through to Finlay in case she was late, before grabbing her bag and gas mask, and joining her.

Lenny drew in a deep breath as their driver pulled up in front of Wanborough Manor, filling her lungs with the crisp, dry air, very different to the thick smog of the capital. Stepping out of London, albeit briefly, was an experience she wouldn't have missed. The rolling countryside punctuated by lazy streams, fields dotted with sheep and cows. If it wasn't for the occasional military vehicle trundling past, she could almost believe that there wasn't a war on.

'Good. We're here. If you can pick us up in a couple of hours, Forbes.'

'Right you are, madam.'

Lenny watched as Marjorie placed the file she was reading back in her briefcase before shutting it with a sharp click. If she'd realised it was going to be a silent trip, she'd have brought her knitting, but an hour with her thoughts wasn't a bad thing, and she would have missed the scenery.

Wanborough Manor was an imposing redbrick building framed by trees and fields. An oasis of tranquillity in an area of unprecedented beauty. That they were here to inspect the premises as to their suitability as a training camp seemed somewhat disrespectful and certainly out of keeping with the bucolic atmosphere.

The gravel drive leading up to the imposing front door crunched under foot, but Lenny was more interested in the army type waiting for them on the top step.

'Major de Wesselow, good of you to meet us. This is my secretary.'

Marjorie didn't introduce her by name but there was no surprise there. Lenny was invisible until she was informed otherwise.

'There's nothing definite, of course,' Marjorie continued, looking out across the gardens. 'On paper the manor seems ideal. The owners are keen to let us have full use for the duration?'

'Yes, dear lady. Plenty of autocratic piles like this going begging currently and the government coin is a hefty one. Enough for a badly needed new roof.' The major gestured for them to precede him. 'This is the seventh I've inspected and the one that does seem the most promising. Close enough to London and with good rail and road links, but far enough away for Jerry not to find without searching high and low first. The current owner, the Earl of Olslow, has headed up to his estate in Scotland. All that's left is an old retainer. I've sent him off to the nearest farm to see if he can rustle up something for luncheon before you head back. It will only be simple fayre but quite sufficient.'

The major was stockily built with a black toothbrush moustache at war with his greying hair. Lenny had met plenty of similar types over recent weeks. Career soldiers who'd fought in one war and were keen to do their bit in the second. She had made a fine art of standing back in their presence. Her function was only as a note-taker even if she had a queue of questions building.

The manor already had a feeling of desertion between its fancy walls and wooden flooring. Faded markings on the embossed wallpaper where family portraits had been removed, and the same on the floor where precious carpets had been rolled up out of harm's way. Lenny trailed after them, her pencil in her hand as she took copious notes, keeping her thoughts firmly to herself.

'I was thinking of ten to fifteen recruits for a period of four weeks at a time.' The major led them across to the central staircase, their footsteps echoing around the empty space. 'The manor has ten bedrooms, but we'll need some of those for the tutors. Two, six bedded dormitories. Two bathrooms, which is one less than hoped for but it's not a holiday camp or a hotel. The attics have already been turned into accommodation for domestic staff and I recommend we continue to use them as such.'

The examination of the formal gardens, surrounded by extensive woods, was no less intense. 'The family have asked if we could preserve the orchard and the rose garden but, apart from that they don't mind what we do,' the major continued, clipping along at a smart pace over a lawn which was already showing signs of neglect. 'The outbuildings are a bonus, as is the swimming pool. There's also a small family church within the boundary wall, which I'm sure will be welcomed by some of our more devout recruits.'

The only part of the garden that was being maintained was the vegetable one, a trug of freshly dug carrots and beetroot waiting to be taken into the kitchen. He led the way up a slight incline, which gave a panoramic view over the surrounding land, his hand raised as he talked through his vision for the future. 'An early cross-country run along the perimeter to build up an appetite for breakfast in the mess. The wooded area to the left of the gate would make a suitable range for weapons practice. Stens and rifles and what have you. One of the reception rooms can easily be turned into a classroom for lectures on intelligence, sabotage, unarmed combat and ordinance. The other we'll set up as a bar.'

Marjorie's eyebrows shot up at that. 'Is that necessary, Major? I thought they were here to learn how to be saboteurs and spies, not sommeliers.'

'Which will involve networking with others in the areas they're dropped into. Being able to hold their beer is a necessary part of that, as is being able to find their way in a blackout after a bottle of the local plonk.' He firmed his jaw, which made Lenny question whether he was speaking from experience. It was something that would be impossible to find out.

They ambled back to the manor, but this time he took them past the Victorian greenhouse and through to the kitchen, where a thin man with dour features was boiling up something on the stove. The trug of vegetables was now on the scrubbed pine table beside a basket of eggs.

Lunch, by necessity, was taken in the kitchen, as the only room with a table and chairs. There was some kind of broth served with the softest bread and duck eggs the size of fists, not that Lenny had time to enjoy it. The conversation continued on a theme once the major was assured that the man was out of the way behind a firmly closed door.

'I like that it's surrounded by woods and high walls,' Marjorie said, placing her fork down and cradling her cup. 'We can have Field Security Police stationed by the entrance to check passes.'

Lenny had been building up the confidence to speak during the tour, her notebook filled with questions that had cropped up along the way. She cleared her throat and asked, 'What do you reckon the pass rate will be, Major?'

'Difficult to say at this stage, but I don't see us passing more than a quarter at any one time. Perhaps four out of the twelve.'

'That low? When we're looking to drop at least four hundred?' Marjorie sounded shocked.

'Better they prove themselves here than end up at the mercy of the enemy.'

Lenny nodded in agreement. Never had training, and the weeding out of unsuitable candidates, been so vital. She glanced at her notebook again.

'And what about those who don't make the cut, Major? It's not just the enemy we need to guard against. If word of this place gets out, we'll be putting those left behind at great risk.'

The major regarded her with interest. 'A very good point, young lady.' He turned to Marjorie. 'I can see why you brought her along.' He straightened in his chair. 'A circuitous route from the train station in a covered army vehicle will be standard procedure. The recruits won't have a clue where they are. They'll also be restricted to the estate. Once they're here, they'll stay for the duration, apart from when on exercise and to attend church.'

'But it's not just the location, is it?' Lenny said. 'What happens to the ones who don't pass? It's not as if we can send them back to their normal lives with all this classified information rattling around in their heads. One rogue agent could put the entire mission in jeopardy.'

Marjorie leant forward. 'She has a good point, Roger.'

'Indeed, she does.' The major tapped his fingers against the table. 'That's why the initial selection process is critical. Your ability to assess recruits, Marjorie, will be invaluable. The genius of our system is that they'll pass through four different training schools. By the time they get here, we'll have already weeded out the most unsuitable. They won't even know why they're here until we're confident of their potential. That should mitigate some of the risk.'

'And for those who still don't make the cut?' Lenny pressed.

'That's something we'll need to consider very carefully indeed.'

The major exhaled, already calculating. 'We'll have to keep an eye on them, which means more staff than I'd originally planned for.'

'We'll also need to censor their letters home.'

'That goes without saying, dear lady.' The major's lips twitched into a grin. 'As does bugging their bedrooms.'

Lenny raised an eyebrow.

'Not for any hanky-panky, I assure you,' he added with amusement. 'What if one of them talks in their sleep? That's a huge liability, no matter how good they are.'

By the time they'd finished, the teapot was dry, and the table empty. The major pushed back his chair.

'Well? What do you think of the place?'

Marjorie surveyed the room with a discerning eye. 'I think it's perfect. I couldn't have chosen better myself.' She glanced at her watch, the tiny gold timepiece the only feminine item in her otherwise austere attire. 'You know that the air commodore will be in post soon? I'll recommend the manor as being eminently suitable. He's bound to agree. If you could start scouting around for tutors and instructors. No scrimping. We'll need the best. We've promised the prime minister that the first operatives will be trained and ready to drop into occupied territory by May at the latest.'

The major exhaled sharply. 'That doesn't give us much time.'

'The enemy isn't going to wait for us, Roger, and neither is the war.'

It was much later than planned when they finally pulled away – closer to five than the two Lenny had expected. At least she'd thought to phone Finlay. The last thing she wanted was to give Ellen even a smidgen of unnecessary worry.

Marjorie was more willing to speak on the way back than she was on the journey out, but only when the glass panel separating them from the driver was closed over.

'You're in agreement that the manor will do, Miss Gallienne?'

Lenny would have liked her to unbend a little and call her by her first name but that was probably too much to ask.

'Absolutely. It will do very well.'

'In what ways exactly?'

'Well, it's near enough to London for us to keep a weather eye on what they're up to, but far enough away to confound the enemy if they get wind of the location. The woods will be ideal for training. What they'll need is good food and, with the farm nearby and the vegetable patch tended, that's guaranteed. We'll work them into the ground but give them the right tools to achieve success.' Lenny glanced down briefly, removing a wayward thread from her dress. 'There's no point in making it harder than it has to be, but the training will need to be stringent. The major seems to have a handle on that side of things though.'

'The reason I chose him.' Marjorie crossed one leg over the other, arranging the hem of her skirt over her knees, her thick grey tights bagging at the ankles. 'The major was in the Coldstream Guards during the First World War. I won't go into his exploits overseas, but they were as extensive as they were medal winning. A good team player who is bound to train alongside the recruits, despite his age.'

They drove in silence for a few minutes, the countryside stretching out on either side, broken only by the occasional farmhouse. The bright afternoon was already starting to darken, heavy clouds rolling in over the horizon.

'Looks like we're in for some weather.' At Marjorie's words, a strange snapping noise cut through the air, followed by a screech of brakes. The car jolted to a halt.

With a flick of her gloved hand, she slid open the partition. 'What seems to be the problem, Forbes?'

The driver glanced over his shoulder. 'Engine's overheating, ma'am. I'll need to take a look.'

Marjorie let out an impatient sigh. 'That's all we need. I have a meeting later that I can't miss.'

Lenny remained silent, watching the rain sheet down the windows, thick rivulets streaking the glass. Forbes would have little protection, his head buried under the bonnet while they remained warm and dry inside. He appeared to be well past retirement age but, with so many men gone to war, Britain had had to fill their jobs in any way they could. She wondered briefly what his story was, before dismissing the thought as none of her business.

It wasn't long before he reappeared, his navy jacket soaked, water dripping from the brim of his peaked cap.

'Afraid it's not good news, ma'am. Problem with the radiator. I'll need to get her to a garage and phone for a replacement.'

'This is intolerable.' Marjorie heaved an exaggerated sigh, making her displeasure abundantly clear. 'Well, get on with it. We'll wait here.'

Forbes hesitated, shifting on his feet.

Lenny spoke up. 'I think I saw a sign back there for Ripley Village. It can't be far.' She offered him a small smile before glancing at Marjorie. 'As Miss Maxse says, we'll wait here. But if you could arrange for a car...?'

Forbes nodded, tipping his cap before trudging back into the downpour.

'I might as well get on with some work while we wait. I do hope he won't be long.' With that Marjorie propped open her briefcase and was quickly absorbed in its contents.

Lenny leant back, her gaze drifting to the rain-streaked window.

Poor Forbes. His smart, polished shoes and thin jacket will be no match for the relentless downpour.

An hour passed. An hour of Marjorie's constant tutting. If it hadn't been for the torrential rain, Lenny would have felt jealous of Forbes and his mission. At least he had an excuse to escape. Instead, she was trapped in the stifling backseat with the relentless, maddening tutting.

Instead of the car she'd been hoping for, there was a tow truck. A rickety affair that might once have been blue but was now more rust than paint.

Jumping down from the passenger seat was an apologetic Forbes, an old raincoat draped over his shoulders. 'I've arranged for rooms at the nearest inn while we're waiting for a replacement. It could be as soon at ten tonight, if the mechanic can arrange it.' Forbes's tone was as respectful as the mechanic's expression. The sight of the gleaming black Bentley tended to have that effect on people.

'Tomorrow will do,' Miss Maxse replied stiffly, though she managed a begrudging, 'Thank you,' as Forbes helped her up beside the driver in the front cabin.

'I'm sorry, miss. There's only the back unless you want to ride in the car while it's being towed?'

'Mr Forbes, as long as there's a hot bath and a warm drink at the end, for both of us, I really don't care.' She lowered her voice to a whisper. 'If you hadn't arrived when you did, I might have chosen to walk the whole distance.'

His eyes gleaned but all he said was, 'It's just Forbes, Miss Gallienne.'

'If I'm Miss Gallienne, then you're Mr Forbes, Mr Forbes.' She smiled briefly. 'Unless you'd prefer first name terms, but I do believe that Marjorie would have something to say about that.'

SIX

**Saturday 21 September, 1940 – On the road to London
8.50 am**

Lenny got what she wanted. She managed to put through a brief call to Ellen before a hot bath, a very satisfactory supper and eight hours of dreamless sleep, which she put down to the country air instead of London's heavy smog. When she woke it was with a rare sense of peace. Had she known it would be the last for a very long time, she might have savoured the feeling.

The car was ready, and with Miss Maxse impatient to get back to London, breakfast was a slice of toast and a single cup of tea instead of the pot Lenny craved.

The drive into the city was forty minutes of silence, until they stopped in Whitehall. Lenny got to step out after her only to pause, one foot in, the other out of the vehicle, Forbes standing back at a respectful distance.

'No, Forbes will take you home. Thank you, Miss Gallienne. See you on Monday, bright and early.'

'Where to, miss?' Forbes, back in the car, idled the engine, his face half turned towards her. She noted he needed a shave and felt guilty at the thought. None of them were as smart as they had been yesterday, after a night with only the clothes they stood up in.

'Richmond. Peldon Avenue. Near the park.'

'I know where it is, Miss Gallienne,' he said gently, indicating before turning the car into the traffic.

The drive was sedate, luxurious even without Miss Maxse beside her. She was just considering slipping off her shoes when an army vehicle packed with soldiers tore past, overtaking them on their approach to Chiswick Bridge.

'They're in a bit of a hurry.' Lenny spoke her thoughts out loud, noticing the unusual number of people milling around, lingering at corners, standing outside gates in small clusters. An absence of children playing in the streets. No children for that matter. All the elements of a usual Saturday morning either missing or shifted, apart from a lazy grey cat curled up in a patch of sunlight.

The car had slowed to a crawl and Lenny did nothing, said nothing to change that as they turned left onto Clifford Avenue, before taking a right onto Upper Richmond Road. Forbes seemed to know what he was doing and, with the turning for Peldon Avenue up ahead, she was nearly home. She would have smiled at the thought, but her lips couldn't seem to follow the command, her attention on the commotion at the other end of the street.

The turning into Peldon Avenue.

Forbes stopped all pretence of driving. Instead, he pulled to a halt behind the first in a line of police cars and got out. Lenny followed instead of waiting, a cold, hard, leaden weight settling in her stomach. That she knew he'd want her to wait until he found out what was happening was irrelevant.

She was halfway down the road when a shout from behind followed her. 'Miss Gallienne. Wait up.'

Lenny didn't hear him or, if she did, it didn't register. As she reached the end of the road, she saw the house on the corner of Peldon Avenue in her mind's eye. The one with the pretty curtains and the pretty wife, who she nodded hello to every morning like clockwork. She didn't know her name. She hadn't lived on the avenue long enough to know everyone. There'd been a party promised. A welcome to the neighbourhood get-together, which hadn't materialised. Something to plan for in the lull between the end of summer and the countdown to Christmas.

Lenny reached out a hand to the brick wall running parallel, her fingers fanning the stone, her arm braced against the sudden wave of dizziness that caught her unawares, her eyes unable to shift from the gap in her vision.

The space where there should have been a house.

'Miss Gallienne.' Forbes finally caught up, his voice a mere murmur. His hand on her arm. A formal touch until she turned into him, her face as pale as frost on a winter's day, her heart an icy lump to match.

'Tell me.'

He eyed her briefly before taking a step back, his head averted from the corner and the hive of noise and activity ahead. Noise and shouts, amidst the silence and sorrow.

'They suspect it was a parachute bomb around midnight. The air raid siren was only able to give a few minutes warning. Some of the families were saved, the ones sleeping in their Anderson shelters.'

'What about number...?' Lenny cleared her throat and tried again. 'What about number 11?'

'I'm sorry, Miss Gallienne...'

'Oh, for heaven's sake, it's Lenny. And I know you're sorry.' She realised she was shouting and, with a shake of her head, lowered her tone. So soft that he had to bend his head to hear it.

'What about number 11?' she repeated. She searched his face, noting the tension in his jaw, the telltale flicker in his cheek. He didn't want to tell her.

Which could only mean one thing.

Her breath caught. She blinked, then blinked again, her fingernails carving crescents into the brick wall beside her.

The bomb had done its job.

Number 11, along with the rest of the street, was gone.

SEVEN

Mr Forbes's first name was Stanley. Lenny learnt a lot about him that Saturday, in addition to his name. Words like strong and steadfast came to mind, the way he shadowed her footsteps as she rounded the corner. He had no need to stay. His remit had been to drop her off at her home and that's exactly what he'd done.

That her home was now a pile of rubble wasn't his fault or his responsibility.

She also learnt that the man was more than he seemed. Working as a chauffeur was only part time, while his weekends were given up supporting the war effort in any way he could.

Lenny wandered down the road, her eyes on her feet as she stepped around, through and over a conglomeration of brick and stone. The noise was unbearable. A cacophony of shouting and grief-laden screams from people she didn't recognise. Soldiers and police. Neighbours and strangers. The people she'd probably said hello to as she'd passed them in the street. They all looked alike, their clothes and faces coated in grey dust, their expressions as one. Desperate and defeated as they scrabbled around on their hands and knees searching through the wreckage.

Smoke clung to the air, thick and acrid, stinging her throat with every breath as she tried to get her bearings. She knew the layout of the street better than she knew herself so why couldn't she tell where one house ended, and the next began? There were no streetlights, trees or other landmarks to guide. If it wasn't for the fact that she knew Peldon Avenue led off Upper Richmond Road, she'd have thought she was at the wrong address.

A building site, without a building in sight.

She was almost halfway down the road when she stopped and turned, but there was nothing to pin her whereabouts in relation to Finlay and Ellen's home. She closed her eyes as the tears fell. If it wasn't for Stanley's strong arm suddenly gripping her shoulder, she'd have sunk to the ground, without a thought for her knees or her dress, the only item of clothing she now owned.

It doesn't matter. None of it matters.

'Come on now, Miss... er Lenny. This won't help.'

'I suppose not.' She raised her tragic face to his serious one. 'What will? I need to do something. If there's a chance of finding them, even a small one, then I'll take it.'

'We'll see if someone can lend you something.' He cast a glance down the length of her from her tangled hair to her smart dress and smart shoes.

In ten minutes, she was wearing a pair of Wellington boots two sizes too big and an old, ragged coat borrowed from a lady in the next street.

The boots flapped against her heels as she moved, but at least they'd keep the worst of the debris from slicing into her feet.

She pulled the coat around her. Then she began to search, Stanley beside her, his smart coat and cap in the car, his shirtsleeves bunched up to the elbow, his tie in his pocket.

Hour after hour, they sifted through the wreckage. Her hands were raw, her limbs aching, but she kept on going, brushing aside shattered crockery, splintered wood, the broken remains of ordinary life.

A lump rose in her throat. She didn't even know if she was in the right spot. If she was searching through her home or someone else's.

They stopped for a drink. Someone somewhere had a kettle on constantly with tea doled out in a variety of mismatched cups.

'Are you sure about the house, Lenny?'

She brushed her hair back with the edge of her hand. 'I'm not sure of anything anymore,' she said, handing back the empty cup and continuing her search.

She'd stopped to stretch, her hands in the small of her back when she zoomed in on what looked like a couple of twigs sticking out of the rubble.

No, not twigs. A pair of blackened knitting needles as if someone had poked them there.

The wool was charred to a crisp, falling away when she pulled the needles from the debris, but it wasn't the wool she was interested in as she wiped them against her sleeve. These were her knitting needles. French ones someone had bought for her. She'd recognise them anywhere.

Her sense of purpose increased now she knew she was searching in the right area, though she didn't know what to do with the needles. Making holes in someone else's coat was out. Instead, she wiped them clean and poked them through her hair and resumed her search, uncaring of what she looked like.

The corner of a photo frame came next, half-buried in dust and brick.

Her brother's face stared out at her, smiling in the way she best remembered.

She sank to her knees, clutching it to her chest before carefully removing it from the broken frame and sliding it carefully into her pocket, her breath coming in uneven gasps.

'What you got there?' Stanley's voice came from somewhere behind her.

'A photograph of my brother. Means we're in the right place. If they're going to be anywhere, it will be in the shelter.'

The ground beneath her feet shifted, her boots skidding on loose rubble. A large sheet of corrugated iron caught her eye a few feet off to the right. One of the sheets she'd helped Finlay fix together. The Anderson shelter that Ellen had been adamant she wasn't using. She could hear the row as if it was yesterday and not more than three weeks ago.

'Money well spent if it saves our lives, Ellen.'

'A waste more like,' she scoffed. 'No one is ever getting me inside that dark, damp hovel of a space.'

'For God's sake, woman, it's built to keep us safe! That's what it's for!'

'Underneath the stairs was good enough for my parents in the last war, and it's good enough for me now.'

He exhaled sharply. 'Well, if you won't use it, then I'll send you to my brother in Scotland, lass. In fact, I think I'll do it anyway. With the wee bairn to think about, I can't take the risk. Arisaig will be perfect for you both, being as it's by the sea...'

'You will not.'

'I will.'

'That's not why we got married!' Her voice rose to a crescendo. 'To be separated like that, to have you send me away like I'm some burden—'

'To keep you safe!'

'If you do that, I'll divorce you,' she choked.

Silence.

Then, softer this time. Desperate. 'Will you use the shelter, lass? Please, I'm begging you.' His voice faltered, falling away to nothing.

Lenny had placed her pillow over her head, but it was impossible not to hear the conversation batting backwards and forwards through the thin walls that separated their bedrooms.

She was about to find out which of them had won the argument.

'Help me lift it. Careful now. They might be inside.' She didn't add any riders as to what condition they'd be in. She hadn't heard any excited exclamations since lunchtime, when a family of three had been discovered in such a shelter, the roof and sides caved in with the weight of rubble on top of the weight of soil. Battered and bruised but alive.

Then she saw it.

A crooked arm.

Lenny froze, bile rising in her throat as she reached out a hand to brush away soot and soil.

The familiar sleeve of Ellen's nightdress. The shape of her hand. Her wedding band a stark yellow hue against the white of her skin – as white and cold as marble.

'Ellen?' Lenny's voice cracked. 'Ellen, love, it's me...'

Silence.

She closed her eyes, willing herself not to break. She could mourn later. There was still work to do. There was still Finlay and Betty.

No. Not Finlay. She scrunched her eyes closed at the sight of his mangled arm, where he must have been trying to protect his family.

A small mewl caused her to open them. A sound so fragile she almost convinced herself she'd imagined it. A thin, reedy wail, muffled beneath the debris.

Her heart pounded as she scrambled forward, pulling at the rubble with renewed desperation.

'No, wait.'

Stanley didn't ask. He commanded. Another thing she learnt about him that day was that he was a leader among men. He probably hadn't realised it until that moment either, the way his expression immediately changed to one of contrition.

'Help. I need help over here,' he shouted. 'Quickly now. Careful how you go.' He glanced at Lenny briefly. 'A baby?'

'Only weeks old.'

He nodded. 'We think there's a baby down there,' he said to the two men who appeared out of nowhere.

'Right you are, guvnor. We'll go easy. Ted, you go that side, and I'll take this one. Out the way, old man. Let us young 'uns take the strain. On the count of three. One. Two. Three.'

A shift of iron sheeting. A calculated removal of which bricks should come first, and which were safe to be left. A torn blanket. And there, tucked into the hollow of Ellen's arms, and protected by Finlay's body – Betty.

Her face was smudged with soot, her tiny hands clenched into fists, her face wrinkled into a tight prune as she opened her bow of a mouth and yelled for her dinner.

Those eyes. Those beautiful blue eyes the exact same colour as Ellen's. As deep as the bluest of oceans. Lenny could drown in their glistening depths. Instead, she wrapped her in her arms, crooning softly.

'It's alright, my lovely. I will make sure it's alright. I promise.'

EIGHT

Sunday 22 September, 1940 – London 8.45 am

The following morning, Lenny arrived at St Thomas's Hospital in Stanley's black Morris 8. That he'd taken her to his home instead of dropping her off at a hotel as she'd asked was just another act of kindness from someone she now counted as a friend. The offer was there for her to spend a second night, but they both knew she wouldn't take it.

Irrational though it seemed, she couldn't cast off the feeling that she'd brought bad luck to Finlay and Ellen's door. First there were her parents and her aunt. Then James, Ellen and Finlay. She was determined not to risk anyone else close to her. Not that she was close to Stanley or his wife, but they were good people who deserved better. She'd left with an old suitcase packed with essentials, that Mrs Forbes had insisted was heading to the Red Cross for distribution among the needy. Lenny didn't believe her but had no way, or true inclination, to decline the items. For someone whose precious possessions included a pair of knitting needles and a curled photograph, she couldn't argue the provenance of the carefully folded, and in some cases new, items of clothing.

The children's ward was noisy in a way that only children can be. But there were quiet corners where pale-faced children dozed, well-loved stuffed animals tucked beneath fragile arms. Lenny took it all in as she made for the desk and the smartly uniformed nurse with a toddler balanced against her shoulder, a telephone to her ear.

'I suppose we can get another four cots in but it's going to be a squeeze. I'm not sure what matron's going to say.' She replaced the receiver, and looked at Lenny with a small smile, though the deep frown remained.

'Can I help you? It's not visiting time, I'm afraid.'

'Yes, sorry. I came to check on Betty Stewart.' Lenny swallowed hard, then tried again. 'I'm the Stewarts' lodger. I was the Stewarts' lodger.'

'You wait there a sec. Let me just pop this little poppet where he belongs. Derek, you be a good boy now. Nursey has something to attend to, but I'll be as quick as I can.'

His wail started up even before she'd left him. Lenny felt like joining in.

'Poor little mite. Lost both his parents in the first of the raids and old enough to know it,' the nurse said when she returned, pushing a box of tissues in her direction. 'Go on, have a good blow. It will make you feel better. Betty is a sweetie. Slept right through her feed, the little darling. She's having her bath. I'll let you in to see her in a sec.' She leant on the corner of the desk, whipping a small notebook from her pocket. 'Now then, what can you tell me about her? Her date of birth for a start and the full names of her parents. The ambulance driver was a bit sketchy.'

Lenny relayed the information, a bunch of tissues pressed to her eyes, ending with Betty's address. Her former address.

'And anything about her relatives? Sorry, I know this must be difficult for you, but I'd like the little dote settled as far from London as I can. Lodging her with foster parents won't be difficult at her age, but family are always best.'

'I don't know.'

The thought of Betty being taken into care was more than she could bear, a steady tide of tears appearing. She'd look after her herself, but a single woman, with no means other than those she earned, wouldn't be allowed. Ellen had never mentioned any family apart from her mother, who was dead. But Finlay...?

The overheard conversation suddenly came back to her.

'Betty has an uncle. Somewhere in Scotland. On the west coast. Near a beach. Sorry, I can't think of the name. Begins with an A, if that's any help?'

The nurse eyed her from under her thick fringe. 'Look, this is totally against the rules but, as you can hear, Derek is about to tear the place down.' She tapped the phone. 'Dial o for the operator. See what you can come up with.'

Lenny clenched the receiver in her hand, feeling a fool. Trying to find a Scot with the surname Stewart among the many hundreds with that name was going to be a disaster. There was also her current homeless state to think of and the fact she hadn't even seen Betty yet.

If I'm not quick, I'm going to be sleeping on the streets tonight, she reminded herself, hurriedly circling the o.

'Good afternoon, how may I connect your call?'

'I'm trying to reach a Mr Stewart. The only problem is, I don't have the number, or his first name for that matter. I know he's somewhere on the west coast of Scotland. A place beginning with the letter "A".'

'Don't worry, ducks. I've heard worse. The west coast, you say. That's a fair stretch of land. Do you have anything more to go on?'

Lenny could hear the sound of rustling on the other end of the line, as if she was searching through a book or a file. 'I'm afraid not. Oh, and very near a beach.' She didn't know if that was important or not.

'Ah. Narrows it down to about fifty villages. Let me check my map.' Then after a moment. 'Here we go. What about Ardfern or Applecross or Acharacle?'

'No, no, it doesn't sound quite right. Ar... something. Aris?'

'Arisaig, perhaps? Looks to be on the coast, near Mallaig?'

'Probably.' Lenny didn't really know but Arisaig sounded about right. 'Do you have a listing for a Stewart there?'

'One moment, madam.' Then, after a couple of seconds – 'There's an Angus Stewart listed in Arisaig. Could that be him?'

'It might be…'

'I'll connect you now. Hold the line, please.'

Lenny froze, her tongue having run away with her. She glanced up but there was no sign of the nurse. There was no sign of anyone. It looked like she was on her own.

'Stewart speaking.'

His voice boomed out, so clear it almost felt as if he was standing beside her instead of 500 miles away. Was Scotland 500 miles away? She didn't even know that.

'Hello, Mr Stewart. You don't know me and I'm not even sure I've got the right name…' She paused, struggling for breath. 'Do you know… are you by chance related to a Finlay and Ellen Stewart in London?'

There was a sudden pause among the crackles. Then his voice, a much softer version with a remnant of Finlay's accent tucked between the elongated vowels. Softer and uncertain. 'Can I ask who you are, miss?'

'Leonora Gallienne. Lenny really. I've been lodging with Finlay and Ellen in Peldon Avenue.' She managed to hold back a sniff, using her hand under her nose instead of a tissue. 'You are Finlay's brother?'

'Aye, that's right. Miss Gallienne. I'm guessing Finlay isn't able to come to the phone?'

Lenny stared at where the nurse was walking back to her, Derek in her arms, a big cheeky grin on his face at getting his own way.

A lifeline when she needed it most.

'I'll just hand you over to the nurse.'

She covered the mouthpiece with her hand. 'Mr Stewart, Betty's uncle. Her father's brother,' she elaborated, in case it wasn't clear. 'I haven't explained about his brother and sister-in-law yet…'

'That's fine. leave it to me.' She took the receiver, nodding towards a room on the right. 'Betty's in the nursery. Having her feed. I've told the nurse to expect you. Mask in the jar outside the door, a clean apron on the hook beside.'

Betty was as beautiful as the first time she'd seen her, and far happier than the last, cradled in Ellen's cold as ice arms. Lenny tried to shake the horrifying image from her mind as she hugged her tight, placing a gentle kiss on the top of her head, unwilling to let her go.

She'd have stayed all day if the clock above the door had decided to stop its relentless ticking. It was Sunday. A day of rest unless you were Miss Maxse and wedded to your job. She knew she'd find her in the office. Lenny was still in need of somewhere to stay tonight. Hopefully Miss Maxse could help with that. There was Mary from the WI Knitting Group to inform too, she remembered. Ellen would have wanted her to know. She'd also be able to provide her with some wool. She'd have plenty of time to make Betty a few things.

'I'll be back later, dear. Be good for the nurses.'

It took two days for Finlay's brother to travel from the west coast of Scotland, and two days for Lenny to strengthen her resolve.

After work she sat in the ward feeling weary, her knitting on her lap as Betty slept in the cot beside her. The noise from the other children barely registered. It was amazing how a few hours among them had inured her to their cries and wails.

At least she'd found somewhere to stay. Miss Maxse had turned out to be the perfect boss. When she'd heard about Finlay, she'd pulled every string available to secure one of the prized service apartments in Orchard Court. They were used to house visiting politicians up from the country but, as one of the War Office's key employees, as she'd called her, it was hers for however long she needed it. That Marjorie had managed to persuade

Dalton to agree was astounding, but he was still in shock at the loss of his right-hand man.

The whole department had been horrified about what had happened to one of their own and had allowed Lenny the time she needed to visit Betty, and to move into her new home. The second part didn't take up as much time as the first, or it wouldn't have if it hadn't been for Ellen and Finlay's cat, Gary. He'd been waiting for her yesterday evening, or that's what it had seemed when she'd instinctively made her way back to Peldon Avenue like a homing pigeon in search of what she'd lost.

Everything.

But the Stewarts' cat had lost everything too, she reminded herself as she smuggled him into her apartment block right under the nose of the snooty concierge. Animals weren't allowed in Orchard Court, but she was prepared to take the risk.

After he'd been fed and watered, she'd stared at the four magnolia painted walls with their dentist waiting room feel before finally moving to the bed, dragging the blankets over her. But sleep wouldn't come. She'd tossed and turned, hearing every creak of the old building, the distant rumble of a passing lorry, the sharp bark of a dog, the uneven footsteps of someone walking home late. All the sounds amplified as if they were occurring in the room with her instead of in Portman Square below. She'd finally fallen asleep as the sky started to bleach at the edges, Gary tucked into the space behind her knees. By morning, her eyes were bleary, her limbs leaden, and the thought of food turned her stomach.

She was hungry now, but it was a deep, hollow ache, the kind no amount of food could fill.

With a sigh, she picked up her knitting, only to place it on the counter at the sound of Betty's grizzle. That the matinee jacket wouldn't knit itself was irrelevant when compared to a hug from Betty.

'Hello. Miss Gallienne? I'm Angus Stewart.'

She looked up into the calm face of Finlay's brother. An older, more serious version of Finlay. Late twenties as opposed to his brother's mid.

'Call me Lenny,' she managed. 'And this is Betty. Betty, this is your Uncle Angus. Would you like to hold her?'

'Er... no.' He cleared his throat, offering a wry smile. 'I'm not that good with children. No practice, I'm afraid.'

'There's no time like the present.' She stood, inclining her head towards the chair, her expression leaving no room for argument.

He hesitated briefly before lowering himself onto the seat.

'Just bend your elbow. Yes, like that. That's the ticket. She's nearly asleep again, poor little love, which will make it easier on you.'

Lenny reclined against the counter, her knitting pushed to one side as fatigue caught up with her. The nurses would have coped with introducing Angus to his niece. They were far better at this sort of thing, but they were also busy with the influx of children since the Blitz. The ward couldn't move for cots and beds. *And Betty is taking up one of them,* she remembered. A precious resource when there was nothing wrong with her apart from needing someone to love her.

She was just thinking of leaving him to it when he lifted his head. 'What about getting a bite to eat? There are things we need to discuss, and it might as well be over supper.'

They decided on a Lyon's teashop, which was both nearby and affordable. It had been Lenny's idea, prompted by the state of her bank balance and the sight of Angus's frayed cuffs and battered trilby. She didn't know what he did for a living. It wasn't the sort of question she felt she could ask. There were far more pressing ones like who would be available to care for his niece, while he was doing whatever he did to earn a crust.

'Ah, that's better.' He settled her in her chair before removing his jacket and scarf, his hat already taking up space on the coatrack by the door. 'I can't remember the last time I've been in one of these establishments. Probably when I was in London and that's over ten years ago.' He caught her startled expression, her gaze on his collar. His dog collar, which he fingered briefly. 'You didn't know I'm a man of the cloth?'

She shook her head, suddenly struck dumb, remembering the way she'd insisted on calling him Angus. What must he have thought. 'I only knew that Finlay had a brother somewhere in Scotland, reverend. The operator did the rest.'

'It's Angus, please. You're not one of my parishioners.' He stopped briefly, as the waitress approached. 'Tea do, and what about eggs on toast?'

'They'll only be powdered,' she warned under her breath, watching him grimace.

'Soup then?'

'Soup would be good, thank you.'

'Now, where was I?' He placed his elbows on the table, only to remove them to his lap with a laugh. 'Sorry, I'm not fit to be seen in company. Living alone has ruined my manners.' He offered a sheepish smile, brushing non-existent crumbs from the table.

'Nonsense. It's something I do on occasion. Nothing more comfortable than sitting with your elbows on the table,' she said, one of her questions answered, another one taking its place.

How was he going to manage running a parish while looking after a newborn?

They picked up their soup spoons and started on their meal, the conversation limited to pleasantries until their bowls were empty. With tea poured, the conversation started in earnest.

'So,' he said, wrapping his hands around his cup. 'You were lodging with my brother and sister-in-law?'

She nodded. 'That's right. When I got the job at the War Office, Finlay was kind enough to offer me somewhere to live.'

He studied her with a raised eyebrow but all he said was, 'You're not from London? I can't quite place your accent.'

'Guernsey. It's one of the—'

'Channel Islands. I know.' He smiled briefly. 'And occupied currently. I'm sorry.'

'There's no need to be. It won't be forever.'

'I hope not. I'd have joined up, you know. I wanted to but Finlay and I...' He shoved his foot out briefly. 'Flat feet. What a thing to stop one from fighting for one's country. You were there that night, I believe?'

The swift change in the conversation from feet to the Blitz had her fingers tense around her cup. 'I was away on business. Got back early the following morning to find...' She stopped, inhaled then exhaled. 'To find that the avenue had been destroyed.'

He swallowed hard, his Adam's apple bobbing in his neck before settling. 'I'm sorry. And you found them?'

She nodded again, pressing her lips together before speaking. 'The shelter took the brunt but... it wasn't enough.' She glanced at him, expecting to see a crack in his expression, something that matched the tightness in her throat, the ache in her chest. But his face was composed, except for a slight firming along his jaw. Angus was clearly a man who'd learnt to keep his emotions well hidden. Probably came with the job.

'And Betty?' His voice was quieter now.

'Under a piece of iron, protected by Ellen, who in her part was protected by your brother.' She concentrated on the tablecloth and the small mark where she'd dropped some of her soup. Instead, all she saw was Finlay, who'd positioned himself over Ellen and Betty so that he took the force of the explosion. The image would stay with her forever.

He settled his cup back in its saucer, his elbows back on the table, not that he appeared to notice, the small action offering a brief respite. 'Thank you. I'm indebted to you for everything you've done, but I'll take it from here. I have a housekeeper back at Arisaig, who is quite excited about the thought of adding a young lady to our small household.' He stared across at her. 'Arisaig is a beautiful part of the world, lass. If you're ever in need of somewhere to stay, or even if you only want to check up on Betty. Well, what I mean to say is that, after what you've done, you'll be treated like family in my home.' He straightened slightly, his elbows back by his side. 'And in the meantime I need an emergency course in baby management, including how to hold her properly.'

Lenny nodded slightly, mostly to herself.

Finlay's brother would do. That was all she could ask.

She blinked. No, there was one more thing, one more loose end she needed to tie off.

'What are your thoughts on the subject of animals, Angus? Specifically, cats?'

NINE

Wednesday 25 September, 1940 – London 9 am

'I'm not quite sure I understand, Miss Gallienne?'

'I'd like to be part of the prime minister's army, Miss Maxse.' Lenny stood squarely in front of her boss, her hands loose by her sides, her gaze direct. She'd practised her speech long enough to have both her words and her manner off pat. 'I'm fluent in French, can get by in German and have no family left to worry about, either in Guernsey or Britain. I might as well allow the War Office to make use of my language skills.'

'I don't think Mr Churchill quite meant you when he set up the Special Operations Executive though.'

Miss Maxse leant back in her chair, her glance considered but not unkind. She'd been given a job to do by the prime minister and she was carrying it out without deviation until the new air commodore arrived to take up the harness. It was up to Lenny to bring her round to her way of thinking.

'I know that you have more reason than most to hate the Germans, but it would be ridiculous to use hatred as a benchmark to identify suitable candidates.' Miss Maxse managed a brief laugh. 'If that were the case everyone would want to join, including me.

The hard truth is that good people like yourself are more useful this side of the fence. Don't ever underestimate the importance of what you're doing, Miss Gallienne. It's the little people like you and me, the cogs if you like, that are keeping the country turning while our men in navy, green and grey are on the front line.'

Lenny was annoyed, not that it showed, thanks to that hour of practising her facial expressions in the bathroom mirror earlier. Miss Maxse was being disingenuous as far as she was concerned. It wasn't that she didn't want Lenny to go. People like Lenny were two a penny in war-torn London. Hardworking women who were trying to do their bit for the war effort. No, it was the fact that she was a woman. In all the meetings so far about choosing candidates, not once had the possibility of a female agent been mentioned. She was going to change that or resign in trying. That she'd promised herself she'd hand in her notice if she was refused was a huge decision and one she hadn't taken lightly.

'The fact is men are in short supply, Miss Maxse, and it's as easy to train up a woman as a spy if she's determined enough. Oh, I know that some women wouldn't be suitable but I'm not one of them. While I might look small, I'm wiry and was always good at sports at school. I also have a brain in my head and a fluency in colloquial French that you'll find hard to beat. Did you know that French was my first language?' she added, conversationally, in French. 'I only learnt to speak English when I went to school,' she ended, switching languages quicker than most people took to blink.

'That's as may be, Miss Gallienne, but I can't think for a moment that the air commodore will agree no matter how proficient you think you are.'

'There's nothing to say that women are going to be less proficient in these roles. In fact, it's women who are going to be able to go under the radar, Miss Maxse. Remember, France is as full of women as Britain is. The men are either off fighting or prisoners of war, or dead. It's the women who are planting crops, ploughing the fields, and caring for their children while their menfolk are at the frontline. Think about a woman like me mingling among the other women, walking beside them in the street, standing behind them in the queue for the butcher, the baker, the greengrocer. A nondescript sort of woman. The kind of women ignored as little more than a wife or a daughter. There are many ways to fight a war, Miss Maxse. Women need to be given the chance to do our bit too.'

'I really don't think…'

Lenny locked eyes with Marjorie. 'All I'm asking is for the chance to prove myself. I'm happy to stay and train up Gloria for my position until the manor is ready for the first lot of recruits. Then it will be up to the major to decide whether I'm suitable. If I'm not, I'll return to take up my post.'

Lenny could hardly believe that a month had passed since that meeting, but the calendar didn't lie and neither did Major de Wesselow, she thought, as he started to speak.

'Welcome to Wanborough Manor, gentlemen, and, er, Nora.' The Major nodded at Lenny, a distinct twinkle lurking in the back of his eye at her pseudonym.

They'd all been issued false identities when they'd arrived at headquarters earlier that morning. Little square folded pieces of paper with the name they were to use for the duration of the course, another layer of security that Lenny hadn't thought of. She'd grimaced as she'd handed back the paper, any romantic notions of the likes of Mata Hari ground to a fine powder. Nora Swann was only a name and one relatively easy for her to remember. It was a derivative of Leonora after all. That she was the only woman among the twelve recruits hadn't gone unnoticed.

'You have four weeks here, under my guidance as well as that of Harold Dennison, my conducting officer.'

Lenny managed to hide a grimace. She'd recognised the man from the train straight away. Harry. James's friend from hockey. He'd smiled as he'd shaken each of the men's hands, before sending a curt nod in her direction.

She'd felt aggrieved until she'd remembered the lost telephone number, which caused her face to flush. Lenny had regretted losing the slip of paper at the time, in the same way she'd regretted ignoring him on the train journey, but she was a different person now. And there was a war on. She decided to ignore him too. A little childish but there were far more important things like getting to know the other recruits, she thought, tuning back into the major's speech.

'At the end of the four weeks, we'll draft a report on your suitability for the next part of your training. For now, you have what's left of the morning to unpack and get to know the manor. Security is tight. You will not be allowed to leave the premises except for church and exercises, and all mail will be censored. Use of the telephone is also forbidden. However, I guarantee good food and a well-stocked bar.' A loud cheer rang out. 'Luncheon will be served at thirteen hundred hours in the mess, where only French will be spoken. After lunch, your training will begin in earnest. Until then.'

Lenny wandered across the room, noting the way the conversation faltered as she neared, the men shifting back as if an invisible line had been crossed. There hadn't been the opportunity to chat on the way down, only a quick swapping of names and all under the careful eye of Harry Dennison.

They were a mixed collection of sizes, shapes, ages and levels of friendliness. She'd already segregated them into two groups. The men who were prepared to accept her and those who thought it a complete waste of time and resources having a woman on the team. She knew she'd have to work twice as hard to be taken seriously.

She smiled briefly. It would be a delicious challenge to prove the sceptics wrong.

'You're a sight for sore eyes, luv.' The tall, lanky Welshman paused before announcing his new name, his brain, as well as his tongue struggling to get used to it. 'I know we've already been introduced but I'm Bill, pleased to meet you.'

'Nora, and likewise.'

'Enchantée, mademoiselle. I'm Georges.' It was the turn of a wiry Frenchman to bend over her hand, landing a kiss in the centre, causing her to laugh.

'Well, I can see you're not going to have any trouble with the lingo, Georges,' she replied, rolling out her French accent for the first time since meeting them.

'I wouldn't have thought they'd have let women in,' Johnny said, folding his arms across his broad chest, his expression not difficult to read. She'd already pegged the short, stocky Londoner as someone to keep an eye on. She raised her shield to his hostility even as her smile brightened.

Rule One. Don't let them in on your thoughts, unless you're sure you can trust them. I'm here to stay until such a time as they ask me to leave.

'Oh, I don't know. Who'd suspect a woman? Certainly not me.' Bill laughed. 'Which is probably why I'm not married and not likely to be. Confusing species, the lot of you.'

'Well, if you'd like any lessons in that regard, Bill.' Lenny grinned, starting to relax for the first time since arriving at the manor. Banter she could manage. 'An instruction manual on all our key points perhaps?'

'I'm not sure I'd be clever enough to follow it.' Bill slapped her gently on the back. 'I for one think you're a huge asset. If any of this lot give you a hard time, just holler.'

'I can't for a minute believe that they will but thank you. That's very much appreciated.'

Instead of lingering, she retreated to her room and unpacked. It wasn't an act of cowardice, more one of self-preservation. The men could get to know each other without the presence of a woman curbing their conversation. There was nothing they could speak about that would be of interest to her. Best leave them to it and join them when the bell rang for lunch.

Unpacking didn't take long. She hung up her few clothes and placed James's photo on the chest, along with her knitting. A blue cardigan for Betty.

She dropped on the edge of the bed, her head sinking into her hands at the sight of the wool. Ocean blue to match Betty's eyes. A sudden image of sweet Betty filled her mind, everything the tiny baby had lost tightening the strings of her heart. Angus had written, inviting her to make Arisaig her home while the Blitz raged over London. She should have gone instead of trying to be something she was not. A soldier.

The first lesson was straight after lunch, with barely time for her coffee to settle. They were taken into a large room with panoramic views over the gardens, but it was the contraptions set out on the long central table that drew her attention. That and the army type standing with his hands behind his back, his face an impassive mask as he watched them paraded in.

'Welcome to your first lesson on Morse code. By the end of your time here, we expect you to have memorised the alphabet, and be able to transmit and receive messages with both speed and accuracy.' The major's gaze swept over the recruits, his tone clipped. 'For some, this will come easily. For others, it will feel like learning to speak a foreign language from scratch. I cannot emphasise enough the importance of mastering this skill. Some of you will be sent into enemy territory as radio operators, which comes with its own set of unique rules. Out in the field, your life and the lives of those around you may depend on it. A single mistake could mean the difference between survival and capture.' He tapped the small metal key on the desk beside him, a sharp beep echoing in the room. 'This is your new voice. Learn it well.'

By the end of the session, Lenny was positive that she'd flunk the final test. The rumour was that they had to be able to transmit twelve words a minute, a herculean task for someone who was taking that length to get a couple of vowels out. Some of the men seemed to pick it up with ease, tapping out hesitant but recognisable letters, while she puzzled over every dot and dash, second-guessing herself before she even pressed the key.

She stole a glance at the others, catching the smirk on Johnny's face as he rapped out what looked like a perfect sequence. Bill gave her a wink and a thumbs-up when she finally managed to send a simple 'E'.

Next came map reading. In Guernsey, an island nine miles by five where everyone knew everyone else, maps barely existed. Longitudes and latitudes were a new concept to Lenny, and the vast stretches of unfamiliar land laid out on the map before her in intricate lines and symbols might as well have been written in more code. This time a silent one.

She frowned at the sheet, tracing the contours and tiny markings with her finger. 'It's not as if I've ever needed one before,' she muttered under her breath.

'Well, you'll need one now, Miss Swann,' the major said, leaning over her left shoulder and making her jump. He tapped a point on the map. 'If you can't read this, you're as good as lost behind enemy lines.'

She swallowed, gripping her pencil a little tighter. Lost behind enemy lines. The phrase sent a shiver down her spine.

Beside her, Bill gave an encouraging nudge. 'Don't worry, Nora. It's just like learning a new language. You'll get there.'

She hoped he was right.

It was going to be a long four weeks.

TEN

After supper, they congregated in the bar, the men bending over themselves to ply her with drinks until they realised that she wouldn't budge on the subject. Instead, all she'd accept was a glass of lemonade before retreating into the corner with her book on coding and her knitting.

Mostly, they'd been good-natured about it, teasing her a little before turning back to their conversation. Apart from Johnny, who was the loudest of the lot, his voice carrying across the room. He made a show of clinking glasses, toasting everyone from the king to the major, his laughter a little too loud when he glanced in her direction.

'What's wrong, Nora? Too good to have a drink with us?' he called, his grin not quite reaching his eyes.

She didn't look up from her book, calmly slipping another stitch onto her needle. 'Not at all. Just prefer to keep my wits about me.'

A few of the others chuckled, while Bill murmured, 'Give it a rest, Johnny.'

But he wasn't quite done. 'Come on, we're all in this together, aren't we? Can't be much fun sat in the corner like an old maid.'

This time she did meet his gaze, her expression steady. 'I'm exactly where I want to be but thank you for your concern.' She could have added, *I'm how I want to be too*, but that was perhaps a step too far. That she had no interest in the opposite sex was her business. They'd only think her anti-men, which wasn't the case. She'd adored both her father and her brother, the very best of men. The truth was, she'd never met anyone who could equal them, in either her mind or her heart. Until she did, she was happy with her knitting and her solitary ways.

There was a beat of silence before Bill ordered another round, steering the conversation away. She exhaled slowly, focusing on the page of code in front of her. She had more important things to worry about than proving herself over a pint.

It was in that short span of silence that Harry peeled off from the group, in favour of her table.

'May I join you?'

'Of course.'

Lenny shifted her ball of wool to make room for his glass.

He took a sip from his beer before placing it down, careful to avoid her wool. 'What are you knitting?'

'Just socks for the troops.' He didn't need to know about the cardigan for Betty. She closed her book and settled it beside her, not wanting to appear rude but unsure of why he'd decided to single her out.

'You women. Always busy.'

'And what of it?' she replied, taking umbrage at his tone. 'I enjoy knitting.'

She also enjoyed her own company, but it would be rude to tell him. Harry was the enemy as far as she was concerned. The man responsible for writing up their final reports. The man who could easily stop her from completing her training.

Her hand clenched briefly. There was one thing she could say. One thing that might crack his calm long enough to reveal what he was really thinking.

'Did you hear about my brother?'

He paused mid sip, shooting her a quick glance before focusing on something in the distance. 'Missing in action. Presumed dead. Yes. I'm sorry. A good man. Has there been any word?'

'Not since the initial telegram, no.'

'I'm sorry,' he repeated gently. 'That must be hard on you and your family.'

What family!

She knit to the end of the needle and started on the next, using the time to gather her thoughts into some semblance of order.

'It is what it is. Keeping busy helps.'

'Hence the knitting and the book. I get it.'

No, you don't, and you never will.

The book on coding was essential if she was going to pass the ruddy exam. In her opinion four years wouldn't be long enough, let alone the four weeks assigned.

After a few minutes of awkward silence, he picked up his glass and drained it. 'Fancy another?'

Lenny stared at her empty glass in disbelief. How had that happened?

'No, not for me. How long do you reckon before they turn in for the night?' She broke off her wool and started to cast on the sock's pair.

She was suddenly bored of the conversation, bored of him. It was all a joke. A game. Johnny and him singling her out. Why? She could guess why. Because she was a woman, although she'd thought better of Harry. The one thing they didn't realise was that she was stronger than the lot of them put together. Having nothing to lose was key. No family. No friends. And now no homeland to run back to. She had nothing but this. She wasn't about to lose it because of some misguided belief that women should stay at home knitting!

She blinked rapidly, the navy wool wavering in front of her, his next words saving her from making a complete fool of herself.

An angry woman was one thing. Angry tears something else entirely.

'As long as it takes. Being able to handle their booze is part of the assessment.' He turned to her, his eyebrow raised. 'You're not drinking, Miss Swann?'

She swallowed carefully before replying. 'I don't, Mr Dennison, and, as it won't be part of my cover, if I'm successful, that's the way it's going to stay.'

'How do you figure that one out?'

She settled back in her chair, her knitting forgotten, her hands resting lightly on top. 'When was the last time you saw an unaccompanied female in a bar, or a restaurant for that matter? And France is no different to here in that regard. A woman alone with a drink in her hand is going to attract the wrong sort of attention. Hardly ideal if one is meant to be slipping by unnoticed.'

Harry studied her for a moment, a flicker of something like appreciation crossing his face. 'Fair enough. Though I imagine there'll be times when blending in means playing along?'

She smiled briefly. 'Then I'll hold the glass and let someone else do the drinking. I'd rather not dull my senses when my life, or indeed someone else's, might depend on my sobriety.'

'Smart thinking, that,' Bill said, joining the conversation. 'I'll wager she's got more sense than the lot of us put together, lads.'

Johnny, who had been nursing his pint, scoffed. 'Or just a convenient excuse.'

Lenny met his gaze levelly. 'You believe what you like, Johnny. It's no matter to me.'

The conversation drifted after that, the men turning back to their drinks and their talk of training exercises. Lenny picked up her knitting again, but she could feel Harry watching her with an odd expression on his face, one she couldn't place. She dropped a stitch but carried on without picking it up. No one would know except her, and she'd sort it out later.

Georges wandered over, nodding at Harry before taking the seat opposite and flicking through her book. He only started speaking when Harry had drifted back to the bar.

'Not bothering you, was he?' he said under his breath.

'No, of course not.'

'Well, if he does, just jab him with one of those needles of yours. That should do the trick.'

Lenny laughed properly at that, the tension easing just a little. 'I'll keep that in mind.' She paused a second. 'If you must know, he was a friend of my brother's. Lost him in Dunkirk.' She managed to meet his sympathetic gaze without faltering.

'I'm sorry,' he said finally. 'Dunkirk was...' He exhaled, his accent more pronounced than ever. 'Hell.'

'You were there?' she said, her fingers tightening around her knitting.

'Yes. Rescued by a tug.' He was going to say more but stopped himself. Lenny lifted her head to find the reason why. Harry was watching them. They'd been warned about oversharing their past. How much had he heard, and what did he intend to do about it?

'So, what are you knitting?'

She laughed in relief, holding up the finished sock. 'What do you think?'

'It's a sock.'

'Correct. Although not just any sock.' She passed it over. 'See if there's anything you can spot?'

He eyed her briefly before bending his head and running his finger over the bumps in the stitching.

'No, sorry. You've got me there.'

'Knitting is made up of two stitches, Georges, just like Morse code but knit and purl instead of dots and dashes,' she said, taking the sock back and running her finger over the raised loops between the smooth stitches. 'I thought I'd work on my coding.' She lowered her voice. 'But don't tell anyone.'

'So, what does it say?' he whispered out of the side of his mouth.

She glanced down at the hidden message, her fingers grazing over the stitches like a blind man reading braille.

'Don't ask me to translate any Morse word for word, I'm not that good yet but I've worked out a plea for news of my brother,' she replied shortly, balling up the sock.

'Very clever.'

It wasn't just a plea, she remembered as she started picking up the dropped stitch. It had taken her all through supper to work out the wording, while the men were trying to outdo each other with the most outlandish tales. As if she'd be interested in who'd downed the most pints in one sitting, or their dating exploits. She couldn't help feeling that Johnny had deliberately hijacked their ambling discussion with the express intention of making her feel uncomfortable, as well as excluded. The laugh was on him. She'd switched off to their banter, instead translating a simple message into code that included all the letters of the alphabet in the style of a child's Victorian sampler.

A Morse sampler that she could convert using simple knit and purl stitches instead of dots and dashes.

James Zachary Gallienne, missing during Operation Dynamo. Updates appreciated by the War Office.

ELEVEN

Friday 29 November, 1940 8.30 am

Lenny knocked on the door, her gaze drawn to the pile of suitcases waiting to be taken to the two vehicles outside. There was no sign of the other recruits. She wasn't quite sure where they were, but tried to not let it bother her. She'd find out soon enough. She straightened her spine, her hands hanging loosely by her side. Her hair was restrained by a mountain of clips in an effort to make it lie flat, instead of springing into a mophead of unruly curls. She'd only been partly successful.

Her hair, along with her nerves, were on their own trajectory as she waited to hear whether she'd passed or failed the course. The early cup of tea had done nothing to assuage her dry mouth or calm her racing heart. Her newly acquired gloss of indifference was only that. A superficial patina.

On the surface, she looked the same in her smart blouse and grey skirt, but underneath everything had changed. After a month at the manor, she had changed. Her body felt different, her skirt loose at the waist, her arms and legs toned, the morning run impacting on muscles she hadn't even been aware of. Their training schedule had made a mockery of the netball and hockey she'd played at school. She felt good and she knew she looked it, but it wasn't the physical demands that had changed her the most. It was the mental acrobatics. Learning about codes, ciphers and maps. Learning to think three steps ahead, to anticipate, to mislead. And, on occasion, to lie.

The one thing the training hadn't provided was any clue as to whether they were going to pass her or make her an example.

Harry had returned to avoiding her after that first evening, while Johnny persisted in his boorish behaviour, but only when they weren't observed. Smirking at her failings and dismissing any proficiency she displayed as either luck or unimportant. If she'd been at the War Office she'd have made a complaint. Here, she had no such luxury. Instead, she swallowed her frustration, kept her head down and resolved that if Johnny was waiting for her to crack, he'd be waiting a very long time.

In the beginning, she'd doubted that she'd ever learn to code or to map read. Her thoughts now were very different.

What would she do if she failed?

'Come in, Miss Swann.'

She lifted her chin before pushing the door open, her eyes connecting with an impassive Harry and a warm, welcoming smile from the major, which meant exactly nothing. The major was a gentleman and always welcoming. The jury was still out on Harry.

'Do take a seat and you can breathe, you know.' The major laughed at his little joke, his attention on her hands before flicking back to her face. 'I see you've neglected to bring your knitting. I think this must be the first time I've seen you without your needles poking out of your bag.'

She managed a smile, unsure if the major's banter was because he was about to fail her or if it could be taken in a more positive light. Her knitting had become something of a joke between the men. Bill had teasingly suggested she make them all balaclavas, while Johnny, ever the thorn in her side, had muttered something about it being the only useful skill she had, the implication being that she'd learnt nothing. If it hadn't been for Harry's constant presence, she'd have been tempted to stab him with one of her needles on the way past. That her knitting had shot her to the top of the coding class was a secret she'd only shared with Georges.

'All packed up and ready for the next part of my journey,' she finally said, hoping that he wouldn't leave her waiting any longer than necessary. All of the recruits had to leave for the station as near to nine as possible, or risk missing their connecting train. To where was still unknown. Orders were given on a need-to-know basis, and apparently, she didn't need to know, yet.

'Harrumph.' He leant forward, sliding a single piece of paper in her direction. 'This is a copy of the report we'll be sending up to Whitehall. I don't mind telling you that we had our reservations, especially with you being a girl so to speak but, well done. Very well done indeed.'

Lenny could barely believe his words, but his smile was genuine enough. She'd passed!

The relief swelled up like a balloon ready to pop, even if her expression remained unchanged.

'Thank you, sir. That's very kind.'

'Kindness doesn't come into it, girl,' he barked. 'Your skill in coding is off the scale remarkable. All I ask is that you keep up the good work. Major Young up at Arisaig is no pushover so don't let me down.'

Lenny blushed as she studied the document, the colour racing up her neck and flooding her cheeks at a speed she couldn't control.

Agent Nora Swann has demonstrated exceptional emotional resilience, maintaining composure in high-pressure situations and displaying a deter-mined attitude despite initial hostility from some of her peers. Her physical fitness has improved significantly over the course of train-ing, showing endurance and agility beyond expec-tations. She adapts swiftly to new challenges,

grasping technical skills such as Morse code and
navigation with commendable speed, and adjusting
seamlessly to unpredictable conditions. While
she works well independently, she has also inte-
grated effectively into the unit, proving
herself a valuable team player by earning the
respect of supportive colleagues, and refusing
to be undermined by dissenting voices.

Given this progress, she has secured her place
in the next phase of training, where further
assessment will determine her suitability for
field operations.

Lenny's pleasure only lasted long enough to be shown to the
car and the three men waiting for her. Bill and Georges wore
welcoming smiles. Johnny's greeting was slightly different, if not
unexpected.

'I don't believe it! Four out of twelve and they only go and keep
bloody Knitty Nora.'

'That will be enough, Johnny, and do hop in, Nora. I don't
want to miss our connection, or we'll never get to Scotland.'

Harry held the door open for her before climbing into the
driver's side, his mood as impossible to read as ever. Lenny
clamped down on a reply to either of them, her teeth making deep
indents into the tender flesh of her lip.

Think about what's important, she told herself, pulling out her
knitting needles and starting on a new pair of socks. *You'll be
seeing Betty shortly and after, think about your future, a future
without either Johnny or Harry.*

Georges leant forward between the gap in the seats. 'I think I
should teach you how to knit the continental way, Nora. That is if
you intend to use it to code when you're away.'

'You use code in your knitting?' Harry darted her a look, before
turning his attention to the tractor that had just pulled out in front

of him, causing him to brake sharply. 'Why haven't you told us before? Is it something we could teach the others?'

'Not blooming likely,' Johnny snorted. 'You're not getting me to take up knitting. That's women's work.'

'You'll do what you're told or leave the team, Johnny. This is about winning the war and not the petty squabbles between the pair of you. I had a mind to fail you both. I still might if you don't sort out your differences. Understood?'

Lenny had never heard him speak like that until now. She waited, her mouth slightly open to see how Johnny would reply.

'In more ways than one, guvnor.'

What?

As a reply it might well have been in a foreign tongue for all the sense it made. She frowned down at her work, annoyed at Georges for letting the cat out of the bag, but far more annoyed at both Johnny and Harry's behaviour. It was her choice to knit or not to knit and as for teaching the others... No!

'Thank you, Johnny.' That Harry was taking his reply at face value was galling.

If she lived to a hundred, she'd never understand the opposite sex. Probably the reason they were called the 'opposite' sex. They certainly couldn't be more dissimilar to women if they tried.

'Well... Nora?' Harry always left a short gap before saying her name, but as the only one who knew her before the war, she couldn't blame him. She wished now she'd taken more notice of James's friends in those days, but it was too late for regrets. She'd racked her brains and still couldn't place him among the ten other players on her brother's team. A melting pot of athletic young men, with muddy knees and flushed faces, was all she could visualise.

Now she had to come up with a reply.

'Knitting is made up of two stitches, Mr Dennison, which means it lends itself brilliantly to disguising messages in the pattern. Gobbledegook to most but not to a knitter.' Her voice softened, as she turned to Georges, the difference in her tone enough to cause Harry's brow to beetle together into a frown. 'That would be fabulous. I didn't even know there was a difference.'

He shrugged. 'Nor do I really, but you hold your wool differently to my mère and grandmère. I'll show you when we stop, but only if you promise to knit me something.'

She laughed, delighted at the thought of working on something other than socks and baby clothes for a change. 'Of course. What would you like? A guernsey like mine?'

'A French fisherman's jumper, in red. Something I will be able to wear with pride when I'm back in my homeland.'

'If you tell me what it's like, I'll make it with pleasure.'

'I think you've made a rod for your own back,' Harry whispered out of the corner of his mouth, as he finally overtook the tractor.

'Pardon?'

'I'd like one too. Just like Georges so I'll be able to wear it in France, but in blue.'

TWELVE

Saturday 30 November, 1940 – Fort William 10 pm

'I'd like a word, Miss Swann.'

Lenny grimaced, but stayed where she was, watching as Bill, Georges and Johnny headed into the bar for a nightcap. She was Miss Swann again too when she'd been Nora earlier, she remembered, trying to work out what she'd done to change that. It wouldn't have been much.

They'd arrived at the Station Hotel only a short time before and been immediately directed into the dimly lit dining room for an indifferent meal of some sort of pie and overcooked vegetables. All she wanted now was her bed, but it seemed as if Harry had other ideas.

'I'm tired. I thought you'd want to join the others in the bar?'

'You thought wrong.' He pushed away from the table and, scrunching up his napkin, dropped it on his side plate. 'And I won't keep you long. Promise. There's a small sitting room next door. Best leave the waitress to clear up.'

'Of course.' She reached down for her bag and followed him out the room, offering a small smile of thanks to the elderly woman piling up dishes onto a wooden tray.

She wasn't in a position to object. The thought of her next report from him was already preying on her mind. She'd only passed one course. Three more to go.

The room was warm with a fire in the grate, and piles of newspapers scattered around the coffee tables. She chose a chair near to the fireplace, stifling a yawn but not hard enough.

'I know I'm a hard task master, but this is important.' Instead of taking the upholstered chair opposite, he pulled a wooden one from the small card table in the window and carried it over, arranging it so that he was sitting at an angle.

'Right, with the others gone, I now have space to hear myself think.' He smiled then, a genuine smile that crinkled up his eyes, causing her to respond with one of her own. She had no idea what he was up to, but she liked this version of Harry far better than any of the previous ones.

'You'll probably think me mad, but I want you to show me how to knit.' He raised an eyebrow, his voice lowered to a whisper. 'Particularly the coding part.'

If Lenny had any illusions about this change in him, they collapsed in a heap at his words.

'Now? It's a little late for knitting lessons, isn't it? What's the urgency?'

'That's something I'm not prepared to say. Come on, Miss Swann. You have me where you want me for once, bearing in mind that it won't last. Tomorrow I'll be back to my usual overbearing self.'

'I really can't wait, Mr Dennison.' Lenny dragged her knitting out of her bag, her eyes gritty from tiredness. 'Have you ever done any knitting before?'

'Nope. I'm a complete novice.'

'Great!' She rested her needles on her lap, her hands set on top, her expression frank. 'The thing is, I've been knitting for years. Ever since I can remember so, while I might make it look easy, some people find it difficult.'

'I perfectly understand.' He smiled again. 'But I'm happy to prove you otherwise.'

'On your head be it.' She started to speak, her needle primed with a fresh strand of wool, her voice matter-of-fact as she slowed down her hands to snail pace instead of hare quick. 'This is how you cast on. A series of loops over the left-hand needle formed by the right. Each loop, or knot if you like, is the foundation for a stitch.' She cast on ten stitches before turning her work, taking a moment to show him the loops. 'As I said in the car, knitting is only made up of two stitches, knit and purl, determined by whether you place the right needle in either the front or the back of the stitch on the left. For the purpose of coding, a dash is a knit stitch while a dot is a purl one.' She shrugged. 'It could, of course, be the other way around, but it's my code so my choice.' She offered him the needles and sat back, her eyes gleaming. 'Your turn.'

'You make it sound so simple,' he grumbled, struggling to hold the needles.

'It is, when you've been doing it as long as I have. Remember, men like Georges, whose mother and grandmother knit, will be easy to teach while men like—'

'Johnny will be impossible.'

'Exactly.' She watched as he fumbled his way along the ten stitches, dropping more than he managed to pick up, before placing his work on the table with a sigh. 'You win this round.'

'Does this mean you owe me a favour, Mr Dennison?'

He sighed again. 'If you like.'

Lenny unravelled the knitting and returned her needles to her bag. 'Oh, good. I'll have to think of something.'

'I can't wait.' He stood, waiting for her to join him. 'I've suddenly changed my mind about that nightcap after all, Nora. Join me?'

'Not tonight but thank you. Don't get too disheartened, Mr Dennison. You can always have another go tomorrow.'

'I seem to have started something I may not be able to finish.'

'Not to worry. Anything worth having is worth working for.'

'As demonstrated by you on the course. Thank you, Nora. Sleep well.'

Lenny made her way up the stairs. She was almost at the top when some instinct made her turn back, only to find him watching her, a strange expression on his face.

THIRTEEN

Sunday 1 December, 1940 – Arisaig 4 pm

Lenny lay back on the bed, her head relaxing into the pillows, her limbs unwinding after the bumpy last leg of their journey between Fort William and Arisaig. And Betty, she remembered, the sweetest of smiles forming even as she pushed the image to the back of her mind. Arisaig House was akin to living in prison with no one allowed either in or out, except under strict supervision. The only spark of hope came with the thought that Angus was the minister, and attending church was written into their programme.

She closed her eyes in bliss. Instead of unpacking, she'd decided on using the time to unwind. Harry had warned them on the way over that their training would go up a notch in intensity. The more rest she could get the better. It was already dark outside, the sun having set on their way up to the house. No reason to inspect her surroundings until the morning, when she'd probably be taken on a route march first thing.

The knock on her door was a surprise. As the only woman in the group, she'd made it a rule to be friendly, but not too friendly with the men. They knew that she liked her own company and, up to now, none of them had sought to change that.

She sat on the edge of the bed, fumbling for her shoes, wondering who it could be. Probably the housekeeper.

It wasn't the housekeeper.

'Mr Dennison.'

'Yes.' He glanced behind her, towards the bed and the indent on the pillow. 'Sorry for interrupting your rest, but I'd like you to accompany me. Please.'

The please was an afterthought, the order clear, not that Lenny was having any of it. She was tired to the bone and spending time with the most frustrating of men wasn't her idea of fun.

She folded her arms, propping up against the door. 'Why?'

'Because it's important.'

'Not to me, unless you can explain why, Mr Dennison.'

He stared down at her, his mouth compressed. 'I need to buy some... supplies and your input is essential to that.'

Lenny was starting to enjoy herself. 'What kind of supplies do you think you'll be able to buy on a Sunday, Mr Dennison? The shops will be closed.'

'Knitting supplies, alright?' He ground the words out between gritted teeth. 'And I phoned ahead to make sure the shop would be open. Don't play awkward, Miss Swann. Major Young is a stickler for recruits not being allowed off the premises when training begins.' He glanced down at his watch. 'Which means we have fifty minutes.'

'I'll grab my coat and hat.'

A wool shop when she'd been managing on wool leftovers and handouts ever since arriving in Weymouth. Lenny planted a serene smile on her face for the five-minute journey, her eyes alight with anticipation, her purse tucked in her pocket.

The shop was set in the middle of a short run of buildings, a butcher on one side, a grocer on the other. Angus had written to her about the beauty of the place. The glorious beaches and stunning scenery, but he'd never breathed a word about the cornucopia of wool to be found in the small, general store. From four-ply, double knit to chunky and in all the colours imaginable.

'What exactly are you looking for, Mr Dennison?' she asked, forcing her gaze from a delightful double knit in a delicate shade of mauve, which would be perfect for Betty.

'Everything we'll need for you to teach what you know to the three men. No, make that five. Six, including you,' he amended, trying not to look embarrassed and failing miserably.

'So, six sets of needles,' she mused. 'Double knit is probably the best, and in different shades so that we can assign different colours to each of them. It will make it easier for me to see how they're getting on.' She went to the counter, only to say over her shoulder, 'I take it you don't mind if I stock up on a few skeins while I'm here.'

'Buy what you like. The War Office will pay,' he added, pulling out his wallet. 'It's the very least we can do.'

'You might regret having said that, Harry.' She sent him a sweet smile before turning her back.

'Don't worry about it, Nora. You're going to have to earn it.'

She picked him up on those words as soon as they were back in the car, two large bags of wool supplies in the boot.

'I can't help feeling you have plans for that wool, which sits outside teaching the men a few stitches,' she said, placing her bag on her lap.

'You could say that.' He crunched the gears as he pulled out of the parking place, one eye on his watch. 'This evening after supper, I'd like you to knit a couple of samples. One in code and the other without.' He sent her a brief smile, as they approached the long drive leading up to Arisaig House. 'Nothing fancy. A square in each will do.'

'What's the hurry?' Lenny was desperate to start on the mauve wool. Just the feel of the soft strands had her heart beating in her eagerness to cast on for the rib. Instead, she'd be knitting boring squares.

'Because I'm heading back to London tomorrow, and I want to take them with me.'

Lenny glanced at him sharply. 'You never said.'

'I don't have to say anything, Miss Swann. You're safe enough with the men.'

Yes, but she'd got used to his quiet presence and his watchful gaze.

FOURTEEN

Tuesday 3 December 1940 – Arisaig House 7.55 am

Lenny raced down the stairs to breakfast, her wet hair tied back in a ponytail. They'd been woken at six and taken on an hour long warm-up jog along the beach before being allowed to cool off in the sea.

Slowing her pace as she walked into the mess, she spotted an unexpected addition at the table. Sir Frank Nelson, Miss Maxse's boss, was chatting with Harry and Major Young as if they were old friends.

That Harry was back and so soon was a shock. That he'd brought company a far greater one.

She slipped into the chair beside Georges, her voice soft.

'Morning. What's the big chief doing here?'

'No idea,' he whispered back, taking his time in heaping marmalade onto his toast. 'But by the way he's staring at this end of the table, I'll bet it has something to do with you.'

Lenny's hand hovered over the toast rack briefly before returning to her lap, her heart skipping a beat. 'Why not you?'

'Because they weren't looking at me until you came in and, as much as I adore you, chérie...' He eyed her uniform and scraped back hair. 'You'll have to admit there's nothing much to see in that get up.' He pushed the dish towards her. 'Marmalade?'

'I think I might have lost my appetite.'

'Eat up, there's a good girl. We have a busy day in front of us.'

'Morning, Miss Swann. Good of you to join us.'

Lenny smiled briefly, taking the seat offered in the small sitting room off the mess, her bag placed neatly by her feet. She settled her hands across her lap, splitting her gaze between Sir Frank and Harry, wondering what could have made the current head of the Senior Operations Executive trek up to Scotland.

'You're probably wondering at the intrigue. Nothing terrible, I can assure you.'

Sir Frank sat back in the wing-backed chair, one leg crossed over the other, seemingly perfectly at ease with the situation. He was an austere, serious-faced man in his late fifties with black hair combed back from a high forehead. Not someone to travel hundreds of miles without due cause. It was this thought more than any other that had her stiffening her shoulders at what was to come.

'Harry has been telling me some interesting things in relation to you and your ability to code.'

She darted Harry a quick look, which he appeared to ignore, his attention on a small notebook in front of him, pen in hand. Of the many things she'd been expecting, from court martial to dismissal, knitting hadn't featured.

All this for a couple of squares, one in code. Ridiculous.

'It's nothing special, sir. Just something to help me to learn Morse.'

'I beg to disagree.' Harry placed his pen down with a sharp tap. 'For such a simple idea, it's ingenious. It opens up many possibilities, Sir Frank, and not just for our field operatives, but for our POWs and their families too. Think about being a prisoner of war stuck in a camp in the back end of nowhere, where everyone is the enemy. You might be desperate to hear from loved ones, or even news about what's happening in the war, but all letters are censored. Then you receive a scarf, or a pair of socks knitted in code.' He spread his hands. 'Not only could it include news about the war, but what about details of their current location? The best escape routes? How to contact members of the resistance afterwards. The location of safe houses. Train schedules and walking routes.' He tapped his notebook briefly. 'I've thought more about it since I met with you in London, Sir Frank, and I truly believe that knitting is the perfect way to impart information while fooling the enemy into the bargain. At some point they're going to cotton on but until then...'

'I must agree with Harry, Miss Swann. You're really on the back foot here if you honestly don't see how useful this will be.'

Lenny pressed back in her chair, completely at a loss as to how to respond. While she could see the advantage in everything Harry said, how would it work in practice? Who would do the knitting? Who would teach them? What about obtaining the wool and the needles, with rationing? Not everyone had a well-stocked store like Arisaig. All important considerations that she didn't feel able to voice in front of the man who was ultimately her boss. But she had to say something.

'But knitting, sir. Really? Most of the men view it as women's work. Won't they object?'

'We're talking about saving lives here, Miss Swann, not crafting. The men will do as I tell them or suffer the consequences.' Sir Frank leant forward, his eyes intense. 'This has gone right to the top. Mr Churchill is of the opinion that your little idea has a real chance of making a huge difference to the war effort. You should be proud of your achievements, not putting barriers in the way.'

'I'm not. I mean I'll do anything I can,' she said helplessly. And she would. It was just the shock that it included knitting.

'Very good.' He smiled briefly. 'I believe you have all the equipment in place to start instruction right away.'

Lenny's eyes widened. 'You mean now?'

'Yes, right now. Lead the way, Harry.'

There was no sign of Major Young in the training room, which wasn't really a surprise. Lenny had known from the outset that he hadn't agreed with her being on the team. Whether that was because she was a woman or because he'd taken a personal dislike to her was irrelevant. His attitude made her more prepared than ever to pass the course.

Six pairs of needles, all size eight, and six balls of wool in assorted colours lay in the centre with Georges, Bill and Johnny eyeing them in the same way they would an unexploded bomb.

She would have laughed but it was far from funny. Teaching someone who wanted to learn to knit was difficult enough. That Sir Frank had decided to join in meant that she was terrified.

Harry was also there, but she wasn't so worried about him.

He still owes me that favour.

She took a deep breath, her eyes trained on Georges and Bill.

'I've been asked to teach you to knit, but not only that. To knit in code. Any questions before I start?'

Not surprisingly they all stayed quiet, although she noted how Johnny could barely look at her, his mouth a thin line of disapproval.

'Good. Knitting is made up of two stitches. A knit stitch, which appears smooth on the front of the garment, and a purl, which makes a little wave. If you examine your jumpers, gentlemen, you'll see that the front is smooth.' She waited a second, watching as they all glanced down at their jumpers briefly, all except Sir Frank who was dressed in an immaculate three-piece suit.

'Right. First we have to cast on. These first stitches, or loops if you like, are the foundation for your knitting. Tension is important. Too tight and you won't be able to knit into them; too loose and the garment will lack definition.' She demonstrated briefly, using a set of needles from the table and a ball of white wool. 'Now, I'd like you to do the same. Cast on ten stitches.'

She wandered around the table, adjusting the position of a needle here and there. She took the needles off Johnny and, bending in front of him, cast on again before watching as he tried to follow, his posture stiff with resentment. 'It just needs a bit more practice.'

Sir Frank's needles lay in front of him, his wool one big knot. Lenny withheld a laugh. 'Would you like me to cast on for you, sir?'

'It seems as if you'll have to. My nanny despaired of me ever tying my shoelaces, let alone teaching me handicrafts.'

'You'll soon get the hang of it.'

After what seemed like an age, and a lot of effort, all of the men had cast on.

'Well done. Next comes the knit stitch.' She demonstrated slowly, taking her time in placing her right-hand needle into the front of the first loop on the left one. Within minutes, she was turning her work and demonstrating the purl stitch. 'Remember that this is only your first lesson.'

'But you make it seem so easy,' Bill moaned, waiting for her to sort out his dropped stitch.

'As will you if you practise, Bill.'

'That's exactly right.' Sir Frank had long given up on his, his wool rewound on the ball, his needles poking through the centre. 'I've suggested to the major that you bring your knitting into the bar each evening. That way Miss Swann will be there to assist you. In the meantime, I'd like you to show the men what you can achieve when you really put your mind to it, Miss Swann.'

'What would you like, Sir Frank?' she replied, her practice square on her lap, her hands resting on top.

'Oh, I don't know. Whatever you think fits the situation.'

Lenny thought a second before looping the wool over her fingers, in the French style Georges had taught her, her knitting needles flashing backwards and forwards. Within a couple of minutes, she cast off the end and set the piece in the middle of the table, the pattern clear to see.

'As it's a demonstration, I've added a new word every two lines but, in reality, if you were making a scarf or something, I'd suggest a little loop over the needle to demarcate the end of a word and the start of another.'

Harry picked up the piece of knitting, his fingers running over the wool. 'If I call it out, Georges, how about you jot it down and we'll see what we've got.' He dug out his notebook and pen from his pocket. 'You can use my diary. Ready?'

'As I'll ever be.' Georges glanced across at Lenny, throwing her a little wink. 'So, it's a knit stitch for a dot, and a purl one for a dash, right?'

'You got it. Why not make it easier, Mr Dennison. K for a knit stitch and P for a purl one. That way it aligns better to dot dash.'

'Good idea. Right, here goes. The first word is:

'KK PPK PKPK K

'The second KKKK KP PK PPK KKK.

'The third. KP KPK K

'The next P KKKK K

'The fifth PPK K KKP KK PKPK KPKKK

'And finally KPP PPP KPK PKP KKK KKKK PPP KPPK.'

Harry sat back, the knitting sample pushed away from him. 'You didn't make that easy, did you?'

'It's not meant to be, Mr Dennison,' she replied, her expression calm even if her eyes were twinkling with hidden laughter. They all turned to where Georges was labouring over his dot dash translation, before leaning back in his chair with a laugh.

'You little minx.'

Harry glanced between them in confusion. 'Why, what does it say?'

'Idle hands are the devil's workshop... sir.'

FIFTEEN

Saturday 7 December, 1940 – Arisaig House 7.55 am

'Time to get up, Swann. You've got five minutes before we start without you. Full kit.' The message was accompanied by a fist thump on the door before the sound of the major's boots faded into the distance.

Lenny didn't dawdle. Jumping out of bed, she ignored the sink, instead starting the laborious process of getting dressed in full kit. Major Young, a kilted officer of the Black Watch, was very different to congenial Major de Wesselow at the Manor, even if their remit was broadly the same. When she'd met him last week, his lip curl said everything about what he thought of having a woman on the team, especially one that had brought about his men trailing knitting wool around the place.

It was up to her to prove him wrong.

Heavy woollen trousers, thick enough to keep out the biting Scottish wind came first. She'd raised an eyebrow when she'd first found the trousers on the bottom of her bed. As a woman brought up to wear skirts and dresses, trousers had taken a lot of getting used to. However, as the men hadn't batted an eyelid when she'd first appeared in them, she'd decided to quash her embarrassment. Practicality had to come before modesty. A coarse army-issue shirt, layered beneath a scratchy jumper that smelled faintly of lanolin came next, followed by a pair of her softest hand-knitted socks under her boots. They were the same leather boots she'd been issued in Surrey, but they still rubbed at her heels despite her best efforts to soften them. The outfit was topped off by a thick canvas greatcoat, designed for endurance rather than comfort.

Lenny flexed her fingers, already stiff inside the coarse gloves, before reaching for the final piece, a heavy rucksack, its straps digging in. Inside was everything she might need if she was lost in the mountains, except for the one essential.

A guide!

She tucked her special lace handkerchief inside her shirt at the last minute.

The major was tapping the side of his leg, when she arrived with ten seconds to spare, annoyance marring his handsome features. Annoyed that she'd made it, or annoyed for another reason?

Impossible to tell.

The sky was as black as ink, the ground crunching underfoot with a thick layer of frost. There was no breakfast. Nothing to help shake off the shadow of sleep. She was still working on tightening her boot laces when he ploughed ahead at a steady jog, not caring whether she followed or not.

They skirted the grounds and made for the village at a steady pace. The few shops were still shuttered, no one about apart from an orange cat lingering by the bins. It dragged her back to Peldon Avenue on the evening before she'd had to leave for Wanborough Manor, Betty asleep on her lap, and Gary, disgruntled at having his place stolen, lying lengthways between her legs. One of the last times she'd felt truly happy.

The sudden rush of emotion caused her steps to falter. That it could be Gary was a thought she tucked at the back of her mind as she picked up pace to make up for lost ground. Even if it was, it would be unlikely that, after two months, he'd still remember her. Betty certainly wouldn't.

The coastal road was long and flat, her breath coming out in short gasps, the noise punctuated by the sound of the tide rushing up the shore. There was no light, save for the dull sheen cast by the moon rippling across the water. No other sound apart from the pounding of her feet. If it hadn't been for the fear of failure attacking her from all sides, she'd have been perfectly at peace in a part of the country she was learning to love.

She hated London.

The suffocating stink of coal smoke and damp, the thick smog that clung to buildings and people alike, turning everything a dull, lifeless grey. The constant press of jostling bodies. The hurried, impersonal glances. And the noise. Shrill voices calling out, the wail of sirens cutting through the air like a knife. The thundering underground.

Surrey had soothed her with its wide green spaces and tall stately trees, but it had been a means to an end. A stepping stone to the next training school.

Scotland was very different. She'd only been here a couple of days to appreciate the pull of the land and the sea, the hills and the mountains. The vast spaces and crashing shores. She'd never considered living anywhere apart from Guernsey, but she could live here.

It might be an idea to stay instead of continuing with her plan. She glanced up to find the road ahead empty. There was every chance she'd fail the fitness part of it, even if she'd tricked herself into excelling in other aspects. They'd told her earlier that she didn't have to keep up, that the men were going to be the quicker runners. It was a race to the finish. A chance to prove yourself. The implication was clear: as a woman, she was never expected to succeed.

She stopped dead, fumbling to remove her gloves before pulling out her map and her compass. The course had been carefully marked. The village and the sea. She could do this. It wasn't difficult. She needed to make for Loch nan Uamh followed by the open boggy moorland of Glen Mama. With a resigned sigh, she carefully replaced the map and set a pace more suitable to her ability. If she didn't win the race, and there was no hope of that, at least she wasn't lost.

It took five hours for her to revise that decision, an hour of which had been spent wandering through a muddy bog sometimes up to her thighs. She'd thought she was in the right place. Glen Mama, with the railway viaduct in the background, a dense thicket up ahead. But there was no path, no sign that anyone had been that way... ever.

She carried on, but her feet were dragging, the fabric of her trousers clinging to her legs. Her boots were a soggy mess where water had seeped through her trousers and invaded her socks, the friction acting on her heels like sandpaper. She knew she was getting blisters, but there was nothing she could do about it. The constant battle with her stupid, uncontrollable hair coming adrift under her cap, meant her cheeks were streaked with mud. To compound matters, it had started to rain. Not the gentle showers she was used to. Thick drops as large as pebbles, and as hard, pummelling her from a great height.

If there'd been a cliff, she'd have been quite happy to throw herself from it.

However, the one thing there wasn't was tears. She was saving them up for when things became desperate. That they were already desperate hadn't quite managed to filter through her cold, numbed brain.

'Stop messing about, Swann, or I'll quite happily leave you behind to rejoin the others in the bar.'

The sound from the trees up ahead was like a voice from heaven, even if the words had been uttered by Harry, the one man she couldn't quite figure out.

Bill and Georges were darlings, steady and good-humoured, while the major was simply doing his job, nothing more, nothing less. Johnny, on the other hand, was a brute, but an easy-to-read one. The kind of man who wore his nastiness like a badge. Men like him were predictable, and predictability made them manageable.

Stay away where possible, and when it wasn't, never be alone with him.

Simple rules she'd learnt in the schoolyard and carried into adulthood.

If a man couldn't be trusted to treat you well in public, he certainly wouldn't in private.

'Yes, sir. Coming, sir,' she shouted, in a loud enough voice to cut through the biting wind and lashing rain. If she'd thought herself fit when she'd arrived last week, she'd been wrong. A twenty-mile trek, with only her compass and a folded-up square of map to guide her, had reduced her confidence to a damp puddle. The only markers left were the lakes and the hills. The snowy mountains and crystal-clear waters. But, with no discernible land-marks, they were impossible to navigate. She'd lost sight of the others hours ago and, with the sun starting to collapse into the landscape, she was starting to doubt she'd escape alive.

'God, you're soaking. What have you been doing? Swimming in it. You'll be lucky not to catch pneumonia.' Harry looked down at her, with the grimmest of expressions, which made her feel smaller, if that was possible. Small and useless.

'Here, take a swig of this.' He passed her a flask, which she pushed back.

'I told you I don't drink and certainly not spirits.'

'You're taking a swig or I'm leaving you here, understand? I knew you'd cause me problems...' There was a pause, just a beat, another unreadable expression flashing across his face. 'The first time I saw you,' he added, his voice strangely quiet, as he unscrewed the lid of the small silver flask and held it to her lips. 'Now drink.'

The liquid burned the moment it touched her tongue, a fiery heat that shot down her throat and exploded in her chest. She coughed, spluttering as she fought for breath, her eyes streaming. 'Bloody hell, what is that?' she gasped, wiping at her mouth with the back of her hand.

'Dutch courage.' He recapped the flask and tucked it back in his pocket. 'Now stop fussing and get moving. Only five miles left. If we're much later, we'll miss supper, and we can't have that.'

The five miles felt like five years, the blisters on her feet ballooning to raw, throbbing welts. Every step was agony, her boots feeling more like instruments of torture than essential kit. By the time Arisaig House came into view, Harry was looking increasingly concerned, his steps slowing to match hers, his usual gruffness tempered by something close to admiration. Her rucksack dangled between his fingers as if it contained feathers instead of the tent, and the other emergency kit they'd been forced to lug around.

Without a word, he stopped and lifted the rucksack back onto her shoulders. 'Count that as your favour repaid in full. You're on your own from here.'

Lenny whispered his name through dry lips. 'Harry.'

She watched him pause, glancing at her from over his shoulder. 'What?'

'You seem to have forgotten that it's up to me to choose how I collect the favour, not you.'

He didn't bother to reply, instead he strode ahead, his tall frame quickly swallowed up by the darkness.

She limped into the hall, exhaustion dragging at every muscle. Her rucksack slipped from her shoulders, landing with a dull thud just inside the door as she made for the nearest chair, sinking onto it with a sigh. She barely had time to catch her breath before Johnny appeared from the bar, a pint in one hand, a smirk firmly in place.

'What time do you call this?' he drawled, turning to the others. 'About to send out a search party, weren't we, lads?' A few chuckles followed, but no one joined in with much enthusiasm.

'You alright?' Georges' voice cut through the noise. He stepped forward, ignoring Johnny as he reached down and picked up her bag. 'I'll leave this outside your door for you,' he said, his tone softer than usual.

She nodded, too tired to do more than whisper, 'Thank you.'

'No, you don't.' The major stepped out from the shadows. 'Part of the rule is a soldier *always* looks after their kit,' he said with a sneer. 'Supper is at seven sharp, which is in exactly ten minutes. If you're not changed and down here by then you can forget carrying on with your training.' He turned back to the bar only to stop, his back to her. 'You haven't seen Dennison have you, by any chance? He seems to have gone missing.'

'Not missing. Right here, sir.'

Harry bounded down the stairs, dressed in his civvies, his hair still wet from his bath. 'Sorry, I'm late. I had a few phone calls to make. Now, who'd like a beer?' He shepherded the small group back into the bar, leaving Lenny time to limp up the stairs, the heavy weight of her rucksack dragging behind her.

By the time she reached her room, she was already tearing out of her clothes, dropping them in a tangled heap on the floor. Her boots and trousers came last. She had to withhold a scream as she peeled off her socks and the newly formed scabs, the wool leaving little tuffs of fibre behind. There was no time to clean the wounds. The pain alone told her they were bad.

She yanked a dress over her head, her face still streaked with mud. A scarf tamed her wild hair followed by a quick drag of a flannel over her skin. No time for lipstick or powder. When she spotted her shoes and stockings, she stared in horror before grabbing her slippers and easing them on – even that was torture.

The gong sounded as she was negotiating the top of the stairs, her hands clawing at the banister for support. She limped into the dining room just as the last echo faded.

Georges was already waiting behind her chair, ready to settle her in place. 'You've missed a bit. A streak behind your left ear,' he whispered.

'Thank you.' As she turned to the rest of the table, the sudden silence told her that she'd been the main topic of conversation moments before. 'What an amazing place, gentlemen. Such stunning scenery.' She picked up her bread roll and started to butter it. 'I've been meaning to ask how you're getting on with the knitting homework I set? I'll be in the bar after, if anyone wants extra help.' She bit into the roll, to the sound of collective groans around the table.

SIXTEEN

Sunday 8 December, 1940 – Arisaig House 7.45 am

Daybreak was a good hour away. The moon was still flaunting its pearly face when Lenny finally surfaced.

She stretched beneath the covers and slowly opened her eyes, disoriented for a moment. Then she remembered: being lost, the blisters, the pain. The boots drying next to the fireplace.

She'd slept well, better than she had in weeks. Better than she had since the bombing, which made no sense. Yes, she'd been over-tired after hiking miles, but the threat of being discharged from the team should have had her up all night. She stared at the ceiling, wondering why she wasn't worrying about what the major was going to do about her. He certainly wasn't the kind of man to let it go.

And there was Harry.

The man made no sense, his actions even less. He'd gone back to ignoring her since that knitting lesson in Fort William, only speaking when he had to. What had prompted him to come to her rescue? She'd worried at first that he was going to tell the others. Use it as a reason to get her kicked off the team.

But he hadn't.

Lenny didn't know what to think. It had been far easier when she was certain she needed to be wary of him, to prepare for his clipped remarks and cold silences. Far easier to keep her distance when she knew which side of the fence he sat on.

Obligation. There, the word was out in the open. The one thing she didn't want was to feel obligated to anyone.

If only she could work out the reason for his actions. If only she could spend five minutes in his mind, just long enough to understand what was going on.

Thought every woman everywhere, she reflected dryly, manoeuvring from lying to sitting. *The opportunity to understand a man's silences, the short ones as well as the long.*

After gathering her towel and clothes, she slipped into the corridor and the bathroom next door, early enough to be first.

Stepping into the bath proved impossible, the pain of hot water on raw skin enough for her to nearly cry out. Instead, she sat at the edge, legs dangling in the rapidly cooling water while brushing out the knots in her hair.

Infection was a real risk with the embedded wool fibres and ingrained mud.

After, she slapped on a couple of dressings and found, to her relief, that she could slip her feet back into her shoes without too much difficulty. If it felt like glass scraping at the backs of her heels, she ignored it.

There were plenty worse off than she was.

Sorting out her heels was only the first of the challenges she faced that morning. The second was waiting for her when she finally managed to hobble into the dining room.

A package on her chair.

For once the dining room was quiet. No quips from Johnny, who seemed suddenly engrossed in decapitating the top off his boiled egg with surgeon-like precision. Bill and Georges offered small smiles of support while the major stared at her as she settled in her chair as if she'd crawled out from under the nearest stone. She stumbled a little at his expression. What had she either done or not done to warrant it? He couldn't still be annoyed with her for yesterday, could he? She'd made the dining room in time for supper, alright with less than a second to spare but that shouldn't have made any difference, and she didn't think Harry had ratted on her.

Looking around, there was no sign of him. As conducting officer, his role was more of an organisational one and seemed to involve lots of paperwork. He rarely showed at breakfast unless he intended to take part in their exercises, and it was Sunday.

'Morning, sleep well?' Georges broke into the silence, sliding the toast rack in her direction.

'Thank you. Like a log. And you?' she replied automatically, ignoring the toast rack in favour of the parcel, which was now on her lap. A parcel forwarded on by the War Office, the original Whitehall address scored through with a couple of black lines.

She turned the package over, noting that the seal had already been broken. That someone had written to her was one thing but that the words might have been examined...

Lenny closed her eyes against the sudden pain. They'd been told on their first day that mail would be both censured and sporadic, arriving from London a couple of times a week. She hadn't bothered with the news then. With Guernsey closed off there was no one left to write to her, apart from Betty's uncle, and she'd told him not to. Now the thought that someone had been rummaging through her stuff felt like the worst kind of betrayal.

Her fingers hovered over the parcel, a slight tremor rippling across the back of her hand. The official stamp was enough. She'd been waiting for further news about James. Now it was here...

First came the scarf, knitted in thick green rib. The scarf she'd made for him, wrapping it around his neck moments before he'd left on the steamship to England.

She fingered the wool briefly before securing it around her throat and opening the letter.

Dear Miss Gallienne,

It is with the deepest regret that I must now inform you that Naval Volunteer Reserve James Gallienne has been declared deceased, following his disappearance in action on 1ˢᵗ June of last year.

Despite exhaustive efforts and repeated inquiries, no further information has come to light regarding his whereabouts. In the absence of new evidence, and in accordance with military protocol, his status has been formally changed.

We recognise the anguish this prolonged uncertainty must have caused, and we extend our heartfelt sympathies to you and your family. James served with courage, dedication, and honour, and he is remembered with great respect by all who knew him.

Enclosed with this letter is one of James's personal belongings: a scarf recovered from the scene and sent via the International Committee of the Red Cross, in line with the Geneva Convention.

Please accept our most sincere condolences.

Yours faithfully,

Captain W. Williams
War Office

The paper trembled in her hands, the words blurring into a grey blob of letters as tears clogged her eyes. A sudden rush of blood caused her heart to thump, her vision narrowing to a pinprick as darkness flooded from all sides, her head a mass of misfiring neurones and disconnected thoughts. The sheet of paper fluttered onto the table from loose fingers as her body dissolved and slid sideways out of the chair, her bones liquid, her brain mush. By the time she hit the floor, she'd lost control of her world and everything in it.

When she came to, she was stretched out on the sofa in the bar, a damp cloth pressed to her brow, her body moulding into the plush fabric. Someone had gone to the trouble of placing a pillow under her head and removing her shoes. A small kindness that, on any other day, might have had her reaching for her hankie. But she was done with tears.

The knowledge that she'd blown any chance of staying on the course after yesterday's performance, and compounded by today's was a punch in the gut, but one she'd recover from. She'd pick herself up and get to France another way. The WRVS was always looking for new recruits, she remembered. It wouldn't be difficult. James was dead and, if she was entirely honest, it was something she'd known since the first telegram. She'd just struggled to accept it. Confirmation of his death wasn't the end of her war. His death, along with that of Ellen and Finlay, would only be the beginning.

It took her a moment to slide back to full consciousness, which she used to take stock. A dull, persistent pounding pressed against her forehead. She must have hit her head when she went down. A headache she could cope with. If anything, it was a welcome distraction from the pain in her heels.

'Ridiculous situation, Harry.'

'More like tragic.'

The sound of voices alerted her to the fact that she had company.

Harry and the major.

She kept her breathing steady, forcing herself to remain still. She hadn't been called bat ears at school without good reason.

'We cannot have someone collapsing in a fit of the vapours at any given opportunity. We'd be a laughing stock among our own lot, and that's not even thinking about the Germans.'

Harry's reply was respectful enough, but only just.

'You don't seem to understand the situation, if you don't mind me saying, sir.' A pause. Then a rustle of paper. 'You must be aware about her brother being missing in action since Operation Dynamo?'

'Her letter?' the major scoffed. 'I don't see how confirmation of his demise makes a difference. Sending someone like her to France is as good as signing her death warrant, and that of anyone accompanying her. Look at yesterday. And don't tell me you didn't go back for her. I have eyes in the back of my head as well as the front. Nothing happens here that I don't know about.'

She heard Harry exhale sharply. 'I agree her fitness isn't that of the men. It never will be, will it? But that's not what we need her for. You have to admit, she's unparalleled when it comes to signalling. Her idea about using knitting to record messages instead of paper and pen when the enemy are looming is inspired.' He heaved a sigh loud enough for her to hear the other side of the room. 'As far as I'm concerned Swann has proved herself to be an important member of the team. So what if I chivvied her along at the viaduct. Did you get a look at her feet when I removed her shoes just now? A bloody mess. I doubt I'd have got half as far with blisters that size. All I'm asking is that we give her until the end of the course. If we continue with a failure rate this high, there'll be no point in carrying on with the operation, and that would be a disaster.'

'Which is as may be, but don't you think it's far preferable to lose men by attrition than at the end of a bayonet or a pistol.' The major let out a laboured sigh. 'I suppose I'll have to give her one more chance, although I do abhor how she's turning my carefully designed programme into little more than a knitting circle. But this will absolutely be her last, Dennison. And no helping her. This will be your last chance too.'

Lenny jerked her head off the pillow.

'Sorry about that, sir. I don't know what came over me. It won't happen again.'

She ignored Harry. It was better that way. Yes, he'd helped her yesterday, but that was yesterday. She couldn't expect him to keep bailing her out and, as the major had made perfectly clear, in France, she'd have to do her own bailing.

'Be sure that you don't, Miss Swann.'

The major stormed out, leaving the door wide open. She was grateful for that.

She didn't spare Harry a glance. Instead she focused on slipping on her shoes, trying to hide her grimace as the raw blisters screamed in protest.

After, she walked back to the dining room, her gaze direct, her teeth gritted against the double assault of pain. Her heels and her heart.

James was dead, as were Ellen and Finlay. It was time for her to pick up the reins of her brother's war and make it her own, but first there was church and the promise of Betty.

SEVENTEEN

Arisaig Church was two miles from the house. No distance unless your feet were slashed to ribbons along with your confidence. That there was a car outside the door when she hobbled into the courtyard was irrelevant. Lenny started down the winding road to the gate only to stop halfway, when the car pulled up beside her. It was Harry in the driving seat, with Georges, Johnny and Bill crammed in the back.

'Jump in, Swann,' he said, leaning his head out the window.

'I think I'd prefer to walk, if it's alright with you, sir,' she said, catching sight of Johnny's smirk.

'Don't be awkward, there's a good girl. We were laying on the car anyway. We need to make sure you're all back in time for lunch so that we can crack on with the afternoon session.'

'Yes, do get in, Swann. It's bomb making swiftly followed by bomb disposing.' Bill chortled. 'Far more exciting than knitting but best not get them mixed up, eh, or there'll be a right to do.'

Lenny did what she was told. Sometimes taking the path of least resistance was easier, even if it was more awkward. She hadn't had the opportunity to catch up with the men since breakfast. By the time she'd returned to the table they'd wandered off, leaving her to finish her meal in silence.

She slid into the passenger seat beside Harry, folding her hands in her lap, her bag by her feet. The men started talking, clearly at ease in each other's company. Instead of joining in, she gazed out the window and started reciting the alphabet. ABCDE until Z before returning to A and starting all over again.

The sight of the church up ahead had her lifting her bag from the footwell, her face composed into a serene mask. Anyone looking at her would be surprised to learn about the emotions surging underneath her tranquil air. It was another one of the expressions that she'd been practising in the tarnished mirror above the sink in her bedroom. It didn't mean that she didn't care about her brother, it meant that she cared too much. Collapsing in front of the men had been a hard lesson, but a useful one. No matter how much she was tearing up inside, she was determined not to show it.

Reciting the alphabet helped.

Seeing Angus at the pulpit as she took her seat beside Harry put her serene outer appearance to the test. He looked thinner, his robe hanging loose, his arms pale sticks in comparison to the ruddy hand she remembered clutching onto his cup in the Lyon's teashop. He'd lost his brother, in addition to gaining a niece and a cat. She'd told no one in Whitehall about his relationship to Finlay, not even Miss Maxse when she'd recommended Arisaig House as being a distinct possibility to accommodate the SOE. While their connection wasn't a secret, she was wise enough to know that it could be used as another mark against her hope to travel to France.

After the service, she joined the queue by the entrance, waiting her turn to shake the minister's hand and hoping that he was a good enough actor to mask his surprise at her appearing out of nowhere. With their mail censored, she hadn't been given the opportunity to warn him beforehand.

The line inched forward, the exchanges predictably familiar.

'Lovely sermon, minister,' the elderly woman ahead of her murmured, pressing his hand.

'Very moving,' another added. 'A comfort in these times.'

'Aye,' someone else chimed in. 'Reminds us to hold firm, no matter what's thrown our way.'

The minister nodded, offering the same calm, practised smile in return. 'We must all do our part.'

Then it was her turn.

'That was a lovely service,' she said, her voice steady.

His fingers closed around hers, firm enough to be reassuring, not tight enough to betray his surprise.

'Thank you,' he greeted smoothly. 'It's always a pleasure to have strangers in our midst. On holidays?' His gaze flickered to Harry, who was standing close enough to hear every word.

'Yes. It's proving to be a breath of fresh air after London,' she replied, trying to steer the conversation onto a topic of mutual interest.

His eyes flared briefly. 'It is that. My young niece is staying with me for that very reason.' He broke eye contact, glancing past her as he beckoned to someone just out of sight.

And then, there she was. Betty. No longer a newborn, but a sturdy four-month-old, dressed in a fur hooded jacket, her cheeks pink and sparkling. Lenny blinked in rapid succession, trying to divert her tears with only a limited amount of success.

She watched, transfixed, as Angus reached for her, lifting her effortlessly, his hands holding her with a confidence that made Lenny smile.

'What a beautiful baby. What's her name?' she asked, watching Betty's tiny fingers curl around the fabric of his sleeve.

'Betty,' he said, then added with a chuckle, 'Or trouble, or pickle, or whatever suits her at the time.'

Lenny laughed.

She lingered just long enough to see Betty's delighted smile before stepping aside, allowing Harry to take her place.

'You seemed on very friendly terms with the minister?' Harry said shortly after, his tone laced with curiosity along with a huge dollop of suspicion.

'He seems like a nice man, although it must be awkward being lumbered with his niece.' She plucked her handkerchief from her pocket and blew her nose briefly, hoping the cold wind would explain her sparkly eyes. 'So, what exactly does this session involve this afternoon? I'm guessing a big bang or two.'

'Only if you do something wrong, Swann.' He lowered his voice. 'The major is no pushover, Lenny, and neither am I.' His stare was hard as he swept between her red nose and her red eyes. 'Any more displays like earlier and I can't protect you.'

Lenny replied without hesitation. 'And I wouldn't want you to, sir.'

Back in the car, she turned her head to look at the view, shielding her expression, as tears slipped down her cheeks unchecked.

Your darling Betty is doing just fine, Ellen and Finlay. A credit to you both, and to Angus.

EIGHTEEN

Friday 25 April, 1941 – London 4 pm

'Congratulations, Miss Gallienne. I have to admit to having had my doubts when I heard there was a young gal in the first group of SOEs, but credit where it's due.' The major smiled, offsetting his words.

Maurice Buckmaster had joined F Section last month, when Lenny had been undergoing parachute training at RAF Ringway. She'd had far more difficult things to concentrate on, like keeping her body steady as she plummeted through the air, and remembering the precise moment to pull the ripcord, than remembering who was in post.

'Thank you, sir.' She stood with her hands by her side. Learning to wait instead of jumping in to fill the silence, was another one of her many lessons over recent months. She knew how to catch trout in a mountain stream, and gut and cook it over an open fire built from just a few twigs. That knowledge sat alongside how to bury a parachute before dawn broke, how to throw dogs off a scent and how to endure the kind of interrogation where silence wasn't just a skill but essential. Where a single misplaced word could mean the difference between survival and betrayal, between saving lives and losing them.

She could honestly say that the only part of her that hadn't changed was her love of knitting, and she'd ended up having to alter that too. Now she fashioned her stitches the continental way, as taught her by Georges. Little mistakes like that could give away the most expert of agent. That he was the proud owner of the first of her French pullovers, in cherry red, seemed to be payment enough. She had nearly completed her second, in pale blue, as requested. There were only the buttons to sew on the shoulder seam. It seemed fitting that she'd finish it later.

The end of something before the start of her new life as a French agent.

Looking in the mirror earlier had been an exercise in surprise. She barely recognised the woman staring back. Gone were the soft cheeks and soft gaze, replaced instead by sharp angles and a wariness of everyone and everything about her. Also gone were her blouses and skirts, replaced by the uniform of a sergeant in the Intelligence Corps. Her gaze lingered on the freshly sewn parachute badge on her left shoulder, the neat stitches standing out against the khaki. It was a small detail, but it made her smile. The final proof that she'd earnt her place on the team.

'Right then. Here is your French ID card and your ration book in your new name. Mademoiselle Léonore Bouchard.' He passed her a set of documents, their edges bent, the cover of the ID card stained with what looked like the ring from a coffee cup. 'You'll note the ageing is congruent with the usage they would have received. We're lucky to have an expert forger among our team over at Leamington Spa.' He smiled briefly. 'There's an additional set, in the name of Georgette Tournier but you can forget about those for the moment. We'll sew them into the lining of your suit-case, for use in case of emergencies along with a couple of L pills, if things get desperate. I'm told if you bite down first, the poison acts more quickly.'

She managed to hide her grimace. 'I'm hoping it won't come to that, but thank you.'

Léonore Bouchard. She rolled the name around her tongue, liking the feel of the words more than Nora Swann, which she'd taken an immediate exception to.

The major sat back in his chair, his hands resting on the arms. 'Now, you're happy with your cover story? I believe our luck was in when Monsieur Brossolette recommended a pension that has a room for you to rent. Booksellers are useful people to know, especially when they're part of the resistance. How about running your cover past me to check you've got the facts right.' He paused, his fingers steepling under his chin. 'Actually, scratch that. Let's pretend I've stopped you in the street and asked to see your papers.' He stretched out a hand and picked up her ID card, idly flicking through it, his demeanour suddenly that of a bored guard on duty.

'Where are you from, mademoiselle?'

Lenny nodded briefly before replying, accepting the brief.

'From Brittany. The very south tip, near Quiberon,' she said with confidence. It had been chosen because she'd visited it as a child. 'A small place called Saint Pierre.'

'I've never heard of it.'

'I'm not surprised. It's very small. Only a few families, mostly fishermen. My father was one. My mother died when I was young. My aunt, well, she raised me, along with my cousins. But there isn't much there for a girl.'

'And what brings you to Paris, mademoiselle?'

Lenny shrugged. 'There is no work back home and little food. My father's sister lives in Paris, a cook for a good family. It seemed like the best chance I had.'

Harry had told her the facts had to hold together and that the best stories weren't stories at all. A girl from a poor family moving to Paris in search of work was a common enough occurrence to have a thread of truth in it. A simple enough tale that would be repeated across France. They wouldn't expect her to speak

Parisian French. If anyone questioned her accent, the rural isolation explained it. Brittany was far enough away from Paris that no one would expect her to sound like a city girl. That she knew Saint Pierre was a bonus. That she didn't know Paris was the main flaw.

'I've been here for two months now.' She shrugged again, this time compressing her mouth into a little moue. 'Work isn't so easy to come by, but I make do.'

'And just how do you make do?'

'By helping Monsieur Brossolette in his bookshop along the Rue de la Pompe. Arranging titles, dusting shelves, manning the till when Monsieur Brossolette requires it. It's interesting work. I enjoy reading.' She knew she was waffling, but all the questions had her pulse racing. As much as she disliked being interrogated, and by someone on the same side, she knew that it was for her own good. If she got it wrong, it wouldn't only be her neck on the line but that of the team. She was a small cog in a very big wheel, positioned within Pierre Brossolette's bookshop because of his links to the resistance.

'And what about your accommodation, mademoiselle?'

She grimaced, intimating that it wasn't much of an accommodation. 'I live in a pension not far from the bookshop, run by a Mademoiselle Levain. A room with a shared bathroom.'

The major pushed the ID card across with a smile. 'Very good, mademoiselle. You can go on your way.' Then, after a moment, he changed back from bored to benevolent. 'I can see you've done your homework.' He laced his fingers together, his smile lingering. 'Mademoiselle Levain sounds ideal. It was clever of Brossolette to find her. Now, there's still the important issue of your clothing and luggage to sort. It's the little things, like English labels on skirts and jumpers, that can easily trip us up. We estimate it will take about two weeks, which ties in nicely with the date of the next full moon. We do like a nice, well-lit night for our jumps. What are you planning to do in the meantime?'

Lenny's smile lit her face from within. Harry had warned them during their last day at RAF Ringway about possible delays, and that their drop would need to align with the phases of the moon. It made sense, more sense than most things did these days. As soon as she'd arrived back in London, she'd picked up the phone and placed a call to Angus.

'With Guernsey closed off, I thought I'd visit a friend,' she said lightly. 'He's a minister in Scotland. I leave tomorrow.'

The major nodded. 'Sounds perfect. But first, I hear you're having a little get-together?'

Lenny wished she had the nerve to ask him where he'd heard the rumour. Like her, Georges, Bill, and Johnny had successfully completed the program. She couldn't quite remember whose idea it had been to meet for drinks before they all went their separate ways. Probably Johnny's.

'The American Bar at the Savoy, sir.'

'A delightful choice. Are you bringing your knitting?'

She laughed. 'Probably not.'

'Very wise. Can't have our best coder sharing her secrets with all and sundry.' He smiled before adding. 'I only wish I could join you.'

NINETEEN

'He said what?' Johnny chortled, crossing one leg over the other. 'That would be cramping our style.'

'I'm not sure what style that would be, old chap,' Bill replied, studying the cocktail list with a bemused expression. 'You should have pressed him. Then he might've paid for our drinks. Two shillings for a beer and four for something called a White Lady. Bleedin' daylight robbery, if you ask me.'

Lenny laughed as she picked up one of the menus, turning to the array of wines. Despite much encouragement and numerous digs, she'd stuck to her principles and avoided alcohol but, since her conversation with Harry that was about to change. It needed to. In France wine was typically served with their main meal of the day. She'd better start getting used to it. That she didn't feel like enjoying herself was immaterial. Starving herself wouldn't help anyone, least of all her brother who was well past saving, God rest his soul. That she'd lost weight was irrefutable. A mixture of the intense training and an inability to eat any more than a few mouthfuls at a time. That had to stop. She had to eat what she was given and be thankful for every crumb.

She studied the drinks menu, running her index finger down the list, recognising a few names, but most were unfamiliar.

Burgundy, Bordeaux, Chablis. How was she supposed to know which to choose?

There were other things that had changed besides her thoughts on drinking. Her relationship with Johnny had reached an impasse, the two of them settling into an uneasy truce. They were never going to be mates, but that was fine. With the way the world was going, she was determined to keep her friendships to a minimum. Signing the Official Secrets Act had put an end to any kind of life outside of the War Office. The Blitz, and everything that had followed, had done the rest.

Looking around the table, she let herself relax. Bill was still ranting about the price of drinks, his hands moving animatedly as he argued his point. Johnny lounged back in his chair, his gaze idly sweeping the room. Georges was on the other side of the table, holding an animated conversation with Harry.

The buzz of muted conversation, the occasional laugh. The air restrained, everyone listening out for the wail of the air raid sirens. She'd have liked to have seen the bar before the onset of war. Before fear had infiltrated the walls and soaked into the soft furnishings, adding a false note of gaiety. Everyone was trying just a little too hard to enjoy themselves.

She shook her head at the idea. The hotel was nice enough but too fancy for her liking. Without the war, she might never have left Guernsey. She'd certainly had no interest in visiting the capital. However, whether she liked it or not, this was her home now and these men her friends. Tomorrow, she'd catch the train to Arisaig and Betty, but tonight, she'd try to enjoy herself.

It was going to be difficult, though, under Harry's watchful gaze, which seemed to find her with increasing regularity ever since she'd passed over the sweater earlier. It made her feel awkward. Agreeing to knit him the jumper had been a mistake, but how could she refuse? That he was being dropped into France at the same time was disturbing but also strangely reassuring. He wasn't there to check up on her, which was a relief. Their paths might never even cross.

Lenny didn't know what to think about that, only that the man seemed to be taking up more than his fair share of her thoughts lately.

She straightened in her seat and lifted the menu again. There were far more important things than Harry Dennison.

'Hey, Georges. I fancy a wine. What do you suggest?'

Bill nearly choked, slapping a hand against his leg in surprise. 'Halle-bleedin'-lujah. What made you change your mind?'

Lenny didn't hesitate. 'The fact that it will make up part of my future life.'

She didn't say more. She didn't have to. They were all in the same situation of having to adopt new roles, not that she knew what theirs were. She was only aware of Harry's because they were on the same night parachute drop into Fontainebleau Forest, and even then, all she knew was the location of his drop, not where he was going after.

'Right, I'm getting these.' Bill rose to his feet only to sit at the sight of the waiter descending. 'Three White Ladies, a pint of beer and a small glass of chardonnay.'

After, the men started a conversation about football, which had her eyeing her bag and the telltale knitting needles poking out the top. She was in the middle of a cardigan for Betty, which she was keen to finish, but there was a time and a place for crafting and the middle of one of the poshest hotels in London wasn't it. She sat back in her chair, her hands in her lap as she circled her thumbs around each other. With her stash of wool nearly depleted, she'd be better served leaving some knitting for the train journey up to Scotland, where she was hoping to stock up.

'Lenny Gallienne. It is you, isn't it? I barely recognised you.'

Lenny jerked out of her reverie to glance over her shoulder at the glamorous woman approaching their table.

'Gloria. I can't believe it. What are you doing here of all places?' She enveloped her friend in a hug before stepping back, her eyes widening at the changes the last six months had wrought in the woman who'd replaced her as Miss Maxse's secretary. A subtle scent, something expensive and floral, tickled her nose.

The last time she'd seen her, Gloria had been dressed in the standard War Office uniform of sorts. A crisp white blouse and a sensible grey knee-length skirt. Now, she stood before her in a slinky, sequinned dress with barely a back to speak of, paired with sky-high stilettos, her mouth a slash of red lipstick.

She refrained from comparing the outfit to her uniform and tightly pinned hair. Gloria looked lovely, but in a way that didn't align with how Lenny liked to dress. She wasn't prudish. Not exactly. Well, perhaps a little. But *old-fashioned* was a kinder term. Someone brought up with a set of values that were hard to shake, no matter how far she travelled from her upbringing.

She looked over her shoulder at the table Gloria had been sitting at. 'You haven't come with Marjorie then?'

Gloria threw back her head and laughed. 'As if Miss Maxse would be seen dead in here, let alone alive. Just with my friend, Jane, for a quick drink or two.' She moved to the side as the waiter approached, a tray balanced above his head. 'Well, I should get back.'

'Why not join us,' Lenny said on impulse. The conversation between the men was continuing along the same dry theme, and chatting with a couple of girls might be just what she needed. Also, it might be fun to see how the men reacted to having a couple of pretty women join their group.

'Boys, we have company. Johnny, grab two chairs, there's a dear.' She watched in amusement as he opened his mouth to grumble only to close it with a snap at the sight of Gloria's blonde hair and pouting mouth.

'Of course.' His demeanour changed in a flash. 'My pleasure.' And to Lenny on the way past. 'I never knew you had such charming friends.'

Lenny grinned at the return to his usual form, and the way he manoeuvred the seating so that he was between Gloria and Jane, leaving Bill and Georges out in the cold. Harry settled back in his chair, an unusual expression crossing his face, so fleeting that she'd have missed it if she hadn't been looking his way. Something she quickly forgot about with Johnny taking centre stage.

'So, Gloria, what brings you here?' he drawled, his voice dropping a shade lower, his arm slung across the back of her chair in a move so casual it had obviously been practised.

Gloria's lips curved, her eyes flicking up at him from beneath heavy lashes. 'Oh, you know. A drink, a bit of fun.' She swirled the last of her drink around the glass before knocking it back. 'Not much else to do on a night like this.'

She watched as Johnny dialled up the charm, and to her amusement, Gloria lapped it up, tilting her chin just so, her eyes bright as she laughed in all the right places.

Lenny turned to Harry, who was watching the whole exchange with a raised brow, his beer glass turning lazily in his fingers. When he caught her looking, he tilted his head towards the door in silent suggestion.

She considered a moment. Gloria and Johnny were engrossed in each other, while Bill and Georges were getting stuck into the White Ladies as if they were going out of fashion. Jane, who she'd only just met and didn't think much of, was toying with the stem of her glass in a vague, amused air.

'Oh, go on then. My knitting is calling,' she said to Georges and Bill, who both laughed at her typical Knitty Nora comment.

'Just as my bed is me.' Harry looped his jacket over his shoulder, his hand cupping her elbow loosely. 'I'll happily escort you home then it's a cup of Ovaltine and hopefully a good night's kip.' They were at the door when he stopped to look over his shoulder at Johnny cozying up to Gloria. 'How well do you know your friend?'

'Not that well. Why do you ask?' she said, securing her bag over her shoulder as he held the door for her.

'Oh, I don't know. Just a feeling I have. We're well out of it.'

Lenny paused, her brows pulled into a frown. 'What about Bill and Georges? Do you think we should…?'

He shook his head, turning away. 'Bill and Georges know how

to look after themselves. It's Johnny who's the problem. An ego that big is bound to get itself into trouble now and again.'

They stepped outside, the cold evening air causing her to shiver. The doorman straightened as they approached, giving a sharp salute at the sight of their uniforms.

'Taxi, sir?' he asked.

Harry nodded. 'Why not? Not sure when we'll be back here again.'

The taxi dropped them off outside her building. Lenny hesitated on the pavement, suddenly unsure. The idea of inviting him up fluttered at the edge of her mind, but she pushed it firmly aside. That wasn't who she was, or who she wanted to become. The Glorias of this world were welcome to all the fun they could stomach.

Harry shifted from one foot to the other. 'I hear you're going up to Scotland,' he said finally. 'Staying with family for a couple of weeks?'

'I can't wait.' Lenny didn't correct his mistake. Angus and Betty weren't family by blood, but they were in every way that mattered.

'Right.' His voice was quiet now. He was obviously in no rush or perhaps he had something he wanted to say. She didn't have long to wait. 'I do wish you'd phoned me, Lenny. There are things I'd have liked to have said before the job got in the way. Really I should have said something back in Guernsey.' He pulled a wry grin. 'Timing has never been my strong point and now it's too late.' Then, with a strange kind of gentleness, he lifted his hand and cradled her face, his thumb grazing her cheek as if he was memorising something. 'Take care of yourself and thank you again for my jumper.'

And with that, he was gone.

Lenny spent a long time standing on the pavement outside the building. She only turned away when she started to shiver, in spite of her heavy coat.

PART TWO

TWENTY

Friday 30 May, 1941 – Paris 8.55 am

Lenny, or Léonore Bouchard, as she was now known, left the security of the pension and paused a moment to take in a deep breath of Parisian air. That the air could seem different between London and Paris amazed her. The streets were as busy and as noisy. It was everything else that was different. The weather warmer, the smells from the boulangerie next to her place of work adding an extra layer of deliciousness. Even the fashions were different. There was no obvious shortage of fabric in the wasp-waisted full skirts, a la Coco Chanel.

A woman cycled past, a baguette under her arm, her hair the exact shade of Gloria's, which sent Lenny's thoughts shooting in a totally different direction.

She often thought back to her last night in London before everything changed. What she would have done differently, if anything. Whether she'd been wrong to stick to her principles.

Like all retrospections, it was a waste of time and effort, but that didn't stop her from mulling over what had happened since that night. The night that Johnny had been kicked off the team.

He blamed her for introducing him to Gloria and she couldn't challenge that argument. After all, it was true. If he hadn't met Gloria, most likely he'd be somewhere in France by now. In his mind, she was the reason he'd lost his place, and all because of his inability to keep his mouth shut when trying to impress her friend. That she'd had no idea Gloria had decided to use her womanly skills to lure unsuspecting recruits into indiscretions, as part of her own war effort, was irrelevant. Harry had sensed something was off about the situation, but neither of them had done anything about it.

Their inaction had cost Johnny dearly.

There had been a time when she might have written to him, offering an explanation he would never accept, but that door was firmly closed. Just another burned bridge in a life increasingly full of them. Besides, Johnny was in the past, and her survival depended on keeping the past where it belonged. She had too much to contend with in the present.

Harry was in the past too, and for that she was thankful. It was too confusing otherwise. They'd met again for some last-minute training the day before their drop. But it had felt like meeting a stranger. Polite. Professional. Detached. There hadn't been a trace of the man she'd glimpsed the last time they'd spoken.

The man who'd cradled her face with surprising gentleness.

That man had gone.

It was better that way, for both of them. That he'd started to haunt her dreams was something she wasn't prepared to admit. If they had unfinished business, then it would have to wait until the blasted war was over.

She slipped her key into the lock of Librairie Universelle, the rusty hinges of the bookshop squealing faintly as she pushed the door open. The familiar scent of new books, ink, and paper greeted her, the same scent as the bookshop in Smith Street back home.

The owners lived above in a cramped apartment while her lodgings were on the same road, just a short walk away. She had a narrow room in a pension for single ladies. Spartan but sufficient. A rickety wardrobe, a creaky bed, a chair that threatened collapse, and a writing desk under the window. More importantly, it was a place to store her suitcase. *Not* any suitcase. The wireless transmitter was tucked beneath her bed, hidden under her faded slips. It wasn't ideal but, until she could find somewhere more suitable, it would have to do.

She was placing her coat and scarf behind the counter when Pierre Brossolette emerged from the recess that separated the front of the shop from the narrow staircase behind.

'You're early,' he said, his voice warm.

'Better than the alternative. Being late or not turning up at all,' she replied, picking up a cloth and starting her morning routine of dusting the counters.

'Quite.'

She'd only been in Paris a few days when she'd learnt that people simply disappeared under the new regime, often never to be heard of again. When families pressed for information, it was always the same.

No news.

Pierre Brossolette was tall and lean, with a domed forehead and a permanent serious expression. A journalist before the war, he'd recently turned to bookselling. He primarily specialised in Russian literature, but the reality was he stocked what the French were keen to buy, from stationery to the classics and everything in-between. He'd also distributed resistance pamphlets but, with the recent arrest of a key member in his network, that had stopped. For now.

His wife, Gilberte, followed him down the stairs, carrying a tray with a chipped enamel pot of coffee and three cups.

'You two always start without me,' she moaned gently, pouring out the coffee and handing them out, her wide smile belying her words. There was no milk or sugar, something Lenny missed.

'I have news, Léonore,' Pierre said, taking his cup. 'Word is the Germans are sniffing around again. We need to get rid of the rest of the pamphlets before the end of the day.'

She glanced towards the counter and the pile hidden underneath, her stomach tightening.

'How many are left?'

'Dozens! Anything still here tonight gets burned.'

The bell above the door jangled sharply.

All three froze.

Lenny turned slowly, her pulse quickening. It was early for their first customer. They hadn't even turned the open sign around, but Pierre was a businessman at heart. In times like these, it was only a fool who turned away money.

A woman stood just inside the doorway, neatly dressed. Unfamiliar. Not one of their regulars, when that was all they seemed to get in the shop these days. The kind of woman who might simply be looking for a book, or who might be looking for something else entirely.

'Good morning.' Lenny stepped forward, her voice steady.

The woman replied with a polite smile, drifting towards the table of books in the centre.

Lenny returned behind the counter and picked up her cloth, conscious of the pamphlets stacked underneath.

After a few minutes of browsing, she eventually selected a copy of *Madame Bovary* and brought it over.

'A good choice, madame.' She wrapped it carefully, keeping up a stream of inconsequential conversation. Primarily about books, and the weather.

'That was close,' she muttered, as soon as the door had closed behind her. 'Do you think she heard us?'

'Unlikely.' Pierre swept the pamphlets into a box and walked to the stairs. 'We'll keep them in the apartment until we can think of how to get rid of them. We've been lucky up to now.'

He didn't need to say any more.

Their luck had run out.

When he returned, he handed over a slip of paper with an address scrawled across it. 'Something else. There's a party tonight at the home of a French collaborator.' He almost spat out the sentence. 'Word is they're short a waitress.'

Lenny's stomach dipped. 'And you're asking me?'

'I'm passing on a request, Léonore. It would help if we had someone on the inside. Just to observe. No contact, no interference. Eyes and ears only.'

Gilberte shared out the last of the coffee. 'You don't have to say yes,' she said gently. 'We'll understand.'

'No, it's fine, honestly. Observing I can do.'

'Thank you.'

The coffee tasted bitter, slightly burned, but she drank it anyway. Cradling her cup she turned towards the front window. Outside, students zipped past on bicycles, blazers flapping in the breeze. Pierre and Gilberte's children would have been joining them if they hadn't been sent to the country for their safety. The sight of the blazers reminded her about what she should wear. She didn't have that much with her.

'What about clothes?'

Pierre pulled a face. 'And when you've finished sorting out what dress you're going to wear, I'd like to show you some photographs of a couple of men we're interested in. In particular Oberstleutnant Karl Botz and Hauptmann Erich Vollmer.'

Gilberte laughed, ignoring him. 'We're about the same size. What's mine is yours.'

'As long as it doesn't have sequins.'

'You have a dress with sequins?'

Lenny glanced down at her plain black dress, one of the two supplied by the War Office and sufficiently aged, the collar and hem faded. Her thoughts veered back to Gloria for the second time that day. 'Do I look like the type to wear anything sequinned?'

'No,' Gilberte said, her eyes twinkling. 'But it's always the quiet ones you have to watch.'

TWENTY-ONE

As maid-of-all-duties, Lenny's responsibilities for the evening would be as many as they were varied, Pierre had explained, in the quiet moments between customers.

'Madame Lumineau doesn't employ a large staff. Work is scarce, and jobs are rationed along with everything else. Not that Madame Lumineau worries herself with such matters,' he elaborated. 'With a large black market to tap into and a large bank balance to fund it, one would hardly know a war was raging inside their luxury apartment, with views over the Eiffel Tower.'

'What about her husband?'

He flicked his hand dismissively. 'Lumineau does what he's told. The price of having a model for a wife, and a fashion house with little business currently.' His tone was dismissive, verging on the vitriolic. He never bothered to conceal his thoughts on collaborators, particularly ones who shared both his passport and his culture. Lenny thought him quite restrained, all things considered. She'd have been far more forthright in her choice of words.

After work, she hurried home to change into the plain black dress Gilberte had lent her, before remembering to tell her landlady of her plans.

She found Marianne Levain in the kitchen. A thin, dark-haired woman in her early thirties with a shrewd gaze but a kindly heart. 'I think the lentils again to accompany the pork, Auguste. They're nutritious and filling.'

'I'm pleased I've caught you, Marianne. No supper for me tonight. I'm off out.' That they had lentils and some nondescript meat most evenings made her glad that she was going to miss supper for once.

'Lucky you, Léonore. You have a date?'

Lenny laughed. 'Hardly. No, I've been asked to waitress at a private party. I shouldn't be back too late.'

'Well, careful how you go. The streets aren't safe late at night.'

'I will.' Lenny hadn't thought that far, but she decided to tuck her knitting in the bottom of her bag. In the absence of a knife, her knitting needles would make a good weapon and easily explainable if she was stopped.

On arrival at the Lumineaus' sleek apartment, she was shown into the kitchen, where she was asked to lay a tray with paper-thin coffee cups and the tall silver pot madame insisted upon. There was also coffee to pour for cook, who was in the process of slicing slivers of onion as a garnish for her mini quiche tarts.

After she'd deposited the tray in madame's bedroom, Lenny escaped to the small washroom in the hall to check her appearance in the square mirror above the sink. With her hair dragged off her face in a tight bun, any wayward curls ruthlessly pinned in place, and a pair of tortoiseshell glasses perched on her nose, she barely recognised herself.

Gloria certainly wouldn't have.

There were many ways to win a war. For her it was all about blending in instead of standing out, she thought, heading for the door, her stomach alive with butterflies, despite her composed outward appearance.

There were also far more urgent matters than Gloria, Johnny and Harry and what had become of them since London. Tonight's drinks party was the first time she'd been asked to do something more important than processing pamphlets, but she was sure it wouldn't be the last. Pierre kept his ears pinned back for opportunities such as this. The ideal cover for a young Frenchwoman to learn whatever she could. What was unusual was that the party would include officers from the German military command.

His informant had shared that the hostess, Sabine Lumineau, was an enigma. A beautiful French model of noble birth who had decided the Germans weren't so bad after all. That she'd gone so far as to welcome Lenny into her home in the form of local labour was a double-edged sword. On the one hand, she would have access to more information than she knew what to do with. On the other, the risk was immense. One false step, one glance in the wrong direction, and she could find herself locked up. Or worse. Oh, yes, there was far worse than having her freedom curtailed.

Locked up meant a prison cell. Maybe beatings. Maybe interrogation.

But worse meant disappearing. Vanishing into the belly of the Reich. A nameless file in a drawer. A train with no return. A camp at the end of the line.

And the tragic part? With no relatives, no one would come looking. Her friends back in Guernsey knew nothing about her life these days and, as far as Angus knew she was still working in the War Office in London. It was easier that way. No one to worry if she made a choice that put her in danger.

No one to miss her if she didn't come back.

Major Buckmaster's words still rang in her ears. His last parting shot, tossed casually into the conversation after some comment about joining them for drinks at the Savoy:

'If they catch you, you're on your own.'

Lenny had been on her own since the arrival of that telegram informing her of James's death.

Oberstleutnant Karl Botz and Hauptmann Erich Vollmer were among the first to arrive, their crisp uniforms immaculate, their polished boots clicking sharply against the parquet floor as they handed her their coats and caps.

Both were tall. Both blond. Both undeniably handsome in the clean, Aryan way that was synonymous with the propaganda newsreels they liked to play.

There was little to tell them apart at first glance. They had the same square jaws, same tailored precision, same cool confidence. But their eyes told different stories. Botz's were a cold, glacial blue: calculating and remote. Vollmer's were darker, almost grey. A charmer right down to the tips of his boot-clad toes. Both dangerous men.

'This way, gentlemen.' Lenny walked across the expansive hall towards the drawing room, offering only the polite, deferential smile of a well-trained domestic.

Reaching the spare bedroom, which had been requisitioned for guests' belongings, she carefully added their coats to the growing pile on the bed. With a final glance at the door, she swiftly slipped her hands into the pockets of Botz's coat first.

Her fingers brushed against a silk handkerchief, neatly folded, and a few coins. She fingered through them, but there was nothing unusual. Next, she moved to Vollmer's coat. A quick, practised sweep revealed another handkerchief, this one slightly crumpled and bearing the faint scent of cologne, along with a handful of centimes and a worn cigarette case. Flipping it open, she noted an engraving etched into the metal, easily translated by someone with an Austrian mother.

For my beloved husband. Until we meet again.

She snapped the case shut, returning it precisely as she'd found it. Stepping back, she took a steadying breath before heading into the drawing room and the tray of drinks waiting to be passed around.

She'd been hoping for more. A map, a note, a plan of any kind. Probably too much to expect.

The drawing room was large, with expansive windows. Light flooded through the glass, picking out the tone of the wood panelling and built in bookshelves. The feel was of timeless elegance and exquisite taste, but it was the view from the windows that drew the breath of the Lumineaus' guests. That the Eiffel Tower seemed almost within touching distance had been a shock the first time she'd entered the room. With the two Germans hogging the window, it now felt like a travesty.

There were twelve guests already with a couple more due. A selection of the Lumineaus' old cronies in addition to the two German officers. Shallow, stupid men and women who didn't realise the risks they were incurring by being in the presence of the enemy.

'And with Operation Barbarossa and the push towards the East happening any day now...'

Lenny's ears sharpened at the words, her posture unchanged, the tray steady in her hands.

'More champagne, Herr Oberstleutnant?' she asked lightly, aware she'd been hovering by his elbow a beat too long.

'Certainly. And you, Erich. It's a rare day indeed when we are able to taste such a fine wine, is it not?'

'We must try and add a bottle or two to our cellars.' They laughed between themselves as they picked up their glasses, dismissing her as she had hoped. No one noticed the serving staff.

It wasn't the first time Lenny had heard the push towards the East mentioned that evening, but the first time that she'd heard the name of the operation. It had come up in a murmured conversation shortly before, as she was handing out a tray of the mini quiches. People ignored the staff, when really they shouldn't, she thought, filing away the information for later. Something big was coming and, if they were openly discussing it, then the wheels were already in motion.

Operation Barbarossa. Hmm. London will be keen to learn that Germany is about to attack Russia. Could change the whole course of the war.

She was walking over to the kitchen for more quiches when the buzzer rang, the chime echoing through the apartment. She dropped her empty tray on the nearest table and took a moment to smooth her expression of any excitement that might be showing. It wouldn't do to appear anything other than impassive. Someone doing their job, a job they hoped to keep.

The man filling the doorway was older, his face dominated by a bulbous nose, florid with veins. His hair was a nondescript grey, the only nondescript thing about him. But it wasn't his nose or his hair that caused her eyes to widen, it was his uniform. His black tunic visible under his leather coat, his cap loose in his left hand, his right resting on what looked to be the handle of a dagger.

She recognised the uniform. They'd had a lesson on the different outfits worn by the German army. They'd even joked about them, clowning around, acting the fool as they marched around the room practising their Heils, their arms outstretched until Harry had intervened. He'd bawled them out for being juvenile. Too immature to recognise the seriousness of the situation they could find themselves in.

Lenny wasn't laughing now. Suddenly she was finding it difficult to breathe, the air sucked out of the space, along with any thought that she could escape the evening unscathed. Surely, he must suspect.

'Good evening. I'm Herr Standartenführer Otto Reiner.'

'Good evening. Welcome to the Lumineau residence. May I take your coat?'

She watched as he clicked his heels, surprised that he hadn't seen right through her little act. His behaviour seemed natural enough as did his expression. The fear in her chest started to fade. Everything was in order, even the way he stepped to one side, his hand now waving somewhere behind him at something not quite in her range of vision. 'And this is my Adjutant, Herr Jakob Meissner.'

Lenny slid her gaze across readily enough, pleased to shift her attention from the SS officer and everything he stood for. The chilling sense that he could see right through her, see that she was a big, fat fake remained.

What do they do with big fat fakes again? Oh, yes. Arrest and torture.

There was no premonition about the young officer filling the recently vacated space. No sixth sense. No feeling in her gut, and why would there be?

Eleven months wasn't enough. Eleven years. Eleven lifetimes and it still wouldn't have been enough to come face to face with the man she'd thought dead these last eleven months.

James.

TWENTY-TWO

One beat. Two beats. Three beats before her brain caught up with her eyes, her heart exploding in her chest.

'Good evening, Herr Meissner.' The words came out easily enough, a variation on what she'd been repeating all evening.

James nodded, causing her first doubts to surface.

Was it her brother? It looked like him, but his expression was stern instead of the warmth she'd learnt to expect. His eyes. His beautiful warm blue eyes were as cold and hard as the glass marbles they used to play with before their childhood had been whipped out of their hands by the death of their parents.

'Let me help you with your coat, Herr Standartenführer,' he said smoothly, reaching out to take the heavy garment and adding it to his own. 'Where would you like these, Fräulein?'

'There's a room. The second door on your left. I'll show you in a moment. Thank you.'

She turned, surprised by her steady voice.

It sounded normal. Ordinary. Perhaps she should look to pursue a career on the stage after this farce of a war was over.

Perhaps not. Her nerves would never manage.

'The drawing room is this way, Herr Standartenführer.'

She forced her feet to move. One step after the other, the

sound of laughter and merriment from across the hall easy to follow, if not listen to. Where before she'd been keen to hear any scrap of information, now she was consumed by a sudden surge of shock spreading through every muscle and bone. The granite-hard block of ice in the middle of her chest split apart revealing some-thing she thought she'd lost. That the rush of emotion had chosen the most inconvenient of times to appear only increased her feel-ings, her spine stiffening in protest.

How dare he pretend to be dead and how dare he pretend to be the enemy.

She stopped, letting the officer walk ahead into the drawing room.

Was James *pretending?*

'Ah, Otto. You made it.' Sabine Lumineau grabbed a glass of champagne from the table by the door and strolled over to them. 'I think you know everyone. Please make yourself at home.' She turned to her. 'See what else Cook has for us, Léonore. I don't want our guests to leave here hungry.'

Lenny nodded, retreating quickly to the door but instead of turning right, she turned left to where James was waiting for her just inside the bedroom.

'What the hell. I thought you were dead.' Relief made her words harsh, but she couldn't help that.

'I could say the same about you.' He put his finger to his lips. 'I have to go, or he'll be suspicious. What time do you finish? I'll walk you home.'

'I don't think—'

'What time,' he hissed, already pulling the door open.

'Nine o'clock, after all the food is served.'

He didn't reply, instead he was back in the hall, his voice raised in greeting. 'You wanted me, Herr Standartenführer?'

'Left my cigarettes in my coat pocket.'

'Here, have one of mine.'

Lenny watched through the crack in the door as he pulled out his solid silver cigarette case and flipped it open. The cigarette case he'd inherited from their Austrian grandfather and which he was never without.

'Thank you, but I prefer my own.'

Lenny was already sweeping across the room at his words, dropping to the floor and sliding under the high bed with only a fraction of a second to spare. She lay there, staring at the underside of the bed frame, listening to the sound of his shoes strike the floor. The rummage through his coat. The click of his case and what must be the sharp flick of a lighter flame. Then silence apart from the thrumming of her pulse in her ears.

She closed her eyes, her hands clenched into tight balls as the acrid smell of German cigarette smoke reached her nostrils. Very different to the cigarettes her brother smoked, or the French Gauloise they'd been introduced to during their final weeks of training. Having never been bothered about smoking, Lenny had asked to be excused. She now realised that would have been a mistake and one the instructor hadn't allowed her to make. But recognising the make of cigarette as being German was of no help to her current situation. In fact, it made it worse. The smell made her want to sneeze.

The hard floor pressed into her spine, as she lifted her hand to her nose, clamping her nostrils shut as she started breathing through her mouth, the feeling of being trapped in this position for eternity as stupid as it was fanciful.

Why the hell is he sitting in here when he could be enjoying himself. What does he know, or suspect?

'Léonore? Where is that girl? Honestly. The quality of staff these days leaves a lot to be desired.'

Sabine Lumineau's words burst across the room, her exasperation accompanied by a sharp intake of breath, which meant she must be just outside the door.

'Hello. What are you doing in here all by yourself?'

'Hoping you'll come and join me perhaps?'

Lenny could hear Sabine twittering in amusement. 'You're a

very naughty man, Otto. I know for a fact that you have a lovely wife and three adorable children back in Berlin.'

'My wife is a very long way away, dear lady, and there are plenty of advantages in having a German lover in your pocket.'

'It's certainly something to think about but not in the middle of a party, with my husband next door,' she replied, her tone dry.

'Of course. My apologies.'

Good for you, Sabine.

Lenny let out a sigh of relief, waiting a moment until their voices could be heard fading out of earshot.

Paris by night was very different to Paris in daytime. The wide boulevards were shrouded in shadows, the plane trees forming an eerie backdrop. The tense silence was only interrupted by the sound of a lone café owner closing for the night.

Paris: the home of lovers, of gaiety, of laughter was lost for as long as the enemy remained.

It was also very different walking by the side of the enemy.

A German soldier.

Her brother.

Lenny matched his pace, her hands resolutely thrust inside her pockets, the rhythm of their steps echoing on the empty pavement. Passers-by glanced their way. Some quickly, some with tightly pursed lips and eyes that flicked away without expression. A couple walking a sleek dachshund crossed to the other side of the street, the lead stretched taut as the little beast dug in, rebelling against the abrupt change to his night-time routine. A man standing on the corner took one look before disappearing down the nearest alley.

'Which number?'

The first words he'd spoken since slipping out of the shadows as she'd pulled the door closed behind her.

'Sixty-five. The one with the arched windows and ornate

entrance,' she added, in case he hadn't heard her low rush of words. His nod was his only reply.

They stopped outside. He pulled out his cigarette case and struck a match, the sharp scent of burned sulphur hitting her nose. She watched as the flame highlighted the grooves and lines of his face. A faded scar on his cheek running under his chin. Tired eyes, shadows like bruises pressed into the soft skin beneath. Still her brother but older. Sadder. More disillusioned.

She reached up and touched his arm. 'What are you doing here, James?'

'Jakob, remember?' he replied softly. 'And I could ask the same about you. All these months, I've hoped and prayed for your safety only to discover that you're working in some menial job down the road.'

Jakob.

Their grandfather's name. The cigarette case. Some of the pieces of his story slotted into place as she stared up at him.

'Tell me what happened?'

TWENTY-THREE

'Going to France by boat was the stupidest idea imaginable, Lenny. You know how seasick I get.' He studied the end of his cigarette, lost in the past. 'I thought it would be okay. I was there on a mission. Those poor men in Dunkirk. Something to divert my mind and my stomach from the swell of the sea, waves so high as to nearly bury the boat. I realised my mistake before we'd even pulled out of the harbour, as did the captain and every sailor on board.'

'I'm so sorry, James,' she said, remembering boat journeys to France as a child and similar bouts of seasickness.

'They were all doing their bit,' he continued. 'Hauling men over the side, under a shower of bullets from low-flying Messerschmitts and all I could do was watch. Then the ship next to us.' He squeezed his eyes shut. 'A direct hit. Broke in two before my eyes, men hurled into the heaving seas. Their cries for help. I leant over the side, trying to pull one in. That's all I remember until the next morning.'

Lenny didn't say anything. Her throat had closed over, blocked with tears.

'I was lying on the beach, on my back. No idea how I'd got there.' He shrugged as if it didn't matter. 'The tide probably. The skin on my cheeks, my forehead, my chest was starting to burn.' He lifted his free hand, examining it as if he'd never seen it before. 'The sand beneath my fingers was as hot as fire. I must have lost my jacket somewhere, maybe when I hit the water.'

He threw the end of his cigarette away, stamping it into the ground. 'I tried to move but the pain was too much. Instead, I turned my head and that's when I saw them. British and German soldiers lying on top of each other, a cacophony of grey, green, and navy. All dead that I could see. A graveyard. Before I realised what I was doing I'd pulled a torn jacket over me, anything to stop the beating of the sun, I lay there, unable to move, my mind finally catching up with the position I was in. A British citizen on a German-occupied French beach. An *injured* British citizen, with no hope of escape.'

He stared down at the ground, so all she could see was the peak of his cap. 'I knew what was to come. Hospital if I was lucky before being sent to one of those camps.'

He squared his shoulders as if bracing himself for the next part. 'I must have drifted off to sleep. When I woke, I found myself in a makeshift army camp, where a male orderly had stripped me down to my underclothes. It was only when the doctor came to examine me that I realised the seriousness of the situation.'

Lenny watched as he chose another cigarette with care, tapping the end against the back of his case before lighting it. There was an unmistakeable tremor in his fingers that hadn't been there previously, but if the nicotine helped... He was smoking too much, much more than he used to but tobacco was the least of his worries, she thought sadly. They'd always been close, closer than most siblings. A bond born out of tragedy and cultivated by a maiden aunt who believed in discipline over affection. It wasn't that she was unkind. She'd been placed in a difficult position on the death of her sister and brother-in-law. To have teenagers thrust upon her, when children had never been part of her plan must have been a shock.

The other part of being close was that Lenny used to be able to finish his sentences for him. Apparently, that was still true.

'I'm guessing the doctor thought you German?'

'How did you…?' He sent her a sharp look then shook his head. 'Never mind. You were always able to read me like a book. How was I to know that the jacket I'd lifted belonged to the enemy? His nationality wasn't at the top of my priorities. Poor devil.' He concentrated on the glowing tip of his cigarette. 'That they thought me one of them! Can you believe it? I'd have been angry if I hadn't been so surprised. I let them patch me up. I had no choice not to. It was after that the fun started. The questions. The jacket had been lost by then and my trousers with it, probably only fit for burning. I was lucky I still had my cigarette case.'

'I don't understand.' Lenny was puzzled, trying to work it out. 'Why didn't you tell them who you were? At least they would have had a duty to look after you.'

He gave her a sheepish smile, one she remembered from their schooldays when he'd tried to do something clever only to fail spectacularly.

'My time to prove myself after making such a mess of things in Dunkirk. If I could get them to trust me.' He shrugged.

'That was very brave of you though.' *If a little foolhardy*, but she kept that last bit to herself. She was in no position to act judge and jury. It wasn't as if she was excelling either. 'There were no clues to give you away?'

'No physical ones, no.' The second cigarette received the same fate as the first, his boot smearing it into the pavement. 'The one thing the Germans are is organised. List lovers the lot of them and that's when my problems started. Not having papers on me was one thing. But no name? That's a different story.' He flipped open his cigarette case a third time but, instead of picking out his next smoke, he tilted it towards her, his finger tapping on the name etched into the metal.

'Feigning memory loss, persistent memory loss meant that they took to calling me Jakob. It made a strange sort of sense. The doctors. The psychiatrists. No one could add to that until Otto Reiner came to visit with one of his bloody lists.' He paused. 'A very long list of all the men missing, and presumed dead during Operation Dynamo. A list that included one Jakob Meissner, one of their unaccounted-for Junker pilots.'

Lenny's eyes filled. She'd never felt prouder of him than at that moment, but she sensed that there was more. That the story had more words, more mountains and crevices to navigate. Being fluent in French and German would have only taken him so far. How had he managed.

Spending the last month in France had been the hardest of lessons, far harder than the six months' training she'd received at the hands of the experts. She'd decided in desperation to cultivate the impression of a country girl, with little brains and no looks to speak of. She lived on the edge of conversations, her knitting on her lap, her mouth drooping slightly open as she recorded anything interesting in her stitches.

Dot Dash. No need to remember. No need to keep notes.

But James would have had no such training. How was he coping and, more importantly, what was he doing in Paris with Standartenführer Otto Reiner?

Instead of reaching out and giving him the hug she wanted to, she stepped a little further into the shadows, drawing him with her. The street was empty, but the windows weren't. No one held on to their secrets for long in Paris. Not these days. Traitors hid behind shutters, and around corners. She would be missed by the other women at the pension if she stayed much longer. Their nightly tisane was a habit she wouldn't be able to break easily.

'There's more, isn't there?'

'Oh, yes, dear sister. There's more.' He glanced over his shoulder, but all appeared to be quiet. When he turned back, she noticed a flicker of fear in his face, the jut of his bottom lip, the pull of his jaw. It was as if the years had fallen away and dropped them back into the middle of childhood where she had led and he'd followed, in spite of the eleven months difference in their age.

'Reiner suspects, although he hasn't said anything. It's there in the way he keeps me close to his side. Always watching, waiting for me to make a mistake. It's getting that the other men are commenting about his interest.'

'In what way?' Lenny opened her eyes, struggling to understand what he was trying to tell her.

'What way do you think,' he hissed. 'In *that way*. Remember what happened to the hairdresser up Fountain Street?'

Lenny blushed, her cheeks flooding with colour. Bertrand the Barber.

Small and wiry, with a clipped moustache and the tendency to hum under his breath as he worked. Then one day he was gone. No explanation, just his name scraped off the glass and another man standing in his place. The shop had never been the same after. No jar of sweets for the children. Nothing.

It had started with muttered whispers behind closed doors. She'd been sixteen at the time and too young to be let in on the secret. Was there even a secret? Then someone spat on his boots outside the fishmonger's. After, she'd overheard her aunt telling a neighbour that he'd been driven off the island, and good riddance. No one talked about it, not properly. But everyone *knew* there was something.

'You're not saying...' Lenny began, then trailed off. She wasn't sure what she was saying or asking.

His laugh was grim. 'I'm saying it doesn't matter what's true. It only matters what they think is. And right now, they think Otto's taken a shine to me, despite having a wife and children back home. It wouldn't be the first time a soldier has used alternative ways to... let's say... manage his personal life.' He rubbed a hand over his face. 'I don't like the way they look at me. Like I'm a willing participant. Not being able to remember things doesn't help.'

'But you're ill with amnesia. How can they be so cruel? They should have left you in hospital instead of putting you to work.'

Lenny pulled out her handkerchief, one of the six supplied by the staff over at Leamington Spa, and blew her nose, her eyes starting to run.

'I'm pretending to be ill,' he reminded her gently. 'And, really, I didn't have a choice at the time. After spending months at one of their military hospitals, it was agreeing to Reiner taking me on or the alternative of being sent to one of their sanitoriums. Can you imagine how I'd have fared locked up?' He turned away, his face in sharp profile and she knew he didn't want to talk about it further. She couldn't blame him. 'But enough about me. What about you?'

Lenny was far more concerned about him than herself. That crack about the men had hit her harder than he'd probably intended. Her beautiful brother, and there didn't seem to be a thing she could do to protect him. Certainly not her news about Reiner and Sabine Lumineau, who would surely conduct any affair in utmost secrecy for fear that the husband might find out.

'There's nothing to tell. I was lucky enough to evacuate just before the Germans came, and working in the Librairie Universelle book shop is a good a place as any.' She brushed off the time since she'd last seen him along with the time she'd spent at the War Office. There were far more important things going on. 'Oh, I did catch up with an old friend of yours, on the train in Weymouth, would you believe.' She decided to bring Harry up as a way to change the conversation. 'He recognised that I was your sister. Harold Dennison.'

'Well, I never. Haven't thought of Harry in ages. A decent bloke. Always thought he had a thing for you.'

Lenny's eyes widened, a rush of sudden pleasure filling her veins. 'What? You never said?'

'Well, I wouldn't. Left it to Harry.'

Men sticking together. She pulled a face in the darkness. There'd be time to think on his words later. Now she had far more important things to discuss. 'What are you going to do, James?'

'There's nothing I can do. I'm fine as long as they think I'm still one of the missing, but I fear that's about to change.'

'Why's that?' she asked, not sure she was ready for his answer.

'Because Jakob Meissner's Junker turned up last month and his body with it, which is great for his family but not so great for me.' He returned his cigarette case to his pocket, getting ready to leave. 'Reiner has come up with another possibility. Another Jakob but he's got a fiancée, and what fiancée is going to fail to recognise their loved one?'

TWENTY-FOUR

Lenny closed the door of the pension behind her, the low murmur of conversation and the chink of teacups drawing her into the lounge.

She didn't want company, but she knew it would appear strange if she went straight up to her room. The habit of the household was to decamp to the lounge after supper for a friendly chat while they worked on their knitting or embroidery. There was no way of getting out of it without either causing offence or bringing on questions she wasn't prepared to answer.

'You're late.' Marianne rose to her feet, placing her embroidery on her vacated seat. 'A little tisane before we break up for the night. There's still some in the pot. I managed to get some lemon verbena to add to the chamomile. It will help us sleep.'

'Yes, do join us,' Maeva said, thin as a stick and prone to sniffling even when she wasn't ill, glancing up from her dog-eared copy of *Les Misérables*.

Claudine, the shy one of the group, gave a nod of encouragement.

To sit.

To chat.

To lie to the women who'd taken her in and treated her with

nothing but kindness, had been one of her first hard lessons in the art of spying. To remain composed when her mind was still reeling from seeing James. She didn't know what to feel. What to think except perhaps cheated.

Cheated.

Blinking, she focused on the group as she mulled over the word. A word that seemed to work as well as any other. Cheated out of the last year due to the bloodiness of war. Cheated out of the last year and with no resolution in sight. Worry about what James was going through and knowing there was no way to help him.

'A tisane would be wonderful, thank you.' She collapsed into the nearest chair and slipped off her shoes. Her smile was more difficult to slip into place but removing her glasses and rubbing her eyes helped disguise any lapse in that department. Pulling her knitting from her bag did the rest.

Marianne poured her a cup of the weak brew from the silver-plated pot on the side table and carried it over. 'You look tired, Léonore.'

'A little.' She thanked her for her drink, aware that the woman was waiting for more.

Marianne worked in the school office across from the book-shop, a nine-to-five job with little to distinguish one day from the other. Lenny envied the uniformity that came with the job as well as being in the presence of children.

'The party went on, you know.'

The women were silent, a change that had her eyeing them briefly, her long eyelashes concealing where she was looking.

There was something going on that she wasn't privy to. An underlying conversation.

She concentrated on her knitting a moment, not that she needed to. A scarf, which she'd only just started.

Knit. Purl. Dot. Dash. Click, clack. Lenny recorded everything that had happened to her from when she'd set foot in the Lumineaus' apartment, almost word for word, her thoughts spiralling in a different direction.

Marianne's room was on the first floor, facing out the front while Maeva and Claudine's rooms were at the back of the building. It was her habit to visit her room after supper to collect her embroidery. It would have only taken a moment at the window to catch the scene below.

The scene under her window.

Lenny's stomach twisted. She'd known it was risky to allow her brother to escort her back. But what choice was there? The streets were dark. The pension quiet at that hour. It had seemed innocent enough. It was completely innocent but that didn't matter when viewed through the eyes of these three women.

French women didn't consort with Germans, not if they wanted to maintain the respect of their friends and their colleagues. In occupied France, even the suggestion of consorting with the enemy was enough to stain a woman's reputation. People talked. People judged. Respect could be lost in a moment. *Fille à Boches* was one of the names they whispered out of the side of their mouth. A girl who'd chosen comfort over honour and loyalty. Comfort over their country. The same rules would apply to Sabine, if she was caught. Wealth and beauty would offer no protection.

Lenny suddenly felt sorry for the woman, but she felt sorrier for herself.

She had done nothing wrong but that wouldn't matter. These women, women she was starting to think of as friends, didn't know the first thing about her. She was in a foreign land, playing by their rules and a mistake had been made. One she had to try and rectify before it got out of hand. The worry was that it was already too late.

'In fact, I think that I might have a problem.' She set her knitting on her lap, letting moisture pool behind her lids. Unshed tears held a power stronger than any words. 'And I'm not sure how I'm going to handle it.'

'Go on.' Marianne didn't so much interrupt as announce the words into the silence.

Lenny took a breath and let her voice tremble as she met her gaze. 'You warned me, Marianne. I was stupid not to take your advice.' She paused a second, pressing her handkerchief to her mouth briefly. 'German soldier. He was at the party. I didn't notice him at first. Not at all really. He's the enemy so why would I?' She glanced up briefly. The rapt face of Claudine. Marianne's composed features. Maeva's deep suspicion starting to thaw.

'Then later he seemed to be watching me. I thought it was nothing,' she continued. 'I was polite. Professional. But after the party, he was waiting outside. He followed me.' She stared down at her lap. 'He followed me all the way home. I told him I wasn't interested. I was firm. But he didn't seem to hear. Or maybe he just didn't care.'

'Did he touch you?' Marianne asked, matter of fact.

'No. No, he just... smiled. As though it was a game. As though I'd encouraged it somehow.' Lenny forced her hands to tighten over her knitting, allowing her knuckles to whiten. 'I don't know what to do.'

The room fell silent. Then Marianne stood, walked across the room, and placed a steady hand on her shoulder.

'You told the right people,' she said quietly. 'Tomorrow I'll accompany you to the bookshop. We'll set up a little schedule with the Brossolettes to ensure that you're never left alone on your walk to and from work. No Boche bully is going to upset you.'

'Thank you, I don't know what I'd do without you.' Lenny heaved an audible sigh of relief to emphasise the point, as she folded her knitting and rose to her feet. 'If you don't mind, I think I'll go up now. Try and get some sleep.'

'You do that. Leave your cup. We'll sort it for you,' Marianne said. 'And don't you worry about a thing.'

Which was easier said than done, Lenny thought as she weaved around the chairs out into the hall, only relaxing when she reached the security of her room. It was all very well Marianne taking it upon herself to act nurse maid, but what about James? How was she meant to help him if she'd effectively been assigned a bodyguard? The truth was, it wasn't her who required protecting. It was him.

With the door closed, she propped the chair under the handle for added security.

While each of their rooms had locks no one used them. She could get away with a stiff door, the warped wood did have a tendency to stick in its frame, but using the lock would only engender a suspicion she couldn't afford. The other boarders hadn't come into her room yet, but there was always a first time.

Sending a message from the pension was a great risk. They'd been warned, more than once, about the mobile units. The equipment that could triangulate a signal in under five minutes. Messages were meant to be sent from remote fields, forest clearings, deserted barns. Not from bedrooms with faded wallpaper and thin walls. But she was prepared to take the risk. Just this once.

The wireless was easy to set up. It only required attaching the aerial, and making sure the leads were secure, while she waited for the low rumble to ease off as the valves came to life.

The message was short. A quick series of dashes and dots. She'd already translated the content into code, just enough to pass along what needed to be said, before adding her personal sign off so that they'd know it was from her.

The push to the East is starting. Operation Barbarossa.

It wasn't much. But it didn't have to be. That wasn't her job. She wasn't the one deciding what mattered; that was for the boffins in Whitehall, poring over every detail in dimly lit rooms.

Her finger hovered as she quickly converted one last line of message into code.

Brother J alive. In need of urgent assistance.

Her hands moved fast now, dismantling the set with the practised efficiency they'd learnt at the manor. She'd been half expecting to hear the faint creak of the stairs, but it was still a shock when it came.

She shoved the wireless back into the suitcase and kicked it under the bed, her hand dragging the chair back as the door handle rattled, accompanied by a belated knock as the door pushed open.

'It's me. Marianne.'

She stared wide-eyed from the chair to Lenny, her mouth open in surprise and distrust.

Lenny would have laughed if she wasn't tense with the thought that it could have been the SS at her door. She'd escaped one enemy only to find another, one far closer to home. Marianne, whom she'd viewed moments before with complete innocence.

The enemy at her door.

Inside her room.

Who would have thought.

With her hand still gripping the chair, the other pressed to her chest as if to calm her racing heart. Her thoughts whirled, searching for an excuse that would explain the chair.

'Thank goodness, Marianne. Go fetch a broom. It's either that or me sleeping on the landing tonight,' she said, her voice a breathless squeak. 'A spider. I swear to God. Bigger than a saucer.'

TWENTY-FIVE

Thursday 5 June, 1941 – Paris 10.50 am

The days rolled into the next week with nothing to break the monotony. Days slipped by behind the counter of the bookshop, while evenings slipped by in the parlour, knitting under the muted glow from the shaded lamp in the corner. She'd finished the scarf, which she'd taken to carrying about in the bottom of her bag. It was far too precious to let it fall into the wrong hands, until she'd arranged for it to be dropped off to the Free Zone where it would be transported to England, via Spain and Portugal.

There was still no reply from London, not that she'd expected one. They'd be more interested in Operation Barbarossa than following up on her message about James. And she had nothing more to give them. After confiding in Pierre about Marianne nearly catching her, they'd agreed to curtail any further evening activities. With Marianne and Pierre walking her to and from the bookshop, there was no room for anything else.

The only part of her that felt free was her thoughts. Her thoughts were her own. Nobody else would want them.

She was in a very dark place about her inability to help her brother – she could see no way out of his predicament.

Thursday morning brought a new delivery of books, which she carefully unpacked, priced, and added to the thinning shelves. There was comfort in the ritual, but her mind wandered as she stripped the window and rearranged the new display of Albert Camus and Jean-Paul Sartre's latest tomes, duster in hand as she stretched across the wooden plinth to polish the far corner of the glass.

Outside, the street was busy as life continued, despite the umbrella of war and everything it meant hovering over their heads. Proud defiant Parisians went about their daily lives, their chins high even if their smart clothes and shoes were showing signs of wear and tear. Women in tailored coats and worn heels queued for bread at the baker's next door, their chatter silenced when the enemy marched by.

Lenny watched them from her place behind the window as she polished the glass and flicked away flecks of dust. She also watched the Germans. A quick glance into each of their faces before returning her attention to what she was doing. She didn't know she was looking for anyone other than her brother until one of them stopped and turned.

The immaculate black tunic topped with its smart cap, Indifferent hair and that nose. Herr Standartenführer Otto Reiner. The man from the party.

James's boss.

She continued what she was doing, giving what she hoped was a passable impression of someone too busy to stop.

It didn't matter. He came into the shop, the little bell above the door announcing his presence, his stare hard and unwavering.

Pierre strode over. She listened to their exchange, her head bent as she worked on a stubborn mark at the bottom of the windowpane.

'Good morning, Herr Officer. Welcome to Librairie Universelle. What can I do for you today?'

'Your assistant in the window. A word if you please,' he replied, his French heavily accented.

'Of course.' Pierre walked across the small space to pop his head around the partition, his expression carefully schooled, his eyes round and wary.

What have you done?

'Léonore, there's a gentleman to see you.'

Lenny smoothed her expression into a uniform blandness, aware of the officer's scrutiny as she climbed out of the window.

'Good morning, Herr Officer.'

He eyed her up and down from the top of her untidy hair to her dusty shoes, his hand extended.

'Your papers.'

'Of course. In my bag.' She slid behind the counter where her battered leather bag was stored. A thin affair, which she used to carry everything. With her papers tucked at the bottom, she ended up having to pile her knitting and scarf on the counter to reach them.

The edges of her documents were curled, the paper worn despite the people over in Leamington Spa only completing them a few short weeks ago.

She watched as he opened them, his movements slow and deliberate. He read both from front to back, his finger marking his place as he lifted his head and barked out questions.

'Your full name and date of birth.'

'Léonore Bouchard. The first of June 1922.' Her voice was steady, her expression calm, her hands behind her back curled into tight fists.

'Place of birth?'

'Saint Pierre.'

'Your parents' names?'

'Marcel Bouchard and Lucie, neé Girard.'

He checked each answer carefully before gathering the cards together, tapping the edges against the counter.

'Where are your parents now?'

'In the cemetery, Herr Officer. Both deceased.'

That drew a frown but not a cessation in the questions. She

stared back at him, her heart hammering in her chest. *This is nothing like Major Buckmaster's interrogation.* When she got back to London she'd be sure to tell him.

If I get back.

She watched as he fingered her knitting before pouncing on the scarf. 'A little warm for a woollen scarf, is it not?'

Lenny's heart shivered in her chest, fear expanding from her veins to her blood and all the organs beyond.

'Absolutely. I only finished it yesterday and will post it today, to my aunt. The winters can be harsh in Brittany.' She dropped her mouth open, her gaze taking on that dazed quality she'd practised in the mirror. 'Do you knit, Herr Officer?'

He continued staring at her.

The sound of the shop door opening and the bell doing its thing caused him to click his heels and turn without further word.

Lenny exhaled, a bead of sweat dripping from the back of her neck to her waist as she gathered her documents and stuffed them into the bottom of her bag, the scarf on top.

The customer didn't comment on the visit, but neither did she buy anything. In fact, she only paused to check that the officer had disappeared around the corner before following him, her back broom-handle stiff.

'Not sure we'll be seeing her again in a hurry,' Pierre said, gesturing for Lenny to get back into the window. The semblance of normality was important, when no one trusted anyone else. 'Never mind, she only ever buys pencils. Must have drawers full of the things.'

Back in the window, Lenny shifted a pile of books from one end to the other to dust underneath, her hands not as steady as she'd have liked. Was his visit a coincidence, or a carefully planned exercise? Reiner could easily have asked Madame Lumineau about her, although she wouldn't have been able to tell him much.

Only her name and her place of work, she remembered, sitting back on her heels, her heart slowly returning to its normal rhythm.

It was enough for him to find her. She'd thought at the time he'd had his suspicions. The man wasn't stupid. None of them were.

If he doubts me, then what about James?

Lenny was desperate for news of her brother, whether good or bad, and she couldn't believe that it would be good. Their meeting had left her torn. Overjoyed that he was alive, but in a deep depression over what he'd endured and what he was still enduring. Not knowing where he was or how to contact him was tearing her apart. She tried to console herself that, if he tried to track her down, it might lead Reiner back to her door and, if he went to the pension... She blinked, still unsure of what to think about her landlady.

Marianne, with her kind eyes and calming voice. Marianne, who had seemed a friend and almost maternal in her ways. But the unannounced visit to her room, as if she was trying to catch her out, had been a step out of sync. Lenny didn't know anything about her. Only that she worked at the school and had no family. Both Maeva and Claudine were open about their homes and their relatives. There was little she didn't know about Maeva's twin sister or Claudine's brother, but Marianne was a closed book. Dead parents back in Alsace and a wish to leave that behind to start a new life in Paris.

It was all a bit nebulous and, well, convenient. Convenient enough for Lenny to tie the end of her sturdiest ball of wool to her hidden radio set and lower it from her open window within minutes of the woman failing to find any trace of the spider. It was a simple enough act to move the suitcase out of sight early the following morning, under the pretext of cutting some fronds from the pots of lavender that flanked the garden path. Marianne's suspicion might remain but, with nothing to feed it, there was little she could do, or that's what Lenny hoped.

With the window finished, she finally clambered backwards, swiping at the dust on her knees before attempting to coax her tight bun back into some semblance of order, two hairpins clamped between her teeth. The shop window had turned into a mammoth job, far larger than she'd anticipated, but a quick peek over the top of the screen that separated the shop from the display, revealed it had been worth the effort.

Satisfied, she jammed the final pin into place a little harder than necessary before replacing the duster where it lived in a box under the counter, adding her apron on top and heading for the door.

'I'm just going to see what it looks like from across the street. Back in a minute.'

'If the queue's not too bad, can you grab a baguette too, please?' Pierre called from behind a large ledger, where he was frowning over the accounts. 'Ask them to add it to our bill.'

'Will do.'

Lenny paused at the door, waiting for a pair of cyclists to pass before crossing the road, her gaze roaming left and right to check for German uniforms. For once the boulevard was clear.

The window display looked even better from across the street. The window sparkling, the new books striking against the black backdrop of the screen. At least the morning hadn't been totally wasted. The bookshop looked better, and she'd learnt a valuable lesson.

To never underestimate the enemy.

Reiner had shaken her more than she'd realised, but her training had helped as had the thought that he'd have arrested her if he'd had any proof. It had been a fact-finding expedition and one she'd passed. If he decided to take a little trip to Saint Pierre, he'd even discover the grave of Marcel Bouchard, and his devoted wife, Lucie. There'd be a daughter too, her name carefully recorded in the local church records. Léonore. No one could quite remember what had happened to her.

The power of the resistance movements in rural communities like the Brittany coast was unstoppable.

With a warm baguette tucked under her arm, she pushed open the shop door, only to freeze on the threshold.

The man had his back to her, one hand resting on the counter in the same way Reiner had only a short time before. But this man was dressed differently. Instead of black, he wore a beige jacket pulling slightly across broad shoulders. Dark blond hair, a touch too long. Cream trousers, a little baggy at the seat. Brown shoes made of good quality leather, but in need of a polish. There were a hundred similarly clad men in Paris. No, a thousand. Any man and every man going about his business. Someone who'd dropped into the shop on the off chance. Maybe even someone captivated by the latest books by Camus and Sartre displayed in the window. Except that there was nothing coincidental about this customer's presence.

When she'd put the call out for help at the end of her last message to London, Lenny had been asking for a miracle. That the miracle had arrived in the form of Harry Dennison was a shock. The kind of shock she didn't know what to do with. They weren't friends. In fact, she'd probably have termed him a passing acquaintance if it hadn't been for her last evening in London, standing outside her apartment, the feel of his hand pressing on her cheek. A man she didn't understand. She understood her response to him even less.

He wasn't a friend, but he could be.

She suddenly recalled James's comment about Harry's possible thing for her. He'd been hovering at the corner of her thoughts ever since.

He could be much more, if only the war allowed.

TWENTY-SIX

Lunch would have been a meagre affair with the baguette and soup stretched between four, if Lenny's appetite hadn't deserted her. With food increasingly scarce for those without money for the black market, it was only the foolish or the ill who ignored the offer of a wholesome meal.

'No bread, thank you,' she declined, for the second time, placing her spoon back in her bowl and pushing it away.

It wasn't only her appetite that had deserted her. Hoping that Harry might drop in at any moment to check on them after her message to London was one thing. Seeing him in person something completely different.

'They picked up Agnès last month, Harold.' Pierre frowned, reaching for the salt. 'That makes three now. They're closing in.'

Talk of Agnès Humbert being locked up in Cherche Midi Prison dropped her back in the present with a thump. They'd barely settled around the table when the conversation had turned to the war. The little bookstore in the heart of the 16th Arrondissement might have had to stop its pamphlet production but, as far as Pierre was concerned, that was only a minor hiccup.

'They're restless,' Harry said quietly. 'There's a shift coming.

The word in London is that they're preparing for something. You were wise to stop the newsletter, but the work must continue.'

Pierre leant forward. 'In that case the networks must be unified. We can't keep going on like this.'

'That's in part why I'm here,' Harry replied. 'London wants a structure. A secure channel between here and de Gaulle.'

Gilberte tutted her disapproval as she passed around small cups of black coffee. 'Secure? When our friends are vanishing overnight?'

Harry's voice hardened. 'If we don't move now, there won't be anyone left to organise. We have a duty to protect our soldiers, moving them out of harm's way before the Germans strike.'

'And if they've struck already? What then? They seem to have all the power, hold all the cards. The Germans are everywhere, Harold,' Lenny said, following suit by using the French version of his name.

She'd spent the last hour trying to focus on the conversation. The news from London. The arrest of Rudolf Hess. The rumour coming out of Bletchley Park of a significant development in their codebreaking efforts that could help them win the war. It was all white noise as far as she was concerned.

The war would be won or lost by the little men and women. The likes of her, James, Bill and Georges were collectively playing their part, but at what cost? She'd already lost her home and her friends in this fight for supremacy. She'd be damned if she'd lose her brother. Not again.

The first time had nearly broken her.

'You mean the message you sent about James turning up.' His tone softened slightly over her brother's name, but they'd been friends. Members of the same hockey team despite their six-year age difference. 'Tell me about him?'

'Yes, do.' Gilberte started gathering the crockery. 'And while you're catching up, Pierre and I will open the shop. Take as long as you like. If anyone comes asking, and I can't for a moment think that they will, we'll say you're busy unpacking our new stock and can't be disturbed. Come along, Pierre. If you can take the cups for me while I deal with the plates.'

'I'm not sure I like your hair dragged back like that, and as for the glasses. I take it you're taking your role of bookseller to heart?'

Harry's words when they were finally alone were almost as much of a shock as seeing him in the shop earlier.

'Excuse me?' As an opening it was as confusing as the rest of her week, what with Marianne, James, Reiner and everything else that had gone with it. She waited in the lengthening silence, watching as he shifted his chair closer to the table, his arms folded in front of him, his gaze unwavering.

'Your appearance,' he said. 'I barely recognise you as the sweet girl who used to turn up to our hockey matches.'

If there was a reply, Lenny struggled to find it. There was more to unpick from his words, but surely now wasn't the time.

'I don't think my looks come into it. We're here to discuss my brother.'

'There's no immediate rush, is there? The Brossolettes did say that they're happy to hold the fort.' He idly brushed at a couple of crumbs, the last remnants of the baguette, as if her reply bored him. He didn't look at her. That, at least, was something to be thankful for. 'You could tell me again why you didn't get in touch when you arrived in London? You had my number. It took me a good couple of weeks to realise you weren't going to bother.'

Lenny lowered her gaze to the table. Her emotions, usually tightly controlled, were in threat of exploding. After Reiner's visit, she was terrified that he'd decided to arrest both her and James. He wouldn't have interrogated her otherwise. Harry looked so laid-back. Completely at ease with the situation. But he had come to her rescue. She could afford to be kind. She was also intrigued enough to delve a little deeper into what was happening between them.

'I left your number on the train which, I might add, I regretted. A friendly face in Whitehall would have helped, then. I take it you are a friendly face, Harold? Oftentimes I've wondered.'

He shifted in his seat, his hands brushing the crumbs into two small, neat piles. An important task that demanded all his attention.

'The best thing I could have done for you during your training was to treat you like one of the men,' he told her quietly. 'That I wanted to drag you away from the danger and horror of the war was the biggest challenge I faced. If the majors had realised...' He gave up on the sentence, his hands still, his gaze averted.

Lenny concentrated on his fingers. Long, slim fingers attached to narrow wrists. She'd never noticed his wrists before. Now she stared at them like a fortune teller in search of inspiration, although there was nothing forthcoming. No words, only the need not to upset him.

She'd always known that she was prim. It was hardly surprising with the rigidity of her upbringing. It might have been different if her parents had been alive, but Aunt Madge was a staunch, God-fearing Methodist. Boys were to be avoided, and mostly girls too. The wayward kind who rolled their hair and stained their lips. Lenny hadn't minded, not really. Her life revolved around her brother and her books. Her only other outlet was the knitting group. Relationships were messy, complicated things and, to the uninitiated, terrifying.

Lenny had never even noticed that he might be interested in her. She'd never thought to look. In Weymouth he'd been James's friend and, after, the man who issued instructions and decided if she made the team. He was older, more polished and experienced. A world apart. She was just the girl who kept her head down, doing the work necessary. She'd suspected that he'd been aloof for a multitude of reasons, never for a moment thinking that he liked her.

She'd cut the wires to her heart when her brother had disap-peared. Now it seemed as if fate had decided to solder them back into some kind of workable order.

'I thought that you...' She trailed off. 'I don't know what I thought. You'll have to excuse me. I've never been in this position before.'

'I can't believe that.'

'Well, it's true.' She took a chance and placed her hand over his, his fingers curling around her palm, on some level aware that he wasn't going to push the conversation further without something from her.

It felt nice sitting with him, more than nice but there was James to consider. The stakes were high, too high for her not to want to talk about her brother. Pierre and Gilberte couldn't help, even if they wanted to. They had no choice but to continue their daily routine, or risk being outed by the Germans as enemies of the regime. With suspicious Marianne shadowing her steps, it was even more vital that no one in the bookshop put a foot wrong.

Harry, as an outsider, was all she had. He might be all she needed.

'I never thought I'd say this,' she said, removing her hand and using it to prop up her chin. 'What are you doing later? Perhaps we could meet up after work to... to discuss whatever this is and, in the meantime, I can tell you about my brother.'

He laughed. 'For someone not very experienced, you do a nice job of asking a man out. I accept but don't make a habit of it.' His face relaxed into a smile, as if a heavy weight had been taken from his shoulders. 'By all means let's talk about James.'

Lenny's relief at changing the subject was short lived. In spite of her training and rigid self-control, she felt her cheeks flood with colour. There was nothing she could do about the terrible mess her brother had got himself into, except try to explain his situation without actually saying the words. She wouldn't know where to begin. It was lucky that James had mentioned Bertrand. At one time he'd been the most popular barber in St Peter Port, which meant there was a good chance Harry would know who she was talking about. There was the scarf too, of course. The scarf that must get to London.

The scarf that was currently in her handbag under the counter in the shop.

'Remember the barber up Fountain Street before the war? The one with the oiled hair and thin moustache?'

If Harry was surprised, he hid it remarkably well. 'You mean Bertrand? I don't see how that's...?'

He stopped mid-sentence. Sat back hard, arms folding across his chest. 'No way. I don't believe it. Not James.'

Lenny flapped her hand at him, desperate to make him understand. 'It doesn't matter what you believe. It's what the Germans believe that counts. Some of them think he's this man called Jakob, who's lost his memory, while others think he's... like Bertrand. Meanwhile, his senior officer, an SS beast called Otto Reiner is trying to prove who he really is. Even going so far as to dig up a woman he says could be his fiancée. James can't exactly refuse to see her without giving himself away.'

Harry lifted his hand briefly to stop her.

'Lenny, you're making no sense whatsoever. Start at the beginning. Slowly.'

TWENTY-SEVEN

Harry didn't exactly laugh, not out loud, but it was there in the crinkle of his eyes and the lopsided twitch of his mouth. However, he must have noticed something in her expression, because his reply was serious enough.

'In short, your brother is doing his best not to be discovered, but everyone seems to be conspiring against him. And if we don't do something smartish...?'

'He'll be arrested. Or worse.' Lenny bit her bottom lip, determined to be brave and failing miserably.

'Poor James,' he said, but in a way which told her that he really meant it. 'He's only a kid really,' he continued, rubbing his fingers along his jaw. 'Idealistic to a fault. Always wanting to save the world and everything in it, when the rest of us know that's an impossible task. Man was born flawed. It takes good men like James to make us realise it.'

He reached across the table and took her hand, laying it flat across his warm palm. She could have removed it, but she didn't. Instead, she waited for him to continue, the air between them thick with the smell of old, musty books and an emotion she couldn't put a name to.

'I'm sorry if I've made you feel uncomfortable,' he said at last.

'It won't happen again. I should have remembered how close you two are.' He curled her fingers into a light fist before sliding his hand away.

'Right then. It's clear that we need to get him out. The only question is how and when. Let me do a little digging about this Reiner person. About us.' He pushed back his chair. 'I'll pick you up outside the pension at seven. There's a little café I know. If I can't make it, I'll leave word with Pierre.'

Downstairs, the shop was busy with a steady stream of customers, drawn in by the new books in the window. An event that was becoming increasingly scarce, but great for business.

Lenny busied herself at the counter, tidying a small pile of books that had been picked up, thumbed through, and abandoned in favour of other titles, the scarf beside her. She put the lid back on their precious store of sealing wax before straightening the brown paper used to wrap purchases. Pierre was a traditionalist, fiercely proud of following the old bookseller's customs. It was a way of life that was disappearing, as the war dragged on and resources ran out.

Harry roamed the shop, picking up one book, then another, flicking through the pages before sliding each volume carefully back into place. Lenny watched him out of the corner of her eye, uncertain of what he was up to, or why he lingered. Perhaps he had unfinished business with Pierre. He'd insisted on taking charge of the situation with her brother and she'd been happy to let him. She didn't know how he intended to proceed, which was probably wise.

There was always a risk in knowing too much.

The little bell above the entrance tinkled, and suddenly it all made sense.

She'd told Harry about Marianne along the way, mostly to rearrange her muddled thoughts about the woman rather than to ask for help. She hadn't said much. She didn't have to. He was clever enough to fill in the blanks. The woman had an agenda. Only time would tell what that was.

Marianne hesitated in the doorway, a silhouette against the

grey street beyond. Her piercing gaze darted from Harry to Pierre before settling on Lenny. There was no smile, nothing to alleviate the suddenly tension-filled room.

Lenny saw all this and more in the second it took for the bell to settle back in its housing. The slight stiffening of Pierre's shoulders where he was sorting through a box of books on the other side of the shop. The way Harry averted his head, concentrating on the book resting between his hands. Gilberte balancing on the top of the ladder, her hand outstretched as she reached for the top shelf. A customer, a man in a brown jumper, placing a book down on the counter with a small thud.

A snapshot of life in an average bookshop anywhere in the world except there was nothing average about Librairie Universelle in the 16th Arrondissement of Paris, or the people who inhabited it.

The bookshop was full of spies, but sadly she wasn't sure if all of them were on the same side.

'Can I help you, monsieur?' Lenny asked, pinning a small smile in place as she tried to engage the customer in the social niceties.

His answer was abrupt, disinterested, rude even, his attention on the small selection of pens and pencils displayed in a wooden box, a five-franc note placed between them.

Lenny widened her eyes, shrugging at Marianne briefly, her meaning clear.

We have a right one here.

Marianne gave a thin smile in return, stepping back to allow another customer through the door. The bell tinkled once, then again, harder, as the door banged shut behind her.

But she wasn't gone. Lenny caught a glimpse of her through the window, standing just beyond the awning, the tip of her cigarette glowing like a small red eye. There was just time to hand Harry the Morse code scarf on her way past before they closed for the evening.

. . .

'The shop was very busy this afternoon. Busier than normal, Léonore?'

There was no artifice to Marianne. The words slipped out as soon as the door to the bookshop closed behind them, but Lenny was ready for her.

'Yes. I'm so pleased for Pierre and Gilberte. They work so hard at trying to make a success of it,' she replied, forcing herself to sound breathless rather than calculating. She took a moment to look first left, then right, scanning the street for any sign of her brother, her eyes wide, her thumping heart adding a little extra tremor to her manner. Let Marianne think she was terrified of meeting the German again.

She was terrified, but for a very different reason.

The pension that had once felt like a safe haven now felt like a trap. She couldn't lock her door without appearing suspicious, and she didn't have the luxury of staying in her room to avoid a confrontation, for the same reason.

Great spy she was proving to be, she thought, keeping pace with Marianne's quick footsteps. She couldn't even send a message back to London with her radio out of bounds, hidden under a loose floorboard in the summer house at the bottom of the garden. All her fancy ideas of helping Churchill set Europe ablaze. The reality was far grittier. If she wasn't careful, she'd find herself locked up and then where would she be? Where would James be? Putting others at risk if they decided to rescue them.

What a mess.

'Who was the man in the brown jumper? I didn't recognise him.' Marianne suddenly demanded, stopping in the middle of the street and turning to face her.

'The man in the brown jumper?' Lenny replied, taking a step back to avoid bumping into the teenager rushing past. The little hesitation was all she needed to think up a reply that might suit Marianne's curiosity. 'Oh, you mean the man who bought a copy of *The Imaginary* just now? Sartre is such a wonderful writer, don't you think? I didn't notice what he was wearing. Why, is it important?'

Marianne tutted as she resumed walking. 'All strangers in Paris are important. There's a war on, or had you forgotten? Sometimes I wonder about you, Léonore, and then I remember. You're a stranger too.'

'Not so strange, I hope?'

'What part of France did you say you hailed from again?' Marianne ignored her attempt at humour. They'd arrived outside the pension, the window boxes of red geraniums adding a splash of colour to the stone wall.

'Saint Pierre. It's on the Brittany coast. A small fishing village, so small most people have never heard of it.'

'Yes, I thought that was the name. How convenient.'

'Not if you live there,' Lenny replied. 'Great place to grow up. Not so great as an adult. Nothing to do.'

They mounted the steps to the pension side by side. Lenny's hand was already on the door when Marianne added, almost casually.

'Oh, before I forget, I asked Auguste to turn your room out earlier. Can't have any unwanted spiders disturbing your rest. It's spick and span like a new pin, and funnily enough no trace of any spiders, or their webs.' She shrugged, one of those expressive gallic ones that Frenchwomen do so effortlessly, a wealth of meaning in the simple movement.

We both know you were lying about the spider, and I intend to find out why.

'Surprisingly she also didn't find your suitcase,' Marianne added from the bottom of the stairs, her pink-tipped fingers lingering on the banister. 'I could have sworn that you arrived with one. A small, leather affair with brass studs. I noticed particularly as I've been looking for something similar for ages now.' She shrugged again. 'Oh, well, I must have been mistaken, just as Auguste must have missed the spider.'

TWENTY-EIGHT

The café on the corner of the Rue de Longchamp and the Rue de La Pompe was packed, its customers spilling out onto the pavement, the wicker tables and chairs full. The striped canvas awning had been peeled back, allowing the last of the evening sunshine to bounce off the wine carafes and tall glasses of pastis. A small slice of Paris where, for once, there was nothing to remind her of the war. No German uniforms. No Germans that she could spot. It didn't mean that there weren't any or, even worse, that there weren't any German sympathisers.

Men and women who acted French but were anything but.

The worst!

Harry directed her through the narrow passage between tables and into the cool interior, choosing a secluded spot at the back, out of the way of prying eyes. They hadn't spoken on the short journey to the café, but he'd taken her arm, his hand a comforting presence after the words she'd had with Marianne.

'What would you like to drink?' he asked, a grin flickering right to his eyes as they both remembered a previous conversation on the very same subject. It seemed a long time ago.

Centuries.

'A lemonade, please.'

Harry lifted his hand to signal the waiter and placed his order before removing his jumper. The scarf stayed looped around his neck, the safest place for it, the strange pattern of knit and purl lost in the weave she'd chosen.

'You're wearing the jumper.'

'Of course.' He patted it gently. 'You were very kind to make it for me.'

'I'm not sure I had a choice, being as you're my boss.'

'Well, I'm not your boss now, Léonore.' He used the French version of her name but, then, they were speaking French. 'I'd like to think that I'm your friend.'

'I can work with that, Harold.' Lenny removed her glasses and rubbed the mark between her nose where they didn't fit properly. She went to put them back only to stop, the glasses dangling from her fingers.

'No, leave them.' He paused. Briefly. Reconsidering his choice of words. 'That is, if you don't mind.'

She folded the arms and placed them on the table between them, feeling a little awkward. The arrival of the waiter with two lemonades and a fresh ashtray was a welcome distraction. In truth she didn't know what she was doing here, or what to say. What could they talk about. Certainly not the war, or any of the other highly volatile conversations that could lead to their arrest if the wrong person was passing by on the way to the toilets, situated at the back of the café.

Perhaps not the cleverest of places in which to sit.

The fact that he knew James meant that he probably knew about her, or thought he did, when she didn't know the first thing about him. A good place to start.

She picked up her drink and took a small sip, the silence between them growing to ocean wide. Lenny would never have taken him for being nervous, but there was something about his manner. The way he was avoiding her gaze, his hand tight around his glass. Maybe he wasn't as confident as he proclaimed, or she thought. Maybe she'd made assumptions about him that weren't true.

Only one way to find out.

'What were you doing when we met at the harbour, Harold? I think you said something about your parents?'

'Visiting Mum and Dad.' He took a quick swig from his glass, trying to disguise a grimace at the sweet taste. 'A good job I did.'

'Have you heard how they are?'

'Only the occasional Red Cross letter. Can't say much in twenty-five words, eh.'

Lenny nodded, remembering the occasional Red Cross letter she got from Mrs Gardiner back in London. That she was alive and coping was a relief. 'Any brothers or sisters? You know about James being my only living relative?'

He nodded briefly, removing his cigarettes and choosing one with care. 'I'm an only child, which makes it tougher on Mum and Dad, especially when I joined up as soon as the war was announced. Little did I think that my year bumming around France after leaving school would stand me in good stead for my future career.'

'You worked here?'

'In the outskirts. A café similar to this one.'

'And no wife, girlfriend or significant other?' She felt brave asking, but the simple fact was that she wanted to know why she was here.

'I'm working on it.' He shot her a boyish grin, so fleeting that she'd have missed it if she hadn't been looking. 'My dating went out the window the first time James brought his sister to watch him play, pigtails and all.' He took his time tapping the ash from the end of his cigarette, seemingly riveted on the task. 'I think he suspected although I never said anything. You were only sixteen, a mere kid to my twenty-two and therefore out of bounds.'

Lenny lifted her hand to her hair and the tight bun, as she thought on his words, a few wayward curls framing her face. She remembered those pigtails. The tightness in her scalp, which felt like Aunt Madge was pulling her hair out in handfuls.

'Six years age gap isn't too much, not these days,' she finally said, glancing at the waiter, who'd stopped beside their table to remove their empty glasses. 'And there's a huge difference between a sixteen-year-old and an eighteen-year-old.' That she'd had her birthday during her training was something she'd chosen to forget. An irrelevance with everything else that had been going on. Now it seemed important. 'How about we get some wine, Harold? White if possible. I'm not sure I'm ready for red yet.'

'You don't have to for me, Léonore.'

'I'm not. I'm doing it for us.'

The walk home was very different from the one to the café. The war was partly to blame. It had speeded up the natural order of things, like dating. A life well lived and well-loved meant something different now. Lenny had been offered happiness on a plate, and she'd decided to grab it with open arms, stuffing herself full in case someone decided to remove it.

They chatted like old friends, catching up after a long absence, their arms linked, their laughter only muffled when they spotted a German in the distance.

'When can I see you again?' Harry stood in nearly the exact same spot as James had a week before, his voice soft, his warm gaze never leaving her face, their hands entwined.

'Would tomorrow be too soon?'

He dropped his head and pressed a soft kiss against her cheek, the smell of his light aftershave tickling her nose. 'If you must leave me waiting that long, then so be it.'

She was still smiling when she pushed open the door to the pension only to find Marianne waiting for her, her arms folded across her chest, her lips pursed.

'Is everything alright?'

Lenny took the time to glance down at her watch, which told her it was still early. Not even nine. The house rule was everyone in by ten, when the door would be locked. A rule they both remembered. 'I'm not too late, am I?'

Marianne ignored that. 'I was worried about you,' she said, her words at war with her suspicious expression. She wasn't worried. She wanted to know what Lenny had been up to and with whom.

'There's no need to be. I told you I wouldn't be in for supper.'

'But where were you? We were worried.'

Lenny wasn't sure what Marianne was up to, but her words sounded genuine enough. 'Just out with a friend. We went to that little café on the Rue de Longchamp.' She slipped off her jacket and hung it on the coat hook, her hands working on unpinning her hat. One of the first rules they'd been taught was to stick to the truth as much as possible unless there was a reason to lie.

'A German?'

Lenny maintained a bland expression, trying to work out where the older woman was going with this. It had been a week since she'd mentioned being followed home. The worst of decisions. Her life hadn't felt like her own since. Someone always checking up on her. If she could put the clock back.

She couldn't do that. Instead, she'd have to brave it out. Give a little, but not too much.

'No, of course not. His name is Harold Martin. I met him at the bookshop.' She tilted her chin a little. 'He's a friend.'

Marianne's frown collapsed into a forced smile. 'Well, next time you meet, you'll have to introduce us. I like to meet the friends of my... young ladies.' She closed and bolted the door behind her. 'It will be exciting to hear about your evening.'

Lenny would have far rather gone up to her bedroom to think about Harry. To relive each word, glance and touch while it was still fresh in her memory. Instead, she retrieved her knitting from her room before settling in her usual chair beside the window.

'Ah, Léonore. We missed you this evening.'

'Out gallivanting with some nice young man, Claudine,' Marianne said, working on her embroidery.

'Really?' Claudine leant forward, her eyes wide. 'Not the German?'

'No. I wouldn't.' Lenny's voice must have held enough of a note of shock for them to believe her. 'Just someone I met at the bookshop. He's called Harold and as French as you and me.'

Claudine settled back, her expression softening. 'That's a relief.'

Maeva clapped her hands in delight. 'A romance, Léonore?'

Lenny smiled, a sweet smile she couldn't hide even if she'd wanted to. She'd spent enough time with the two women to know that they both lived difficult lives in a Paris that didn't seem like their home anymore. Claudine's brother was a prisoner of war in Germany while Maeva couldn't be sure where her twin sister was. Reputedly somewhere in the Free Zone, but she hadn't heard from her in months.

'I'm not sure. Hopefully so. He seems... very nice. A gentleman,' she added, picking up her knitting and arranging her wool just so.

The collective sigh from all three women told her that she'd played the conversation just right.

TWENTY-NINE

Friday 6 June, 1941 – Paris 4.50 pm

Lenny had felt a quiet sense of anticipation all day. Her thoughts had gone rogue, taking a detour from the troubles of her brother and concerns about the escalating situation between the Vichy government and what de Gaulle was up to in London. She was here to do a job and all she could think about was Harry and what outfit she could cobble together from her limited wardrobe. Her mind refused to concentrate on the seriousness of what was happening across Europe, instead favouring more vacuous mental pursuits. She'd already decided to arrange her hair in a loose chignon, instead of her trademark tight bun. Her glasses, however, would have to stay in case she met someone she knew.

The bookshop had emptied out around three and, for the last two hours, all she'd served was a teenager in need of art supplies for a school project. Since then she'd mooned about dusting dust-free shelves, trying to decide between her navy or her black dress, a floaty scarf tied around her throat to soften the harsh neckline. She felt guilty, but it was easy to console herself that Harry was in a far better position to help James than she was.

And as for the rest.

France seemed to be teetering on the edge of a cliff. The resistance had taken a hit with the recent spate of arrests. They were all living for de Gaulle's next radio broadcast from London. Waiting for his next move. Until then, Pierre wanted her to continue at the bookshop and curb everything else. Reiner's visit had unsettled him. It had unsettled her too, but not enough to dislodge the budding excitement at the thought of seeing Harry.

Lenny glanced down at her watch, wishing the hands would move quicker. Gilberte was upstairs, so she was alone and bored. She wandered over to the window and peered out at the street for something to do. The sky was darkening, thick grey clouds scudding across the rooftops. People hurrying instead of the leisurely stride she was getting used to.

No one rushed in Paris unless they were late, or if it was raining.

One umbrella, then two appeared. Within seconds, the boulevard was transformed with brightly coloured umbrellas and the shop filled with the sound of hurrying feet as the clouds opened.

Just my luck.

The words had barely left her mouth when the door was pushed open. Pierre and Harry rushed in, laughing as they scattered water across the clean floor.

'Five minutes later and we'd be drenched.' Pierre slipped off his jacket, holding his hand out for Harry's. 'I'll hang it upstairs. You can borrow one of mine. We're about the same size. I'll ask Gilberte to put together some bread and cheese. The sooner we leave the better.'

Lenny watched Harry as he removed his hat and jacket before sweeping his hand through his hair, barely aware that Pierre had walked to the back of the room and the steep staircase beyond.

'Hello there.' Harry walked towards her, his hands outstretched, his smile tender.

'Hello yourself.' Lenny took his hands, her heart jumping as her gaze roamed his face. His blue eyes creased with laughter lines and the way his eyebrows arched in the middle. The slight dimple in the centre of his chin. That he was still wearing her jumper, the scarf looped around his neck. She noticed it all and more in the second she stared up at him.

'What have you two been up to?'

'Oh, this and that.' He dropped her hands at the sound of Pierre clattering down the stairs, his smile collapsing into a frown. 'Pierre and I have a package to deliver this evening, which means...'

Lenny shook her head briefly, disappointment and worry displacing her happiness. There was a war on and there was James.

The sound of a truck rumbling past had her glancing to the window, the small space of time allowing her to bring her thoughts together.

'Then we'll take a rain check.' She nodded in the direction of the window and the sheet of water covering it. 'Not a bad thing, considering.'

She wanted to ask what they'd be doing tonight. She wanted to know if there was an update from London about James, but she couldn't. He'd tell her when there was news and not before. Instead, she turned to Pierre and where he was stuffing a map into the side pocket of his bag, his car keys on the counter along with a spare jacket and a couple of umbrellas, Gilberte hovering in the background, holding a baguette wrapped in a tea towel.

'You might as well lock up, Léonore. It's unlikely we'll get any more customers with the weather.'

Lenny did as Gilberte asked, her ears tuned to the conversation carrying on behind her in soft French as she took her time in twisting the key and sliding the bolt in place.

'You will be careful. There's bound to be road checks. What time will you be back?'

'Not until the evening, ma chérie. I'll try and get a message through if something untoward happens.' Lenny turned and watched them head for the back door. At the last minute Harry stopped and turned, his expression a mix of seriousness and wonder. Then he winked.

She remembered that wink right up until she walked outside, where Marianne was waiting to escort her home.

THIRTY

Friday 6 June, 1941 – Paris 6.50 pm

'I said pass the salt, if you please?'

Lenny lifted the white pot and placed it in Marianne's outstretched palm without bothering to reply. She wasn't sure how many times she'd been asked. By the tone of Marianne's voice, more than once. It didn't matter when compared with everything else that was going on.

Marianne was in a position of safety while James was being hounded by Reiner, and Harry...

She stared down at her plate, the lentils swimming in front of her. Gilberte had let slip just before she'd left the shop that Harry and Pierre were escorting a downed RAF pilot to Montluçon, just South of the Free Zone in Vichy France. Lenny didn't begrudge them helping the crashed pilot, but she was frantic with worry.

Now that I've found Harry, I don't want to lose him.

The weather didn't help, the air heavy with rain and the threat of thunder in the yellow-edged clouds. Instead of changing out of her work clothes, she'd sat by the window and watched the deluge. The garden was awash with water as was the summer house. There hadn't been an opportunity to rescue her transmitter, and it looked as if there wasn't any point. The summer house had more holes in it than boards. A stupid choice in which to hide her case, but she'd been in a panic.

'When do you think this rain will stop?' Maeve said with a sniff, clattering her knife and fork onto the centre of her plate, her hand rummaging up her sleeve for her hankie.

'Not until the morning,' Claudine replied, taking a refined bite of sausage and starting to chew. She only spoke again when she'd dabbed her mouth with her napkin, leaving a small splodge of lipstick on the white linen. 'At least we're in the dry and the warmth.'

Lenny didn't reply. There were many things she could have said about the weather, but there was no point. Marianne would pounce on her in the same way she had since she'd arrived back from work.

Why aren't you changed? What have you been doing all this time still in your work dress?

Lenny had just shrugged as she'd slipped into her chair. Marianne was as likely to believe her about watching the rain as she had about the spider.

Instead, she concentrated on her meal. If she saw another lentil she'd scream. Surely to goodness there had to be something else to eat. They were in Paris after all. Alright, war-torn Paris but it was still the culinary capital of the world. What was wrong with a bit of cabbage or even a few carrots? Anything other than lentils.

Her head started to throb, a sudden onset of pain that had her place her cutlery back on her plate, her meal barely touched. As she placed her hand back in her lap, she noticed that it was trembling. A strange observation. Her eyes narrowed to thin slits, the air suddenly thick and heavy, the pain intensifying as the headache clawed through her brain with a relentless determination. She didn't know what had brought it on apart from worry about James and now Harry. She wasn't prone to headaches. Not since she'd lost her parents. Then, for a few months she'd barely slept for the agony in her mind, but that had been years ago. Her aunt had taken her from doctor to doctor. The small cartons of tablets had started gathering on the bathroom shelf only for the headaches to miraculously disappear at the end of summer. Hot, blistering pain one day and an unexpected coolness the next. The memory had faded, only to bounce back in full colour with the first shard of pain.

'*Léonore. Léonore?*' The voice came from somewhere above. Muted, distorted. Maeva's.

'*Do you think she's alright?*

'*She's awfully pale.*'

'*Barely touched her food.*'

'Come on, chérie. Let me help you upstairs.' She recognised Claudine's perfume as she pulled her to standing. 'That's it. One foot after the other. Soon have you tucked up in bed.'

When she woke, it was late. No light breaking through the slight gap in the blackout blind. It was also quiet. No pitter patter of raindrops against her windowpane. The only sound the occasional vehicle rumbling past. She lay there taking stock of both her surroundings and her head. The pain was still there but lighter. An ache instead of a thump. Manageable instead of incapacitating.

Stress probably.

She would have stayed in bed, enjoying the silence before sleep finally claimed her if it wasn't for the pressing need for the bathroom.

Instead of putting it off, she used her arm to lever into a sitting position, a smooth movement in case the pain ratcheted up a notch. She only pushed to her feet when she realised that the headache appeared to be under control. The candle came next. The precious nub of wax in a saucer, but she didn't want to bang into anything.

While the landing was in darkness, there was a glimmer of light shining at the bottom of the stairs, which meant it wasn't as late as she thought. Checking her watch was useless. She'd forgotten to wind it.

She hovered from one foot to the other, trying to decide what to do, her ears picking up the soft beat of something on the radio.

There was an opportunity prodding her, if only she was brave enough to take it. A little snooping while the three women were ensconced downstairs with their knitting and embroidery. Bedtime was usually ten fifteen, after their ritual tisane. If only Lenny could be assured of the time but, with the old stairs creaking like a branch about to snap, that wasn't an option.

Before she even realised what she was doing, she found herself outside Marianne's room. Her ear pressed against the wood for a second, her hand slowly starting to turn the handle.

She'd been in Marianne's room once before, when she'd lent her a book. One of the books that Pierre had allowed her to take from the shop. The fact she'd never returned it was something Lenny had only just remembered. An excuse in the event she was caught.

As the owner of the pension, Marianne had kept the best to herself. Two rooms at the front of the house, their windows overlooking the broad boulevard beyond. In the dim light cast by the flickering candle, her gaze settled on the bureau beside the window. A dainty affair with cabriole legs and marquetry finish.

The folding top revealed pigeonholes stuffed with bills marked paid, and yellowed receipts. Lenny didn't know what she'd been expecting, but something more exciting than the same detritus she'd found in her aunt's desk. She closed the lid, holding her breath a second but all was silent.

The drawers came next. The first two followed the same pattern. A ledger detailing her household expenses. A half-used book of postage stamps. Three fountain pens with broken nibs, tied together with a scrap of ribbon. A lacquered box had her heart skipping a beat only to disappoint when it revealed a pile of buttons.

She approached the bottom drawer half-heartedly.

It probably contained the woman's stash of embroidery wools, or stockings for darning, along with her supply of Nazi memorabilia. At that point it would have taken a lot to convince Lenny that Marianne was, in fact as partisan as the rest of them and, at first glance she was right. A Nazi armband along with one of their pins.

A carefully folded flag, which she ignored, the sight of the upper-most fold turning her stomach.

Here was the proof she'd been looking for. Confirmation that she wasn't safe.

She gnawed her lower lip, her headache revving up a notch. She had nowhere else to go apart from the Brossolettes' and, with the enemy closing in fast, there was still her brother to consider. He was in a far worse position than she was. Marianne might have her suspicions but what proof did she have? A spider and missing luggage wouldn't hold up against Lenny's impeccable documents, forged by the best in the business. Besides, if she wasn't French, at least she had Austrian ancestry on her mother's side.

She was pushing the drawer back in place, when some sixth sense had her reaching in to feel the underside in the way she'd been taught at Wanborough Manor.

Their tutors had hailed from many walks of life before being recruited, which meant their training was all encompassing. That it included someone who'd spent his formative years living a life of crime, shouldn't have been a surprise. What Lenny didn't know about breaking and entering wasn't worth knowing. She'd excelled at lock picking and, as for safe cracking, she'd come top of the class. According to Johnny, her small hands had been an unfair advantage.

The envelope was old and faded, the paper crinkling between her fingers. She slipped it inside her dress and, with the drawer back in place, hurried to the door, her ear pressed up to the narrow gap.

The creak was soft but unmistakeable, the old staircase doing its best to alert her to what was coming.

Lenny only had seconds to spare. With a flick of her hand, she slipped through the door, pulling it closed behind her, her fingers on the handle to ease the lock into place, her other hand clutching onto the candle in its chipped saucer. There wasn't time for anything else except to turn in the direction of the bathroom, her bladder reminding her the reason for leaving the comfort of her bed.

It was Marianne carrying a tray with a cup and saucer, the distinctive smell of her favourite tisane filling the small space.

'I was just bringing you a drink.' Her expression was wary, her eyes flitting between where Lenny was standing in the middle of the landing and the bedroom doors behind. 'You look better but you should be in bed.'

Lenny remained calm despite the tumult that was her brain.

Is the envelope tucked down far enough? Did I close the desk drawers? What about the door?

She wanted to shift her gaze, but that had been the first lesson the ex-con had taught them. The easiest way to get caught was to look back instead of moving forward. What was done was done. She had to trust that she'd done enough.

'You are kind, Marianne. I needed...' She allowed her gaze to shift to the bathroom, instead of saying the words, the pink of her cheeks adding weight to her embarrassment. She might be an expert safe cracker, but there were still things that women didn't discuss and going to the loo was one of them.

'Oh, of course.' Marianne managed a prim smile. 'I'll leave this in your room. We're coming up to bed now anyway.'

'You really are very kind. I'm sure I'll be better in the morning.' She headed to the bathroom only to stop and turn. 'What's the time, Marianne? My watch has stopped.'

'Ten fifteen. Bedtime.'

She nodded her thanks. Bedtime, but not for her. Not yet.

Lenny did everything that she normally did before bed. Her routine was ingrained. The brushing of her teeth and her hair. The smoothing of a little cream on her face from the tin of Mixa, which had been included with her small supply of French make-up. The setting out of her nightdress. Little actions that were meant to soothe in preparation for sleep but didn't. She was too concerned with what was happening outside her room. The usual noises from

Maeva and Claudine. Nothing from Marianne. What was the woman up to? What had she found, if anything?

The tisane remained in the cup. She wasn't going to drink it. Instead, she decided to tip it out the window. A little dribble of liquid on the wall wouldn't be noticed after the rain they'd had.

After, she sat on the hard wooden chair, her feet pushed into her slippers, her dressing gown around her shoulders. It was warm for June, the shower having done little to relieve the humid air, but she still shivered, her dressing gown held together by a tight fist.

She waited for the house to fall silent. The air to settle as the three remaining women shifted in their beds in search of sleep. It was bad enough to have taken the envelope but to be caught with it would be catastrophic.

When she was as sure as she could be that all was well, she quickly replaced her clothes with her nightdress to keep the illusion of normality. Her dress was positioned on its hanger and her camisole and slip folded ready for the morning. If anyone crept in to check on her, they'd find everything in order.

Her watch said midnight. Time enough.

She positioned herself in bed and gently removed the piece of card from the envelope, one eye on the door and the other on the discoloured document, folded and folded, the edges as fragile as tissue paper.

A birth certificate in the name of Marianne Levi. Father: Rubin Levi. Mother: Rachel Cohen.

THIRTY-ONE

Saturday 7 June, 1941 – Paris 8.30 am

Lenny arrived at the bookshop half an hour earlier than usual but, after a night of tossing and turning, she'd given up on thoughts of both sleep and breakfast. With the way her stomach was rolling, she'd only see it again. To be so completely wrong about Marianne had shaken her world. She'd been convinced she was a collaborator when the opposite could be said to be true. The similarities between their lives couldn't go unnoticed. Displaced from her home and everything she'd known, her parents heaven knew where.

Someone living day to day under the watchful eye of the enemy.

'There you go.' Gilberte placed a cup of coffee before her along with a croissant, her hand resting briefly on her shoulder, the birth certificate on the table between them.

'I don't think I can.'

'A sip won't harm,' she replied, settling in the chair opposite, a cigarette between her fingers. 'You look as if you haven't slept a wink worrying. A little coffee and something small to eat will do you good.'

'I can't believe how stupid I've been.' Lenny lifted her head, blinking rapidly, her eyes gritty from lack of sleep.

'An easy mistake to make in these times, where neighbours and friends are pitted against each other, chérie. I wish Pierre was here.' She took a deep drag, blowing smoke in a stream above her head. 'He's had more dealings with her than I have. Not much but enough to have believed that the pension was the best place for you when you arrived.'

Lenny was desperate to ask about Harry. When she hadn't been thinking about Marianne and James, she'd lain awake thinking about him. Where he was and what he was up to.

For someone who hadn't liked the man until recently, she was amazed at the complete U-turn in her feelings.

'Have you heard any news?' she said finally, trying to be subtle.

Gilberte shook her head. 'I won't until they're back. It's safer that way, with the telephones monitored. Don't worry, they're wily as foxes those two.' She reached across and patted her hand briefly. 'You'll soon have your Harold back.'

Lenny felt herself blush, but Gilberte was her friend, and Harry's too. 'That obvious?'

'I'd have had to be blind not to see the sparks flying when you're together. It was the same with Pierre and me.'

Lenny would have liked to ask more. To learn everything there was to know about Harry, but Gilberte stubbed out her cigarette, her attention on the document between them.

'The question is what are we going to do about you and Marianne?'

'I know!' She grimaced. 'The worst part is that I don't feel safe. Marianne could still report me any time she likes, especially if the Germans turn their attention in her direction.'

'But I don't think she will. In fact, I'm certain of it.' Gilberte tapped the edge of the birth certificate, her face pulled into a frown before relaxing into a small smile. 'Why don't you go back to the pension and own up? I know it won't be easy but, if she does intend to go to the Germans, at least it will give you time to plan what you do next.'

Lenny winced, knowing she was right, even if the thought scared her witless. 'If you think I should?'

Gilberte gathered the plates together as the clock chimed nine. 'Sometimes it's best to go on the offensive. She won't be expecting it, which will be in your favour. Go now without even thinking about it, while I open the shop. That way your explanation will come across as spontaneous.'

The sound of someone tapping on the window had Gilberte rushing down the stairs, Lenny trailing in her wake.

'Bonjour.'

'Morning. I've run out of ink.'

'Of course, Madame Graillot. Blue or black?'

'Red.'

Lenny slipped through the open door and retraced her steps, her footsteps slow, her thoughts ponderous. When she'd decided to fight for her country, it had been right after finding Finlay and Ellen and on the back of losing both her brother and her island to the enemy. Not exactly the right frame of mind in which to decide her whole future. She'd have been better throwing a dice or tossing a coin. At least she'd have given herself a better chance of making the right decision.

No amount of training could have prepared her for the likes of Marianne. A month in France and it felt as if her world was crumbling around her. Yes, she'd found her brother but what else had she achieved. What part had she played in the war effort? One message about the possible German push to the East. How much longer could she carry on if Marianne decided to report her? The truth was that she couldn't. Pierre and Gilberte were key figures in the resistance movement but, so far, all she'd done was make things difficult for them. If the enemy came for her, it wouldn't take long for them to work out the Brossolettes' involvement.

Marianne was sitting at the kitchen table smoking, the remains of her breakfast in front of her. By the look of the overflowing ashtray, she'd been doing a lot of smoking that morning.

Lenny paused in the doorway, glancing at where Auguste was peeling potatoes by the sink. A nice enough woman in her early sixties, who tended to keep to herself.

'I'd like a quick word if I may?'

'Of course.' Marianne nodded to the chair opposite, her face a mask of composure, apart from a little firming of her jaw.

'In private.' Lenny tilted her head slightly in Auguste's direction, her meaning clear.

'Auguste worked for my parents before accompanying me to Paris, Léonore,' she said, her voice holding a note of censure. 'There is nothing you can't say in front of her.' She stubbed out her cigarette and picked up her cup instead. 'I take it you're here about my birth certificate?'

Lenny hesitated before sliding the document from her pocket and placing it on the table. 'I really am truly sorry. Your past is none of my business.'

She watched as Marianne picked up the square of card, her fingers running over the image as her eyes traced the words. 'The past is called that for a reason, Léonore. Some things are best left there.' She lifted her head, and Lenny saw tears streaking down her cheeks. 'We can't fight the enemy by living in it.' With those words, she ripped her birth certificate into tiny pieces before pushing away from the table and throwing them in the stove.

'But... what about...?' Lenny was shocked, her eyes on the stove and where the paper was burning to ash.

'I have forgeries. Very good ones. Birth certificate. Ration Book. ID card.' She patted her arm briefly. 'Don't look so worried, Leonora. In a way you've done me a favour. If someone like you could find it so easily, I dread to think what might have happened if the Germans had. My poor attempt at betraying my ancestry with the enemy flag would have been easily dismissed for what it was. Camouflage.'

Lenny's heart skipped a beat, her mind honing in on Marianne's use of her name. Leonora instead of Léonore.'

'You know about me. Since when?'

'I've known all along, petite.' She smiled briefly. A kindly smile that lit her face from within. 'Spiders and missing luggage were only the icing on the cake. The way you roll your r's is nothing like any of the Bretons I've ever met. You were always more than you pretended. Your presence here today only confirms my suspicions. English?'

'British. From Îles de la Manche. Guernsey.'

She placed both hands on the edge of the table and stood to her feet. 'Well, Léonore, from Îles de la Manche, you'll be pleased to know that we're both on the same side. The less I know about what you're up to the better but, if you need anything, anything at all, I will do everything in my power to help you and your British friends.'

'Thank you.' Lenny was near to tears but managed to hold them in check as she made for the door.

It was time she went home and left the war to those who knew what they were doing. That she could have ever thought this woman was the enemy...

'Oh, just one thing.'

Lenny turned back. 'Yes?'

'Your suitcase. What happened to it?'

The most incriminating evidence of all. If it fell into the wrong hands, she'd be finished. 'Under the floor of the summerhouse – some of the boards are loose.'

Marianne laughed. 'Indeed, they are. Good job you told me. I'm planning on getting them replaced in a few weeks.'

THIRTY-TWO
JAMES

Saturday 7 June, 1941 – Paris 3.15 pm

'Ah, Jakob. Hard at work, I see.'

Reiner appeared before him as if by magic. A combination of rubber-soled shoes and a fleetness of foot that his fellow comrades didn't have.

James would have liked to ignore him, but that was impossible. Translating British propaganda leaflets into German wasn't a life-or-death task in the scheme of things. The man had a habit of singling him out, while ignoring the rest of the team, which never went unnoticed. James was beginning to think that he was doing it on purpose. He could cope with the odd laugh at his expense, but over recent weeks the taunts had been accompanied by the odd punch. The banter now bitter threats.

'Why you. What do you have that we don't? Let's see, shall we?'

He'd taken to avoiding the common areas. He'd also taken to ensuring that he was alone and behind a locked door when he was in the bathroom, but his luck couldn't last.

Reiner had been singling him out since the first day he'd visited the hospital, he remembered, placing his pen on the desk and standing to attention. He'd been sitting in the common room idly flicking through a magazine when Reiner had been taken on a tour. A propaganda exercise, with a film crew in tow, showing the world at large that the Germans were caring for their own poor wounded soldiers. But his wounds had healed. He hadn't lost a limb or half his face, like the soldier opposite. He looked as good as any other serving soldiers, better in some respects, due to the generous food rations.

When Reiner had stood in front of him, demanding to know what was wrong and why he wasn't fit to fight, the doctor had stumbled his way through a long, fancy stream of words that all meant the same thing.

Amnesia.

'I thought you might like to know that we've finally tracked down your fiancée.' Reiner slapped down an identity card, propelling him back to the present. 'I'll grant you it's not a great image, but there's a little something about the jaw and the hair, don't you think?'

James peered down at the image of a smooth-cheeked man with swept back hair, his heart pounding under his regulation vest and shirt. The image was grainy, the features difficult to make out. Underneath it gave his eye colour, blue, and hair colour, blond. It could be him at a push, or any of a thousand other young men.

'Jakob Keller. Ring any bells?'

James tilted his head back to look him in the eye, doing his best to school his features. 'It certainly looks like me, and the eye and hair colour are correct so...' He let his words tail off on an optimistic note.

Reiner grinned, teeth flashing. 'As well as the name, don't forget. Well, your fiancée will be arriving by train in...' He made a show of flicking his cuff back and checking the time. 'Twenty minutes. I've taken the liberty of arranging for you to meet her. No spectators, apart from me. I think it's best that way. After all you've been through. After all she's been through too. Remember what the good doctor said about meeting your future head on being the best way of finding your past.' He tapped the image of Jakob on the thin card. 'If this isn't you, we'll think again.'

James forced his mouth into a smile because it was expected of him. An excited soldier about to meet the love of his life when the truth was very different.

He wasn't married. There was no wife, girlfriend or fiancée in the background. More importantly, he had no story to explain why he wasn't this Jakob Keller. No ready excuse as to why his fiancée wouldn't recognise him, along with the strong belief that Reiner was quickly losing patience.

That was surely as complicated as it came. It was too late to wish that he'd dug his grandfather's cigarette case into the sand before he'd been rescued.

What next? Detention in some traitors' jail before a bullet to the brain, if they thought him German, or transportation to one of the camps if they found out the truth. That he'd been conning them all along, even if it had started out as a mistake.

James swallowed hard, his mouth dust dry along with his thoughts. The worst of it was he couldn't argue his case. He had to sit back and take it, while thanking him into the bargain. Thank Reiner for ruining his life a second time. He'd much rather he'd left him to rot in an asylum. At least there'd have been an end of sorts. Was madness an end. If not madness, then the opportunity to jump off a wall. Perhaps it was something he should have considered sooner. Choosing his own ending instead of having it chosen for him. The result was bound to be the same.

'How wonderful,' he finally managed, unable to think of anything else to say.

Reiner slapped him on the back, hard. 'It's my pleasure to do this for you, Jakob. Just managed to squeeze it in before picking up a young girl for questioning.' He shifted the pile of pamphlets, aligning them so that their edges lined up to the corner of the desk. 'In fact, you were with me when I first noticed her. A Mademoiselle Bouchard. You must remember her? The waitress with the glasses and no looks to speak of when we had drinks around at the Lumineaus'.'

James felt his stomach heave, his pulse a loud erratic thump in his ears. 'I can't say that I do, sir,' he finally managed.

'Really? Won't make a spy out of you, that's for sure.' Reiner's pale eyes held his gaze without blinking. 'There's something about her that doesn't add up and I'm determined to find out what.' He waved a hand to where James had placed his jacket on the back of his chair. 'Grab your coat. We don't want to be late for your dear love.'

THIRTY-THREE

Saturday 7 June, 1941 – Paris 4.25 pm

The train was late. Not interminably so, but late enough for the flowers to start wilting in his tight fist.

Flowers were one of the things the Germans couldn't halt on their march across Europe. They couldn't change the weather or the oppositions' fighting spirit, just as they couldn't stop the bulbs from sprouting through the tight soil.

The French loved their flowers. The bright, gaudy kind in jewel colours. All the cafés and restaurants had vases full of artful arrangements and window boxes stuffed solid. Anything to attract customers into their premises, when resources were limited and food and drink were priorities instead of pleasures.

However, flowers were the last thing on James's mind as he walked towards the Gare Saint-Lazare Railway Station. Thoughts of escape and of rescuing Lenny were uppermost but, with Reiner glued to his side, he knew he'd have little chance of executing such plans. Reiner was carrying a gun and they both knew that he'd use it.

The flower seller, more of a beggar really in tattered clothing and a crooked hat, seemed to wilt as they approached the entrance to the station. Instead of the cherry smile and quick repartee she was making with the Parisians, there was a tense silence. An awkward dropping of her head as she stared at her basket of flowers.

James noticed but said nothing. He'd witnessed the other soldiers as they'd ridiculed the locals.

Why pay when we can get it for free was the mantra he'd heard repeatedly since arriving in the city, whether they were talking about flowers, wine or women. They disgusted him, but he was more disgusted with himself and his inability to act, his unwillingness to challenge them for fear of retribution. So, while he hadn't thought about flowers for his *fiancée*, now he pounced on the idea like a drowning man in search of rescue. Shoving his hand in his pocket, he pulled out his wallet.

'The purple if you please.'

She lifted her head, and he saw her eyes glazing with fear.

'Certainly, sir.' She chose carefully. The best of the bunch before waving her hand away at the sight of his money. 'No. No charge.'

'But I insist, you must take it.' He selected a one-hundred-franc note, partially concealed by his hand, his back to Reiner as he stooped closer. 'Go to the Librairie Universelle bookshop, along the Rue de la Pompe in the 16th Arrondissement and tell the young woman there she's about to be arrested. Please, madame. I'm begging you,' he added, his halting German accent morphing into fluent French.

One beat. Two beats, her eyes never leaving his before she whipped the note from his fingers and pressed the flowers into his hand instead.

James watched as she stumbled away, the swirl of passengers exiting the train station folding in around her. He would have followed except for Reiner tapping him on the shoulder.

'Flowers. Perfect. She'll like that.'

James switched his attention back to him, the flickering look in the flower-seller's eyes burning a path to his brain. He knew that the French hated them, and they had every reason to. But, sitting behind his desk in the hotel, working his way through the pile of pamphlets and newsletters, he'd been protected from what it was really like to be the enemy in Paris. She'd taken the money, but had she believed him? The worst of it was he would have no way of finding out. He had his own troubles to face.

'I hope so.'

'She's lucky we allow her to continue plying her trade,' he drawled. 'Scum, the lot of them.'

The noise from the steam train chugging along the track brought him back to his present difficulties, and the tightly clasped flowers, the stalks squashed to a pulp. He relaxed his grip, the heads starting to droop over his fist, his gaze on the train ahead, the image distorted by the trail of grey smoke. There were many things he wished for in those last few seconds. Most of them were unachievable like sitting on the shoulder of the flower seller to ensure she did what he'd begged her. His last wish, just as the train pulled to a stop was for his fiancée to have decided to run away with someone else.

There were plenty of handsome, blond soldiers milling around to catch the eye of a discerning young woman.

Why would she want to wait for him?

Was she young?

James frowned. He didn't know the first thing about her, not even her name.

There was no way that she'd be able to recognise him and, he certainly wasn't able to recognise her. They could quite easily pass on the platform without acknowledging each other.

'Stand back. Let the passengers exit first, if you please.' The porter, a busy-looking man with a wiry moustache and shiny suit, rushed about opening doors and generally getting in everyone's way. The train was full, primarily of soldiers who appeared to be getting younger by the second, their uniforms pressed, along with their regulation hair. Only boys really, he thought, who should still be at school instead of being sent to fight the enemy. He took a step back, watching as they got into line and started filing out of the station.

Too many to take up posts in Paris, so where were they off to? What were the Germans up to?

James turned back to the train, as he rolled the question over in his mind. He might as well gather information while he still could.

'Jakob.'

James lifted his head from where he'd been wrapped up in trying to remember the number of soldiers and the different uniforms they'd been wearing.

A woman was running along the platform, dressed in a flash of baby pink, her high heels skimming the pavement, a small, battered suitcase dangling from one hand.

Could this be her?

Her blonde hair was pulled back from her face. That was the last image he had before she launched at him, raining kisses against his cheek before pressing her mouth against his.

What on earth...

He froze, one hand by his side, the other holding the flowers.

She loosened her grip but only slightly. Her gaze roamed his face, her expression telling him in all the ways possible how precious he was to her.

'Jakob. Oh, my dear. I thought you were dead. We all did.'

James felt her slip her arm through his, taking the lead. If she hadn't, there was a strong possibility he'd have stayed where he was, his mouth opening like a suffocating fish.

He caught sight of Reiner watching them and began to collect himself.

'Splendid. Absolutely splendid.' Reiner raised his hand as if to clap him on the back, only to think better of it and drop it to his side. 'I knew we'd work it out in the end, Jakob. Well, I'll leave you two to get reacquainted. Don't worry about work today, or tomorrow. Have a holiday and...' He gave him a little nudge, his voice lowering to a heavy whisper. 'About your accommodation. Don't worry about that either. There's a room arranged back at the hotel.'

James stooped to pick up her case because it was expected of him, his gaze on where Reiner was rushing out of the station to his waiting car, the flower seller nowhere to be seen.

As they left the platform, he didn't notice the bruised flowers scattered over the platform, their fragile mauve petals stamped into the pavement by hurrying feet.

THIRTY-FOUR

LENNY

Saturday 7 June, 1941 – Paris 5 pm

The rest of the day at the bookshop followed the same pattern as the morning. A few sales of their ever-popular pencils and pens to the school opposite. Some book sales, not many. Lenny was busy enough to be kept going. Not much time in between to chat about the things that were important.

Pierre and Harry arrived back at five, when they were about to lock up for the night. The noise of the back door opening made Gilberte stare across at where Lenny was turning the sign over to closed.

It was either Pierre and Harry or intruders.

'Bonjour.' Pierre planted a kiss on Gilberte's mouth before doing the same to both of Lenny's cheeks. 'It's nice to be home.' He sniffed the air, the slight smell of sausages and beans making its way down the stairs. 'Mm cassoulet. My favourite.'

'Bonjour, ladies.' Harry paused a moment to drop a kiss onto Gilberte's cheek before standing in front of Lenny. 'Miss me?'

'A little.'

He smiled. 'A little is better than nothing. I, on the other hand, missed you a lot,' he said, reaching for her hand. 'Are you free tonight? I thought we might continue our conversation over a meal.'

Lenny felt a deep glow bloom in her chest. There was so much she had to tell him, things he'd understand. Things he'd be able to help her make sense of. But it wasn't only that. It was the way he made her feel.

'That would be lovely. I just need to go home to change.'

The sound of the door opening had them all turning in surprise.

'I'm sorry. We're closed for the evening.' Gilberte swept forward, her expression composed at the sight of the unkempt flower seller standing in the middle of the shop, wilting flowers hanging over the edge of her basket.

The woman turned to leave, only to stop and, raising her hand, point at Lenny. 'You're about to be arrested.'

'What?' Gilberte grabbed onto her arm, drawing her back inside. 'You can't just come in here and—'

The woman pulled away, rubbing her arm. 'I can do what I want, when I want. A German soldier at the railway station. Gave me good money to pass the message on, which I've done.' She cackled briefly, her beady eyes switching between Lenny and Harry. 'Perhaps your lover, mademoiselle.'

Lenny's legs gave way, her head spinning and the shop with it.

James.

THIRTY-FIVE

JAMES

Saturday 7 June, 1941 – Paris 5 pm

James and his so called fiancée were sitting outside a little café down a side street off the Boulevard Haussmann, a five-minute walk from the station. If it wasn't for his present company and fear about what Reiner was up to, James might have been enjoying himself. The café was homely, the tablecloths bright and the girl opposite pretty. It was all very different to his usual routine being stuck behind his desk, the work piling up beside him. Ever since Reiner had plucked him from the hospital, his days had followed the same pattern. There was no point in taking the leave owed to him. He had nowhere to go and no one to spend it with. Safety meant avoiding any situations where he might reveal the truth about his past.

He frowned, the woman opposite replaced by an image of his sister. Where was she? Hopefully in hiding if the flower seller had done what he'd asked. He'd certainly paid her enough. Most of what he had.

'Don't worry, Jakob. I know you don't remember me. Hardly surprising as you've never set eyes on me before today.'

She withdrew her gloves, white to match the collar of her dress and lay them on the table between them.

'Pardon?'

He'd been trying to arrange his thoughts into some sort of order. Now he didn't know what to think.

'I know. It's all a bit much, Jakob. Of course, as your beloved I'm going to call you by your first name, and you should do the same.' She smiled. A sweet smile that brightened her face and lightened her eyes. Young, and pretty, with a broad forehead and high cheekbones. She held out her hand as if they'd only just been introduced. 'I'm Mademoiselle Gisela Roche, and your boss doubts that you're Jakob Keller. I don't know who you are, but what you are is in danger. I believe much danger indeed.'

James quickly glanced around but they were alone, the narrow street free from pedestrians. The only person in shouting distance, if not hearing, was the proprietor, currently polishing glasses behind the counter. No threat there. James shifted his chair slightly so that the entrance was behind him and the street ahead, something he should have thought of when he'd sat down.

Never put your back to the enemy.

'You have me at a disadvantage, mademoiselle... Gisela,' he finally said, dropping a cube of sugar into the bitter coffee. To say that he was floundering was an understatement. It felt as if someone had dropped him into an alternative universe, without a set of instructions, very much in the vein of H.G. Wells's *The Time Machine.*

A phrase his father used suddenly popped into his mind as he stirred his coffee, something he hadn't thought of in years.

Keep your friends close but your enemies closer.

She spent a moment opening a small patent bag, withdrawing a packet of cigarettes and selecting one, her hands small, her fingernails shaped. 'Would you like one?'

German cigarettes were something he'd had to get used to, along with German beer and German food. After a year, he gave a pretty good impression of someone who enjoyed whatever was put in front of him when the reality was very different. Give him a pack of Players cigarettes over Ernte 23 any day.

'Please.' He took one from the packet offered and, lighter ready, watched the flickering flame bouncing off the sheen of her hair. 'Why exactly are you here pretending to be my fiancée, Gisela?'

She took a deep puff from her cigarette, tilting her head back to reveal a long column of throat before releasing the smoke in a smooth stream above her head. 'Now that's the question. I could tell you that I'm following dear Otto's instructions. They were certainly as clear as water. Find out exactly who this Jakob is and what he's doing because, if he's a Frenchman, then I'm Dutch.'

James nearly laughed at her passable impression of Reiner's voice. He might have under different circumstances.

'So, why the change in plan, Gisela?' he said, confused as to what she was up to.

'There's something about you I like.' She shrugged. 'Call it an instinct that you're not as bad as I've been led to believe. Are you bad, Jakob?' she said, her expression veiled by a thin haze of smoke. 'Ever killed a man, or a woman for that matter? I'll know if you're lying, so don't bother.'

'Of course not. What do you take me for?'

James left his cigarette to burn between his fingers, his gaze intent. Trying to get a straight answer from her was proving tricky. Every time he closed in, she slipped away. It was like trying to trap a butterfly without a net.

She stubbed her cigarette out and picked up her cup, cradling it between her fingers. 'Difficult to say as we've only just met. What your boss *takes you for* is another matter.'

James felt the colour drain from his cheeks as a wave of cold washed over him. He'd been hoping to extricate himself from his current situation and make for the bookshop to find out about Lenny. Now that was impossible.

His arrest was looming.

He had to go. But, instead of moving, he decided to hear her out.

Stay. Wait. Then make a move.

That he didn't know what was happening to Lenny played a big part in that decision.

'What did Reiner say? How do you know him?' His voice was steady, something he was thankful for. The table helped. Underneath, his knees were pressed tight together to stop them from shaking.

She inclined her head, the sweet smile back. 'Otto and I are old acquaintances. Let's just say he employs me on occasions like this to test the loyalty of our esteemed servants of the Reich. So, here I am.' She spread her hands. 'He's asked me to grill you in any way I feel fit and, yes, that does include making use of that hotel room he mentioned.'

James's cheeks heated under her gaze.

Gossip had been rife in Whitehall about a certain calibre of woman to avoid. Women employed for the specific purpose of smoking out spies in what he'd heard called a honey trap. Using their faces and their bodies to lure men to their doom like sirens of old. How Gisela could debase herself in such a fashion was unthinkable. But why lie? What was there to gain.

'And you've decided to tell me all this for the goodness of my health?'

'Hah, very funny.' She chuckled. 'I'm telling you because, despite everything, I don't believe all the good Herr Reiner tells me and some men... some boys, need a second chance.'

'How old are you, Gisela?'

'Older than you,' she parried, selecting another cigarette, this time not offering him one. 'But younger than you might think. I grew up fast. I had to with no mother and a father...' Her jaw hardened. 'And a father who should never have had children.'

James leant back, folding his arms across his chest, trying to see beneath her smooth mask, but it was like staring into a crystal ball and seeing right through to the other side.

She lit the end and took a sharp puff, her face relaxing in pleasure. 'You must realise that life for a single woman in Germany right now is hard, Jakob. No one has any money and not much food. When Herr Reiner contacted me about a job, I seized the opportunity to, well, let's say embroider my life a little.' She studied her hands, the light catching her hair and turning it into a shining halo of silk. 'When I saw you on the platform, I was going to pander to your amnesia. See how long it would take you to slip up, like dear Otto instructed, but...' She lifted her head. 'I couldn't do it. I thought that you'd be the same as the Hitler Youth, stomping around spreading misinformation like a disease but you're not. I don't know your story or what you've done to upset him, but Reiner wants me to come up with the goodies. Your life laid on a platter along with your head. I, on the other hand, don't give a fig about your past.' She leant forward slightly, a hint of gardenias filling the air. 'I don't really care about your future either, if I'm honest. Only what's in it for me.'

Ah, the crux of the matter, he thought. *It always boils down to money or power in the end. The question is how much and whether I can trust her?*

He picked up his cup of cold coffee and drained it before lifting his hand to attract the attention of the bartender.

'Red or white?' He turned to look at her.

'Pardon?'

'Wine.' He managed a brief smile. 'I'm in need of a drink and it will keep the bartender happy.'

'Red then. Thank you.'

The wine arrived with an obsequious smile and a demand for payment, which James complied to without a murmur. He knew he was hated by the Parisians. There was nothing he could do about that. They'd spit at him if they didn't think it might land them in prison.

He took a cautious sip, grimacing at the vinegarish aftertaste, the sour flavour causing his throat to close. Just as he thought. Pig swill. Expensive pig swill at that as he remembered the number of francs he'd had to fork out.

'So, what are you suggesting then?' he said, pushing his glass aside. 'Because I don't think you've quite thought this through. What do you think Reiner is going to do when he finds his fat little pigeon has flown the coop, in search of freedom?'

'I don't think I quite...?'

James tapped her engagement ring briefly, wondering for a second who it had belonged to. It looked genuine enough, but he was no expert. More of a fool to have got himself into such an impossible situation.

'What's going to happen when he finds me gone and you still here? Think he's going to take kindly to the fact you allowed me to escape? You are going to allow me to escape or is this a trap?' James could see by her expression that she'd acted on impulse. Nice of her but foolhardy.

He opened his grandfather's silver case and withdrew a cigarette. A Gitane. French but slightly more to his palate, although he was thinking of giving up. Didn't know why he'd started in the first place. Lenny had been able to stand firm when they'd been passed around by their friends.

Weak-willed and weak-bellied.

With a snap of his wrist, he clicked the case closed and placed it on the table, taking his time in choosing what to say.

'I take it you live near here and the train station was all part of the act?' He waited for her nod before continuing. 'Then I need to get out of Paris and quickly, or was that your plan all along?'

'I don't know what you mean.' She was sitting back in her chair, one leg crossed over the other, her skirt pulled into place over her knee, her stockings a thin sheen of silk.

Silk!

Stupid of him not to notice. He wondered what she'd had to do to earn them.

James watched the thin trail of smoke tracking from his cigarette, and tried to still the trembling of his fingers. Had she noticed?

The evening was taking on a distinct chill, a warning that curfew was on its way. The street was starting to fill. Shopkeepers and employees on their way home. Some would stop at the café for a quick drink, but not with him sitting there. He smiled briefly at the sight of the bartender wringing his hands.

It was time to leave but where could he go?

There was nowhere and that was the problem. No one he could go to without Reiner finding out.

Leaning forward, he stubbed out his cigarette. 'If I'm to believe that this is a trap I can escape from then I'll need some proof.'

'Excuse me?'

James tapped his finger on the table, in the same way he'd recently tapped her engagement ring.

'Empty the contents of your bag.'

He felt a heel but feelings like that might very well get him killed. In a world full of people there was only one person he could trust, now Lenny wasn't available to him, and that was himself.

The bag was little more than a large purse. A flat oblong with a zip at the top and a long strap. Instead of removing the few items one by one, she upended it, pouring the contents in a pile in front of him before sitting back, her expression mutinous.

'Thank you.' He flicked her a brief smile, before picking up a small compact and opening the lid.

The bag contained a lipstick and a handkerchief when he'd suspected a gun or a knife. There was also a small bunch of keys and her identity and ration card. When he checked the name, it was just as she'd said. Gisela Roche. Blue eyes. Blonde hair. Aged twenty-seven.

His eyebrows shot up. She barely looked his age let alone eight years older.

'Right.' He tilted his head for her to repack her bag, his hand in his pocket as he tried to remember how much money he had on him. 'How much?'

'This.' She tapped his grandfather's cigarette case with the tip of her fingernail.

'No!'

He eyed her in horror. The one thing he'd never part with.

She leant forward, her lips pulling into a sneer. 'You're not in a position to argue, Jakob. By now your girlfriend will be under arrest and, I reckon Otto will come searching for you straight after.' He watched as she checked her watch. 'You probably have five minutes, no more. The cigarette case for your freedom is a very small price to pay.'

James's eyes widened at the words, the hardening of both her expression and her voice a surprise. Seconds before he'd thought her twenty. Now she looked twice that, wrinkles where before the skin was silky smooth. If Reiner had been following him, the likelihood was that he'd had him followed here.

Nowhere to run. Nowhere to hide, but at least he had to try. After all, he knew she wasn't armed. The metro wasn't far. He could lose himself among the other pedestrians heading home for the evening.

With the street empty, he surged to his feet, shoving the case into his pocket.

The gun appeared out of nowhere. A small pistol, small enough to be concealed in her pocket. One second her hand was empty, the next she had the barrel aimed at his head, right between the eyes.

'Bloody hell!'

With a jerk backwards, he scraped his chair along the pavement and, with his hand on the edge of the table tipped it in her direction before running into the bar, much to the astonishment of the bartender.

'Monsieur?'

'Get down, now.' He spoke in French, perfect French with the Breton accent of his ancestors, his hand outstretched as he pushed him to the floor before shielding him with his body, his eyes squeezed tight. The man underneath him started to recite a prayer and he was tempted to join him. Praying was about all he could do in his current situation.

The first bullet whizzed past their heads imbedding in the wall beyond, as did the second and the third in rapid succession. He was starting to think that Gisela wasn't a very good shot when he felt a dart of pain on the side of his hand where the next bullet grazed the skin. He opened his eyes briefly, following the blood seeping from the wound. A scratch. He let out a breath, knowing that his luck couldn't last. The bartender must have been of the same opinion as the prayers changed in both words and tempo. He would have smiled if his lips were up to it.

The fifth missed again, this time sending a shower of plaster on their heads from the ceiling above.

'How many bullets left, monsieur?' the bartender said, his voice a low growl, anger pushing away shock.

'No idea. Three. Four maybe.'

There were four. The following two missed. *She really was a terrible shot,* he thought, as the next bullet found its target, digging deep into his shoulder.

The stab of pain brought a gasp. He'd barely drawn breath when the final bullet found its target, only this time almost exactly one inch lower.

'My life for a cigarette case. Not the best of trades.'

THIRTY-SIX

James pressed his hand against his shoulder, the pain a searing heat akin to someone stabbing him with a hot poker. He didn't lose consciousness, but it was only by biting down on his lip, until the metallic taste of blood stopped him.

He was losing enough of the red stuff to want to keep whatever was left.

'Monsieur?' The bartender poked his head up from where he was hiding behind the bar.

'Has she gone?' James asked, feeling the blood drip through his fingers. He knew there wasn't time to waste and, as he wasn't dead, he'd best try and see if he could keep it that way.

'Yes.' The bartender sounded cautious, uncertain, but then he had a German soldier in his café with two holes in his shoulder.

'Good. Grab a cloth. Something clean if you have it to press against the wound.' He tried to move his arm only to find he couldn't, an excruciating stab of pain almost causing him to faint.

'But... you had a falling out with your girlfriend?'

James knew how it must seem and, staring at the bartender, he also knew he only had one chance to get it right. The man looked patriotic. He'd certainly acted that way earlier when he could barely meet his gaze.

But would he be brave?

It was all very well supporting France, but it would be far easier for him to hand him over to the enemy.

The argument batted back and forth, when the truth was, he didn't have a choice.

If the man was a collaborator, he was dead. Without his help, he was also dead.

He took a deep breath, trying to find a way through the pain. 'Look, I'm British, and that German woman is about to come back with a barrack full of the Boche.' He paused a second before adding with a note of desperation. 'Can you help?'

The man transformed before him. He ran around the counter, grabbed a tea towel from the pile and pressed it against his shoulder, before hurrying into the back and shouting. 'Marie, hurry. Quick.'

It almost seemed as if he'd been waiting for this moment, the way he took charge when a thin woman with a cautious smile appeared.

'Marie. Take him out the back, quickly now. Monsieur, my wife will escort you to my friend's house.' His expression changed, his gaze shifting to the entrance briefly. 'It's best I stay. Maurice will take it from here.' He walked beside him into the kitchen and the door beyond. 'Good luck, my friend, and thank you for helping our little country.' He went to grab his hand only to stop at the sight of the bloodied rag clutched in place. 'I think you'll live. An inch further down and it would be a different matter. Come back one day, eh, when we've crushed them. I'll break out the good wine.'

Maurice lived two streets away in an apartment over the butcher's. Two streets wasn't far: James felt like he'd completed a marathon by the time Marie pulled him to a stop.

He leant back against the wall, watching as she stooped to pick up a pebble and aimed it at the window. He didn't know if it was a secret way of communicating. Probably, the way the man peered out the window before hurrying downstairs to let them in.

'Marie, you'd best get back,' he said, when she'd hurriedly explained. 'Monsieur, this way.' He led him behind a thick canvas door, which separated the front of the shop from the back. 'Sit here. I need your coat and shirt, and we must be quick. I'm sorry, but I may hurt you.'

James nodded, his tongue sandpaper dry, his mouth unable to get any words out.

The blood loss and pain combination had caused his brain to fog, but at least he was away from that bitch. Reiner was clever in choosing such a mild-mannered woman to do his dirty work for him.

At least she was a poor shot!

The air was cooler in the back of the shop. There were hooks hanging from the ceiling, some with carcasses. The floor was sawdust. The butcher block in the centre was stained black in places, a variety of knives and saws lined up and scrupulously clean.

'Lean forward.' Maurice pressed and prodded, causing the room to spin and a wave of nausea to hurtle up James's throat.

'Shattered collarbone, hence your arm. Wouldn't have happened if you'd been a pig. Much smaller collarbones,' he said hurriedly. 'Missed your major blood vessels. No sign of any bullets. Good. Lost some blood, of course,' he continued, mostly to himself. 'But a little blood goes a long way. You've been lucky, very lucky indeed,' he finally said, pressing a fresh wodge of fabric over the entry and exit points. 'I'm going to have to strap you tight. It will stop the bleeding for now, but you really should be seen by a doctor.'

James grunted. He didn't have time for that. It sounded like the man knew what he was doing. It would have to suffice until he reached safety. The next problem. His uniform jacket was ruined, but what was the alternative.

Maurice was one step ahead of him.

'Marie tells me you're British and therefore as welcome in Paris at the moment as a bad smell, which means we have to get you out.'

James blinked. The seriousness of his situation was finally catching up with him. Being injured was one thing. It was enough for his addled brain to cope with, but he couldn't stay here and put more people at risk.

'I have an idea. One moment please.' Maurice scurried away, his feet barely touching the floor. He was back within a minute, clutching a pile of clothes to his chest, a woolly hat on top. 'These are my son's. About your size. We need to get you changed quickly. Everything off, even your underwear. We don't want anything to give you away as a German.' He started to help him with his vest, before helping with the belt buckle. James let him, embarrassment mingling with the pain.

'Your son, won't he mind?' he asked.

'Lost him. Battle of Saumur. He was only nineteen. Too young to be part of this madness.'

'I'm sorry,' James replied quietly. There was so much he wanted to say, but the reality of the situation was that there were no words that could help this man. The only thing that would was for him to get his son back.

Life was hell and this man was right in the middle of it.

'Not your fault.' Maurice stood back, eyeing his handiwork. 'Not a bad fit. The shoes are a little big, but I've tied the laces tight. A scarf for your arm. There. Now, what about documents?'

James tilted his head in the direction of his uniform, his shoulder starting to feel a little easier under the tight bandage. He'd rescued his cigarette case and slipped it into his pocket. It was the one thing he couldn't part with, despite the risk. He'd come this far with it. His lucky charm. 'Ration book and ID card. All I have.'

'Will have to be burned. Don't worry. I'll deal with it. Better to have lost your papers than have to explain German ones when you're not wearing the uniform. In the meantime, I know just the place to hide them.'

He bundled up the uniform and placed it in the bottom of a metal bucket under the butcher block, making sure to squash it down flat. James wasn't sure what he was up to until Maurice uncovered the bucket beside it and upended the contents. 'There. It will be a brave German who decides to sift through the contents of my slop bucket. In fact, I'll probably leave the uniform,' he added on a laugh. 'My friend at the farm won't mind and I'm sure his pigs won't either.'

James had never expected such kindness from a stranger. It made him want to weep. The man was putting himself in danger by having him in the shop. He didn't know how long it had been since he'd left the café, but probably edging onto half an hour or so. Time enough for Gisela to have mobilised assistance and got word to Reiner. Time for him to leave, if only he could summon up the energy.

Maurice seemed to have the same idea. 'Quickly now. You need somewhere to sleep tonight, but not here.' He helped him to his feet. 'Think you can manage?'

James gritted his teeth as he put one foot in front of the other, trying to match his step.

Another door. Another street. No lights to be seen behind the closed shutters.

'Make your way to the metro. There's a ghost station. Champ de Mars. It was shut down a couple of years ago. The beauty of it is that it's only a couple of stations away, although you'll have to change lines.' He stopped a second, listening, and then James heard it too. The sound of running feet not far away. 'The station next to it is École Militaire,' he said, the words coming out in quick succession. 'You should be safe enough there tonight. Have you any money on you?'

James gulped, thinking about his wallet.

The pigs will be eating like kings tomorrow.

'Afraid not.'

'Here.' Maurice dug his hand into his pocket and pulled out a pile of francs. 'Go, and may God go with you.'

THIRTY-SEVEN
LENNY

Saturday 7 June, 1941 – Paris 5.10 pm

'I'll go with her.'

'I think that's best, Harold. She's in shock, poor love.' Gilberte said. 'Pierre, grab her bag and coat. I'll throw a few things together upstairs.'

'You mustn't. I'll be fine,' Lenny said, from where she'd slumped into a chair, her voice cracked and uneven.

Harry knelt by her feet, his hands warm against her cold ones. 'We started out together and we'll end it together. Lenny, look at me.' He placed a finger under her chin.

She met his gaze, seeing compassion and kindness in the blue of his eyes.

'Good girl. If we don't leave now, we're putting Pierre and Gilberte, and the whole of the network at risk. Here, let me help you with your coat.' He lifted her arms as if she was a child and she let him, unable to rid her thoughts of what was happening to James.

It was clear to her that he'd been the German the flower seller had been talking about. Something must have happened, something urgent and important for him to get the woman to go to the bookshop on his behalf. But what?

'And your bag, let's loop it across your shoulder. Perfect. Now, time to stand. Lean on me. That's it. We'll go out the back way, it's safer.'

She heard hurrying feet on the stairs and Gilberte's voice. 'Here you go. I think I've thought of everything.'

Harry walked her across the shop, urging her on. 'That's it, Lenny. The sooner we leave, the safer it is for everyone.'

There wasn't time for more than the briefest of goodbyes as they snuck out the back door, Pierre checking the lane first for signs of the enemy.

Her last image of the shop was of Pierre and Gilberte standing in the doorway, his arm looped around her shoulders, their faces pale with worry.

James walked into the metro station, keeping an eye on the two German soldiers standing in the corner chatting. He didn't recognise them, but seeing them was a sharp reminder of the position he was in. He wasn't one of them, and now he didn't have the papers to prove it. So far, the station resembled any other station at rush hour but that couldn't last. If he knew Reiner like he thought he did, then the enemy was only minutes away. For the SS officer to go to such extremes as to get Gisele to find out his secrets was unbelievable, but also the kind of trick that he might pull. Reiner was desperate to know who he was, but too stupid to work it out for himself.

If he hadn't been able to make him crack in six months there was every reason to believe that he couldn't.

James leant against the nearest wall as he took a long painful breath and checked in his pockets, finally withdrawing a handful of coins.

The pain, a constant ache, was compounded by the tight, constricting bandage around his chest and a weakness in his legs.

His gaze swept the platform and stopped cold. Harold – his teammate from the Guernsey hockey club – stood with his arm protectively around Lenny. Seeing his friend here in occupied France was startling enough, but the tender way Harry held his sister suggested far more than a chance encounter. James felt his world tilt, before settling, his eyes closed in silent thanks for Lenny's safety. He would never walk past a flower seller again without buying a bunch of their best blooms.

Pocketing the coins, he followed them through the turnstile and into the tunnel, not bothering about where they were heading or what they were up to. Anywhere was better than hanging around in the station waiting to be arrested.

The train rumbled down the track, screeching to a halt. The carriages were packed, but the 16th Arrondissement was a popular if expensive place in which to reside in central Paris. The doors opened and a pile of well-dressed men and women spilled onto the platform, to the aroma of sweat mingled with some exotic perfume that caused his eyes to water and his head to reel. He needed to sit and quickly if he wasn't to embarrass himself in front of all these people.

Harry and Lenny held back until the passengers had exited when, like a wave, other passengers moved in to take their place.

James held back too, until just before the doors were about to close. Then he slipped inside.

There was standing room only, but he noticed that Lenny had managed to secure a seat. Harry was standing over her, his hand holding on to the bar beside him.

'Léonore and Harold. How delightful,' he managed, planting a wide smile on his face as he grabbed onto the nearest bar, the carriage starting to sway underneath him. 'It's ages since I've seen you both. How was the honeymoon?'

'Ja... Jacques!' Harry was the first to respond, quickly amending James's name to a French alternative. 'Wonderful. I can't believe it's you. How have you been?'

'Oh, so so. Still recovering from my injuries, but enough about me. It's so good to see you.'

The conversation was in rapid colloquial French. Easy, friendly and familiar. A performance solely for the benefit of the other passengers, but James had to get his message across. His body was starting to droop, his arm a dead weight in its makeshift sling. If he didn't rest, then the decision would be taken out of his hands.

'Jacques, you must have my seat. I insist.' Lenny suddenly lurched to her feet, her expression one of relief as she crossed to the other side, squeezing in between a businessman in a natty hat and a woman with a shopping basket, a baguette poking out the side.

James leant back and closed his eyes, the exertion of the last few minutes draining away what little was left of his energy.

They'd put on a prize-worthy show for their captive audience, when mostly people didn't make eye contact on the underground let alone speak to each other. They'd probably be alright for a couple of stops, before they had to change trains.

Keep moving. Make it difficult for Reiner to find you.

THIRTY-EIGHT

LENNY

Lenny glanced between Harry and James, starting to wake up from the nightmare she found herself in.

Her thoughts spiralled, fragments of their last conversation coming back to stab her. Reiner trying to catch him out and the difficulties with the other soldiers at the hotel.

As someone used to the outdoors, James had a ruddy complexion, even in the depths of winter. Now his face was deathly pale, and his arm in a sling.

She watched him out of the corner of her eye. The way he didn't move. His chin to his chest. She wondered if he'd fallen asleep. She didn't want to think of an alternative reason for his sudden stillness.

More people got up to leave, which meant that she was able to take the seat next to him. Harry quickly slipped into the place vacated by the woman opposite before the carriage refilled. This time the passengers included a couple of soldiers, with girls on their arms.

Lenny could have screamed. That was all they needed.

The enemy only a few feet away.

The soldiers seemed in high spirits, passing a bottle of wine between them. The woman with the basket pursed her lips in annoyance, but no one said anything. In fact, the passengers sank into a tense silence as they all avoided looking at the foursome making merry at the other end of the carriage.

'What about coming home with us for a bite to eat, Jacques?' Lenny's voice was low, the words chosen carefully in case anyone was in earshot. 'Then we can have a proper catchup.'

'Sounds like a plan.' He didn't bother opening his eyes. She wasn't even sure if he could.

One of the girls started to giggle, only for the other one to join in and, in the soaring noise that followed, Lenny managed to communicate her intention of getting off at the next stop.

All it took was a flick of her eye and Harry's firm nod for the plan to be set in stone.

James managed to struggle to his feet, but his balance wasn't there. Thinking quickly, Harry wrapped his arm around his back while Lenny copied his action on the other side.

'This is just like old times, Jacques. Such a joy for Léonore and I to bump into you.' Harry continued a string of inane chatter as they made their way along the platform, waiting for the space to clear of passengers. They wouldn't have long. Only a few seconds before more passengers started to queue for the next train.

'There, a bench. Let's rest a minute.' The bench was one of those short ones, with space only for two. Harry stood in front of them, his back to the entrance, shielding them from anyone arriving, his hands in his pockets. Nonchalant. As if he didn't have a care in the world. Lenny admired him his acting skills.

'What happened, James?' she whispered, patting his good hand only to see him wince.

'Careful there. That one's been nicked by a bullet. Same with my shoulder.' He managed a smile, more of a grimace really. 'Good job she was a bloody awful shot, or I wouldn't be here right now.'

Lenny struggled to breathe; her hands curled into fists, her face averted from any onlookers watching the scene unfold.

James shot.

No. Focus on the fact that he's still alive to tell the tale. He needs help urgently and it's up to us to provide it. That's all that matters.

Not quite all.

The platform was starting to fill and there were more Germans. Five big, strapping blokes scanning the area, scrutinising faces and clothing. Searching. For her or her brother? It was impossible to tell. Lenny's gaze clashed with Harry's. They had to do something but, with James incapacitated, their options were limited.

'Quick, stand up.' Harry's voice was a breath of sound, but with a steely undertone that she wasn't going to ignore. She'd barely risen when he grabbed her around the waist and pulled her into his lap before starting to nuzzle her hair. 'I'm not going to apologise for this, Lenny,' he said, shifting his hands to cradle her face and lowering his mouth to hers.

There was no time to think. Her mind and her body froze in disbelief that he'd launched himself at her, even as common sense broke through the icy layer.

The Germans are watching. The only action possible.

There was a sound of a raucous cheer somewhere behind her, followed by a shout in German, which sounded like *be sure to give her a kiss from me.*

How dare they!

'Just relax, alright. It will be over soon, I promise,' Harry mumbled against her mouth, his arms shifting her slightly, his hands now splayed across her back, deepening the kiss.

The kiss. Her first kiss.

What a thought. A kiss born from this madness, and yet the warmth. The heat. A budding inferno rising deep within. Singeing and scorching. She let herself relax into it, relax into him, a small moan gathering in the back of her throat.

He only eased away when the sound of clipped footsteps faded into the distance, before stealing in and placing the gentlest of kisses against her mouth, his hands shifting back to her face, his blue eyes meeting her astonished ones.

'The first kiss was for them. The second is from me. I've wanted to do that ever since I first saw you.'

Lenny stared back at him, her emotions a puddle at her feet as her heart expanded to fill her chest, rational thought impossible.

He'd only kissed her because of the Germans, but it wasn't that he'd kissed her.

It was how.

Her eyes roamed his face, from his suddenly concerned expression to the slight bruising on his lips, knowing she had to change how he felt.

She pressed a finger to her lips before tapping it gently against his, his worry giving way to a grin.

She hated that this was how she'd always remember her first kiss, but she didn't hate him. She couldn't.

THIRTY-NINE

They reached École Militaire Station shortly after, managing James between them. With curfew approaching and the crowd at the metro starting to thin, it was the only option open to them.

Their story changed when James fell into a deep, troubling sleep. Troubling because they couldn't rouse him.

Harry looked across, making a drinking gesture with his hand and Lenny picked up on the cue.

'We shouldn't have opened the port, ma chérie. Should have learnt our lesson after the last time.'

'He never learns.' Lenny raised her eyes dramatically at the disapproving woman opposite, eliciting a small smile and soon the conversation flowed. Tales of similar heavy lunches, invariably ending in bad poetry and missed trains.

Arriving at the station was the easy part. One glance at the wall-mounted metro map confirmed what James had told them before losing consciousness.

Champ de Mars, the disused ghost station, sat between École Militaire and La Motte Picquet Grenelle.

Then they waited on one of the benches, James propped up between them, Harry's hand resting gently on her shoulder, a comfort when she needed it the most. The threat of Reiner hung heavy as did whatever could have happened to James.

'It will be alright, dearest. Sleep is probably the best thing for him currently.'

She tilted her head slightly so that it rested on the back of his hand.

The station cleared slowly of passengers, some loitering as they searched pockets for tickets, some chatting with friends. A final train rattled past but didn't stop, its windows fogged. It would have helped if they'd known the pattern of the metro. When the platforms were cleaned. When the bins were emptied, but they could only guess. It made sense that a station attendant would come down to check that all the platforms were deserted.

It was now or never.

Without a word, they carefully lifted James over to the edge and, with one final look around, lowered him onto the track bed. After, Harry positioned James across his shoulders before easing to his feet.

'I'm sorry. You'll have to take my rucksack as well as your bag.'

'It doesn't matter.'

The only space to walk was between the rails, the surface uneven and littered with rubbish, loose stones and a dead rat, which caused Lenny's heart to jolt.

They moved quickly, as quickly as the darkness would allow. A thin rusted chain barred their way. It took seconds for Lenny to unclip it. She paused briefly, before taking the time to clip it back in place, the rucksack a dead weight on her shoulders.

The platform light quickly dissolved into the shadows, the darkness ahead a thick, dense black full of strange scrabbling noises. Lenny knew what they were. She'd seen the dead rat. She wanted to turn back. Stupid and impossible.

She closed her eyes briefly, hoping it would help only to find that it made it much worse. Then came another sound, a scurrying sound so close she stopped. Her heart slammed against her rib cage, the musty air impossible to soften her sudden gasping breaths. She clamped a hand to her mouth to choke back the scream as something ran over her foot before scampering on ahead.

Dear God.

She repeated the words over and over, a silent whisper, her mouth shaping the sounds rather than speaking them. Noise in the tunnels travelled. Even whispers echoed, bouncing off the walls. Instead, she set her gaze on Harry up ahead. If she stretched her hand out, she could touch him, but she didn't. Instead, she followed, one step at a time until she thought she saw something up ahead. A shape in the dark. She squinted trying to make it out. A thin crescent of muted gold.

'I think we've made it,' she called softly.

'About time.'

Moments later, she placed the bags on the platform before turning back to help Harry with James. There was a sense of relief that they'd made it, but that's as far as it went. Reiner would only be one step behind. Lenny had been running on fear ever since the flower seller had burst into the bookshop, spilling her story. That had drained away to be replaced by a strange lethargy.

The platform was only safe as long as no one discovered them.

'What about that alcove in the corner,' she finally said, squinting in the darkness. 'It's a little out of the way.'

'Great idea.'

They managed to settle James before they were plunged into a thick inky darkness. It was cold, and they had a sick man on their hands with a high temperature. Lenny made a makeshift pillow out of her jumper and lay it under his head, then she draped her coat across his shivering body, feeling helpless.

'Come and sit a minute, Lenny. He probably needs to sleep.'

Lenny didn't have to wonder at the weight of the knapsack when she saw the contents. 'Gilberte must have given us her dinner and half the contents of her cupboard.'

He chuckled. 'Not quite. There's a bottle of water in the bottom along with a knife and a flashlight.' He slapped the knife across his palm before re-sheathing it and tucking it into the side pocket.

'If only we'd known about the flashlight earlier,' she grumbled, pulling out a still warm pile of sausages wrapped in greaseproof paper. 'It would have made that tunnel walk far less scary.'

'And it would also have alerted the guard that he had a couple of waifs and strays in his tunnel. Here, have a swig of this. It will warm you up.'

'This' was a flask of what might be either brandy or whisky. Lenny's foray into the arena of hard liqueur had started with that flask in Arisaig and ended with some wine in a little café somewhere in Paris. It was a memory which brought a host of others along with it, including the moment Harry had walked her home and had pressed a kiss against her cheek.

'I don't think so. Maybe later.'

Harry had done so much for her and James. She knew that spies weren't meant to think in terms of action and reward, but he was quickly becoming so much more than a friend. She intended to do something about that when she had the opportunity.

'I want to see if I can wake James first,' she said. 'He needs a drink, and I need to see that wound.'

'Right. How about if I lean him forward? If we prop the torch at an angle, we should be able to see what's what.'

James stirred briefly when she manoeuvred his arm out of the sling, but fell quickly back to sleep. The bandage was stained with blood, but not sopping, which was probably a good sign. She managed to slip the jumper back on, leaving his arm tucked next to his chest before rearranging her jumper under his head.

'What he needs is a doctor,' she said. 'But that's not possible, is it?'

'Let's wait until the morning and I'll see what I can rummage up. At least they're not looking for me, which gives us some degree of flexibility.' He sank down, his back to the wall, gesturing for her to join him.

Lenny didn't have any reason to object. Something had shifted between them since London. Not just in the way he looked at her. In the way she felt about him.

She didn't lean into him when they settled down for the night, she was far too shy for that, and he didn't offer the comfort of his shoulder.

It was enough that he was close by.

FORTY

Sunday 8 June, 1941 – Paris 4.25 am

It was the cold that woke her. She stared up at the faint outline of the domed ceiling, waiting for her eyes to adjust to the dark. It was completely silent. Their own private sanctuary deep under the busy Parisian metropolis. She could almost believe that they were safe. Reiner surely wouldn't have the interest or resources to follow them indefinitely.

Her body slowly started to come alive after a night on the hardest of beds. Her left hip was aching along with her left shoulder and there was a twinge in her neck. There was also a heavy weight across her stomach. A line of warmth from shoulder to knee.

Lenny took a moment before turning her head and staring into Harry's face, smooth in sleep. A hint of the boy he'd once been under the deep grooves of the man he'd become. It was a rare opportunity to examine his features, one by one, imprinting them on her memory. Heavy eyebrows. Creased lids hiding the intensity of his gaze. An average nose. No hook or crook to mark it out as anything special. Firm lips. Often stubborn but so soft.

Her breathing stuttered along with her heart and suddenly she was looking into his eyes. Mesmerised by their colour. Their depth. Their tenderness...

'Morning.' His voice was soft, a breath against her cheek. 'This is nice. The perfect way to wake.'

Lenny didn't know what to say or how to say it. Her reply had packed up and left, deserting her when she needed it most. Instead, she smiled. It would have to do.

His response was immediate, his arm tightening, drawing her close, his mouth only a whisper away. 'It was worth that nightmare trek in the tunnel just to see you smile at me like that. I thought you didn't like me.'

'I told you before about losing your telephone number. That was true.'

'But would you have phoned it?'

'Probably not.' She smiled again. 'You have to remember that James and I had a very sheltered upbringing, which didn't include talking to strangers, even if they did play hockey with their big brother!'

'Ha.' He stretched back his neck, muffling his laughter and exposing a long stretch of throat, his pulse beating rapidly at the base. 'That's put me in my place. I hope you don't think of me as a stranger now?'

She concentrated on the way the skin trembled over his pulse. Beat, beat, beat, in tandem with her heart rate. The truth was, she didn't know what to think.

A kiss. Then another one. Each one successively deeper, his hand shifting from her waist to her head, cradling her in place.

So, this is what the other girls meant. This tide of passion that sweeps away common sense.

Lenny had always been a wallflower. The shy girl turned shy woman until her brother's disappearance had changed her. There'd been no time to think of anything else. Now, with the sound of her brother's regular breathing somewhere behind her, and the day barely started, there was nothing to distract her except fear.

She didn't fear Harry, not anymore.

She could only be truly scared of what she couldn't see.

The enemy.

What they'd do if they finally caught up.

Not if. When.

Lenny knew they were trapped. Harry might be able to sneak out to get help, but her brother was in no fit state to be moved.

She opened her eyes, only to find Harry staring back at her.

'You know I love you, Lenny? I've loved you since the first time I saw you, standing on the sidelines muffled up like a mummy, cheering on James. It's my dearest wish to be with you for as long as we get.'

In the old days it would have been forever. That wasn't a promise to make in wartime, she thought, holding his gaze which was suddenly and surprisingly so very dear to her.

Dear Harry.

If forever meant only now, then she needed to wring it out for every last drop.

FORTY-ONE

Lenny was feeling happy, happier than she should be, given their situation. They were propped up against the wall, their limbs entwined when James called out. Only a hoarse whisper but enough to broaden her smile to a wide grin as she hurried to his side.

'How are you feeling?'

'Hurts like hell, but a lot better after that sleep. The butcher reckoned the bullets went right through. I just hope I can believe him.'

'Butcher?' She helped prop him up on his good elbow before offering him the last of the water.

'Don't ask! What about you and Harry?'

'We're fine, aren't we, Harry?'

'Absolutely.' He had a large sheet of wood in his hands, which he propped up beside the alcove, keeping a small distance between them.

'What's the wood for?'

'Found it closing off the other end of the tunnel.'

'You went back in the tunnel with the rats and God knows what else!' Lenny stared at him in horror. 'Are you mad?'

'Probably. But with James out of action I thought it might come in handy in front of the alcove.' He squatted down on his haunches, his hand touching hers in the fleetest of caresses. 'What about it, James, old boy? Think you can walk out of here, if we help?'

'I'll give it a bloody good try.'

Lenny glanced between them, before focusing on Harry, tentatively in love for the first time. Tentatively because she wasn't sure if the label was quite right yet. Describing something so new and unknown with a word of only four letters seemed impossible but, if it was love, then she wanted the feeling to last. There were going to be obstacles in the way, not least the fact that two of them were wanted by the SS but, surely they deserved a little luck.

Reiner hadn't caught them yet.

'Now, what about breakfast?' she said. 'Anything left in the bottom of the bag?'

It was in that tiny fraction of time between one thought and the next that they heard shouting and the stamping of feet along the tunnel. Not just one or two men.

An army.

Harry was the first to move. Snatching the rucksack and throwing it in James's lap, followed by her bag, her knitting needles poking out the top.

Lenny froze, her feet and her heart glued to the floor, her eyes wide with panic and fear.

No!

'Here, quickly now.' Harry handed her the contents of his pocket before pressing her back into the alcove, the sound of the stamping feet growing louder, but still a distance away. It was only then that she finally realised what he was going to do.

His ID and ration cards. The only way to identify him.

'No, Harry. No.'

'Yes. It's the only way. They'll be looking for James, Lenny. I'll do instead.'

She grabbed his arm, her fingers digging into his skin, desperate to hold onto him and stop him leaving. Her voice breaking. 'I can't let you... I love you.'

'It's not up to you, my love.' He lifted his hand to her face, his touch fleeting, but a touch she'd remember forever. 'You've given me more happiness than I could ever have imagined.' His mouth met hers, the kiss featherlight, his hands positioned on her shoulders as he manoeuvred her backwards, before sliding the wood over the entrance, hiding them from view.

Boots hammered against stone.

German voices cut through the darkness.

The gunshot when it came was brutally loud, brutally final.

In the suffocating quiet that followed, Lenny's world shattered.

PART THREE

FORTY-TWO

Lenny rammed her fist into her mouth, biting down hard on her knuckles to stop the scream ringing out. Her world splintered into a thousand pieces.

Picture after picture flicked across her mind. Scenes she couldn't see and could barely imagine.

Harry lying across the tracks like a crumpled doll. Being dragged through the tunnel with no thought for the amazing man he had been only seconds before.

Her dear love.

A sound drew her right back into the alcove, her expression one of horror at where James was trying to stand, his face ashen, his eyes twin pools of shock and grief.

Harry had given his life for them. She wasn't about to let that mean nothing.

She flapped her hand at him, willing him to stay still, to not make a sound as she pressed her ear up to the slight gap where wood met wall.

'Good. We've got him. Now it's only the girl.' She recognised the voice immediately as Standartenführer Otto Reiner. A man she'd quite happily kill, if it wasn't for the risk to James.

Too many lives had been lost already.

'Search the station. Leave nothing uncovered,' he shouted.

The sound of feet trampling over the tracks filled her world. She closed her eyes briefly, her hand now spread flat against her chest, fear filling her veins and pumping through her heart.

There was only a thin piece of wood separating them from discovery. Reiner wouldn't arrest them. He'd shoot to kill.

All Harry's efforts in vain.

No. stop it. Pull yourself together.

She bit her lip hard, the sharp metallic taste of blood driving the thought away. If there was any hope of survival, she had to keep strong. Grieving could come later.

A shout echoed through the tunnel.

'Quick. We think we've got her, trying to exit at the next station.' Closely followed by the sound of what seemed like a platoon of soldiers trailing off into the distance.

Lenny glanced down at her hand, where she'd crushed Harry's documents between her fingers. Instead of smoothing them out, she shoved them in the rucksack along with Harry's flask. He'd thrust it at her for a reason. A little Dutch courage. By the look of James, she was probably going to need it.

She stuffed her bag on top before grabbing Harry's jumper.

She wouldn't leave it behind.

Lenny couldn't remember their journey to the next station. Her mind was stuck in a loop that started and ended with the gunshot.

The dark. The sound of scurrying rats. The shift of rocks under her feet, as she pressed James forward, her hand clamped across his back, taking as much of his weight as she could. She knew it must have happened that way, but she couldn't recall any of it.

She was a machine, running on leftover fumes as adrenaline started to dissolve, only to be replaced by fear with grief curdling at the edges.

The first thing she remembered was the end of the tunnel, the glow of the platform arching beyond.

She pulled James to a stop beside her. They leant against the wall, heaving for breath after almost running along the track.

The platform up ahead looked deserted, but for how long?

Lenny didn't know when the trains started but it must be soon. That her watch only said twenty past five was a shock. She knew it was still early, but for everything that had happened to be squeezed into such a small time frame seemed surreal.

Her life was over, and it wasn't even daylight yet.

'One last push, James,' she whispered carefully. 'Think you can manage to clamber onto the platform, if I help?'

She watched as he gritted his teeth, his face bathed in sweat. His sharp nod told her everything she needed to know.

Climbing onto the platform used every last scrap of energy they had. With her hand on James's back, she shoved him up the side before throwing the rucksack and following him, grazing her hands and knees in the process. They collapsed on the nearest bench as the first train rumbled into the station, its doors discharging a few early passengers.

She watched dispassionately as they moved to the exit. A motley crowd of people going about their daily lives, with no thought of what had happened on the next track along. She could barely believe it herself.

The train finally moved, revealing what it had been concealing on the far wall.

Welcome to Grenelle, along with a large image of the Eiffel Tower.

'We need to get out of here.' James rested his head back, his face grey, his hair a mess.

'First things first.' Lenny rummaged through her bag for her comb. 'Let me.' She stood in front of him, combing his hair and wiping his face with her handkerchief before he could object.

'I can do that.' He sounded annoyed, his eyes closed against the glare of the lights.

'It's done.'

She started on her hair, one eye on the empty platform, a pile of pins in her mouth, her wreck of a hat in her lap. After, she emptied the contents of her purse into her pocket before stuffing her comb and hankie on top.

'Here, hold my knitting and don't drop any stitches,' she cautioned, repacking her handbag with her ID card, her ration card and her empty purse. 'There. All I need is a bin and we'll be able to exit the station, and get rid of Léonore Bouchard at the same time.'

The platform was starting to fill again, a couple of German soldiers causing her to unwrap her knitting and start on a new row. The woman on the next bench smiled across at her as she worked on her crochet. She smiled back.

'We'll move as soon as they go.'

'To where? You're forgetting that we don't have a ticket.' He glared at her, anger and annoyance adding a much-needed splash of colour to his cheeks.

'We don't have a ticket, darling Jacques, because your stupid girlfriend left her handbag on the train.'

FORTY-THREE

'You're sure you'll be alright? I won't be long.'

'I'll be fine.'

Lenny paused briefly to glance back at the café. James looked to be engrossed in the newspaper, his head tilted to conceal most of his face, a coffee he didn't want by his elbow along with a glass of water, which he did.

It would have to do.

She hurried along the Rue de La Pompe, her attention on the school up ahead and not on the bookshop across the road.

Returning to Librairie Universelle was out of the question even if she could see the door from where she was standing. It was also foolhardy to be anywhere near the Rue de La Pompe, she reminded herself.

Any sane person would have left the 16th Arrondissement, along with Paris, for the relative safety of the French countryside.

But Lenny wasn't anyone. She had an injured brother and no documents if the Germans decided to stop her. However, there was a perfectly good set hidden under Marianne's summerhouse.

She walked into the school and approached the counter with a smile, her outward composure relying on the rigorous acting lessons she'd undertaken. Her nerves were shot, her future a huge unknown with only one thing certain.

No Harry.

She managed to pull herself together with a little shake of her head, her hand curled into an iron fist in her pocket.

'Bonjour. Apologies. I know it's inconvenient, but I would like a brief word with Mademoiselle Levain, if it's not too much trouble. It's important.'

The nun eyed her with such an air of gentleness that Lenny felt her carefully constructed defences crumble and her eyes start to smart.

No acting lesson could teach her how to hide her grief now that help was only a whisper away.

'Certainly. Come this way.'

She followed her along the corridor past closed doors, the faint noise of children's voices in the background, her breathing a laboured gasp as memories picked holes in her gossamer thin composure.

'Take a seat, my child. Marianne will be with you shortly.' Lenny heard the door close and, collapsing into the nearest chair, buried her head in her hands, tears seeping between her fingers.

If only she hadn't come to Paris. Harry would still be alive, and James would have sorted himself out. She'd only made it worse. She'd made everything worse. First Ellen and Finlay and now Harry. How many more people was she going to lose? People she loved.

She didn't hear the door opening behind her, only Marianne's soft words as she drew her into a hug.

'Whatever has happened?'

'I can't...' Lenny hiccupped to a halt, pressing her hands into her eyes, the weight of her failures crashing down on her. There were things she had to do, like getting James the medical help he needed and all she could think of was herself and everything that was wrong.

Harry, who'd given his life for her.

A life that was worthless.

'It will be alright, Leonora. I promise.' Marianne rested back on her heels, her gaze eye level. 'I will do everything in my power to make it so.'

'I don't think that you can. It would take a miracle.'

'And I'm just the person to provide it, ma chérie. Many helped me when I fled to safety. Now I will help you.'

FORTY-FOUR

Monday 9 June, 1941 – Perpignan 12 pm

Lenny sat beside James on the train, barely able to believe what they'd been through in the last two days. Two days ago, they'd been trapped in a metro tunnel with Harry's blood on the tracks. Now they were hundreds of miles from Reiner's reach, alive only because Marianne and Pierre had risked everything to save them.

Within an hour of arriving at the school, she'd directed them to a safe house on the next street. A tall, narrow building that housed a seamstress on the ground floor, the stairs leading to a poky attic with grubby windows, a broken stove in one corner, a double bed in the other.

'I'm afraid it's not much.' Marianne smoothed her hand across the blanket before turning it back and helping James with his jacket and then his shoes. 'I'll get food and water to you somehow, along with your papers. The doctor should be with you shortly. A good man.' She hurried to the door, before adding. 'I'll try and get a message to the Brossolettes. It's dangerous with the Germans still looking for you, but if anyone can help you with the next bit, it will be Pierre.'

They had to take a train to the south, the first leg of their journey out of France and back to safety.

If they made it.

The train was crowded with an assortment of French and Spaniards now they were close to the border. They were lucky to get a seat in the packed carriage, instead of having to stand in the corridor along with a party of Germans, their rifles slung carelessly over their shoulders.

'I can't wait to meet your parents.' Lenny cradled James's hand in hers. Her gaze switched from the fields of grapevines to his face as the train pulled into the station, thinking about what a good night's sleep had done for him. He would need all the strength he could get.

'They're going to be enchanted,' James managed, playing along.

Lenny knew a lie when she heard it. A glance in the mirror when she'd washed her hands in the rest room at Montpellier Station earlier had confirmed it. She'd aged ten years in two days. All she needed was white hair to complete the picture.

Shifting a couple of hairpins had done nothing to improve matters.

They joined the small queue to exit the turnstile, continuing their gentle chatter for the benefit of the soldier standing over the ticket inspector.

Surely Reiner couldn't be looking for them here.

'What does your brother look like? I know he's younger, but is he fair or dark?' Lenny asked, in an effort to revive their flagging conversation.

'Nothing like me.'

Lenny chuckled, her chin tilted up at him, her peripheral vision tracking where the soldier was concentrating on the nervous-looking man ahead. Her skin crawled with fear, her feet two blocks of iron that refused to move. Welded to the pavement.

'Your papers.'

'Of course.'

They slipped past, slowing their pace when what they wanted to do was run. Run as fast as they could to the mountains in front of them. The mountains separating them from freedom.

The Pyrenees.

Perpignan was sweltering, the heat of the noon day sun beating down on them as they exited the station. They started walking up the street, their pace slow as they scanned the buildings, the name of the bar written on the back of her hand.

'Bar du Figuier. That's fig tree, isn't it?' she asked, after thirty minutes of fruitless searching.

'If you say so.'

Lenny stared across at him, noting the tremor in his jaw and a flicker of pain in his eyes. He'd seemed fine, but they'd finished the last of their water back on the train, and surely it must be time for his painkillers, not that he'd tell her. He hadn't spoken much of anything since the metro. They could chat in front of others, but to each other? A wall had risen sky high since Harry's death, one she didn't know how to breach.

Harry had been his friend. Did James blame her? It wouldn't matter either way.

She blamed herself.

He needed to rest, or she'd have a collapsed man to add to her current list of worries. There'd be no help from the shuttered houses with their flat roofs and wrought-iron balconies, swathes of brightly coloured flowers weaving their way up the walls.

Spain and the promise of freedom was close, if only they could find the café Pierre had told them about.

She tripped slightly, the muscles in her calves on fire, sweat dripping down her back in the oppressive heat. They needed a long cool drink, but didn't have the nerve to ask where to get it. The bar was the meeting place for the local branch of the resistance, a fact the fewer people knew the better, but to wander about in the sun was mad as well as foolhardy. They were the only ones outside.

As easy to spot as an escaped lion and just as alarming.

'Come, let's find somewhere to rest.' She gently manoeuvred him across the street to a park, settling him on a bench in the shade of an overhanging tree. 'I'll be back shortly. Don't move and try not to speak to anyone.'

She watched him briefly before turning away, fear fluttering in her chest. His eyes were closed against the sun, the beads of sweat on his forehead emphasising the pasty colour of his skin.

She'd find the café and bring help.

'Excuse me.' She finally came across a couple of small boys playing football in a side street.

Perfect. Far less likely to be suspicious of a woman on her own.

'I wonder could you help. I'm meeting my friend at Bar du Figuier and...' She shrugged. 'I seem to have forgotten where it is.'

They laughed at that and a little at her too. Within minutes she was in possession of a garbled set of instructions, which had included a lot of arm waving. She'd nearly offered them money for their help before thinking better of it.

Directions to a stranger could be easily forgotten. Money not so much.

The café was tucked away at the end of the street. Weathered stone with dull brown shutters and a wooden sign over the door with Bar du Figuier written in what once must have been red lettering but was now faded to pink.

Lenny opened Marianne's old bag, pretending to look inside as she tried to work out what to do. Pierre had given her a name and a place. Michel at the Bar du Figuier.

She'd trekked from one end of France to the other, but on the word of someone she'd trust with her life. In the dim light of the attic, she'd struggled to tell Pierre about Harry. She'd never forget his expression of pure sorrow or the way he'd pulled her to him as she'd sobbed into his shoulder.

She sniffed back her tears as she closed the bag with a snap.

Her thoughts always found a route back to Harry, no matter how hard she tried to control them. At some point, she could see herself drowning in them but that wasn't now. She had to get James out of France first, which meant the bar and whatever lay inside its dark interior.

Walking into a bar unaccompanied was something she would never have dreamed of doing under normal circumstances. Etiquette forbade it, but etiquette couldn't account for the pickle they were in and it certainly wouldn't save them. Instead, she squared her shoulders and lifted her chin before walking inside, her gaze fixed on the short, wiry man behind the bar.

She ignored the sudden silence. The immediate cessation of chatter.

'Bonjour, Uncle Michel, I've arrived a week early,' she said, her voice pitched low, unable to hide her smile at the way his eyes lit in acknowledgement at the carefully worded coded message. Before she knew it, he'd swept around the counter and was kissing her on both cheeks.

'Little Léonore. I can't believe it's you.' And then in a louder voice. 'My niece from Lyon. How long has it been?'

'Too long.'

He puffed out his cheeks, nodding in the direction of a table in the corner. 'Your aunt will be overjoyed to see you.' He hurried into the back, yelling as he went. 'Collette. Hurry. You'll never believe who's here, and a whole week early.' And in the emotional reunion that followed, they placed a pitcher of water on the table between them, while a tearful Collette took over the bar.

Lenny didn't have to fake her own tears, they ran down her face unchecked as she explained softly about James and where she'd left him.

'Your things. Of course you left them at the station. No point in dragging them here in this heat. Madness. I will go directly. Collette will show you to your room, ma belle.'

FORTY-FIVE

Wednesday 11 June, 1941 – the Pyrenees 11.25 pm

Lenny stared down at the lights of Perpignan twinkling below her in the distance. She'd just said goodbye to her new friends, knowing that it would be the last time she'd ever see them. Once she left France, she would never return. It was a promise that she was determined never to break.

Turning back, she steadied her boots on the rough ground, her attention on where the guide was helping James, a stout stick in his good hand. Everything looked different in the pale light cast by the moon. The terraced vineyards now they were in the foothills, interspersed with small mountain streams from the sheer rock face looming up ahead. At least there was a path, rough-hewn into the landscape by centuries of shepherds caring for their flocks, but something to follow.

The going was only just manageable. Without her training in Arisaig, she wouldn't even have attempted it, or perhaps she would. She didn't have a choice.

'We stop. Change shoes. Drink.'

The shepherd produced espadrilles from his rucksack along with two canteens, one full of water, the other wine. Lenny and

James shared the former, watching with rounded eyes as their guide drank deeply from the latter. They couldn't say anything. If he decided to leave them, they'd be finished.

'Alright, James?' she said, handing him a couple of painkillers, before untying her boots and slipping the espadrilles over her thick socks.

'Fine.'

He wasn't, but there was nothing she could do about that. Michel had told them it was unsafe to stay longer than needed. A night and a day to rest only, before a night ascending into Spain. They could only start to relax when they were safely on the other side of the border.

It had started to rain by the time their guide stood, the mist reducing visibility to only a couple of feet ahead.

'The mist helps as we near the top,' he whispered, pointing at a dim flicker of light in the distance. 'Germans patrolling the ridge. A comfortable bed awaits when we reach Spain.'

Lenny followed his arm, her ears picking up a muffled sound. A sound that turned her blood to ice.

Barking.

She started walking, her feet slipping on the wet rocks, her head throbbing as the air thinned. The only thing that kept her going was the thought of James plodding on ahead.

If he can make it then so can I.

They crawled over the last peak at six, the shepherd begging them to hurry. Lenny eyed the ridge, her face rigid with fear as she tried to get her limbs to work. The sky was already starting to bleach around the edges in a blend of navy and grey when he handed them over to their Spanish guide. The last she saw of him was as he disappeared over the top, almost running over the rocks now he wasn't lumbered with his charges. She hadn't thought to thank him and she couldn't now. He'd never told them his name.

'It is best that way.'

. . .

Lenny slipped on her borrowed dress and shoes, her hair still wet from the shower. Five days staying in Barcelona as the guest of the Consul General and she could barely put one foot in front of the other, let alone one thought.

The room was luxurious, with expensive fabrics and mahogany furnishings. Tall, shuttered windows opened up onto a courtyard with distant views of the Mediterranean beyond, the air full of the scent of oranges from the trees below.

She sat on the end of the canopied bed, staring at the wall opposite, remembering every step of their journey.

The twenty-six-mile trek across rough terrain to reach the fort town of Figueras, walking at night and sleeping rough during the day. James was barely able to speak by then, let alone do more than stumble. The guide propped him up on one side while she tried to support him on the other. The hay wagon to Barcelona had been a blessing and not before time. The doctor at the English hospital had told her that, if they'd been any later, they wouldn't have been able to save him.

He was only just about well enough to travel now and, as much as she hated having to put him through any more, the Consul General had advised her that their early departure was advisable.

'*Not everyone in Spain is content with neutrality, mi querida.*'

She finally moved, slipping on her borrowed jacket and pinning her borrowed hat to her hair. Her bag came next. It held her ID papers, Harry's flask, her knitting needles and a couple of balls of wool. Marianne's way of helping her to pass the time on her journey across France and beyond.

The wool was grey. Two skeins of rough homespun yarn. She ran a strand through her fingers, unable to summon up any of the joy she used to feel at the thought of starting a new project. There was nothing. Not a beat or a flicker. She'd lost so much in France. Knitting seemed to be a part of that.

But their journey wasn't over, and it would pass the time. A living record of what had happened and where her failed trip to France had taken her.

She draped a pale blue jumper over her shoulders, her fingers on the wool. His jumper was a comfort when nothing else was. A part of Harry in the loops and twists.

The next part of their journey should be easier. She hoped that the Consul General hadn't been lying to her about that. A taxi to Madrid where they'd rest the night, before being taken on to Seville. After, a long journey to Lisbon before a passenger plane to London.

France. Spain. Portugal. London and, when the war was finally over, Guernsey.

She'd never leave her island again.

PART FOUR

FORTY-SIX

Wednesday 25 June, 1941 – Whitehall, London 10 am

'You're looking well, Lenny. More rested than the last time I saw you.'

If she hadn't felt dead inside, she'd have laughed. She knew how she looked and well wasn't the term, but it was irrelevant. Just as she didn't care about the war anymore, she didn't give two hoots about the trench-like shadows under her eyes and her ghost-like skin. Every time she fell into a fitful sleep, she found herself in the middle of the station, the sound of that single gunshot dragging her back to consciousness. She was scared to go to bed. Instead, she sat by the window while the rest of London slept. Four sleepless nights and her hands were starting to shake.

'Thank you, sir.'

She smoothed her skirt over her legs, a normal movement for someone whose life had exploded so spectacularly. If it wasn't for Marianne and the Brossolettes arranging for their safe passage across the Pyrenees she didn't know where they'd be. That she didn't care wasn't worth dwelling on. She was only here because Major Buckmaster had demanded it, not because of any sense of duty or loyalty to the cause.

She'd left all that behind in a disused metro station somewhere in Paris.

'And your brother. I hear he's ready to be discharged?'

'In a couple of days, yes.' James, who'd bounced back after a good rest and a second course of sulfonamides for the blood poisoning that had nearly killed him. He was even talking about going back to work at the War Office. Lenny couldn't think of anything worse.

She'd done her bit for the war and ended up making a complete mess of it. If she'd stayed in London working for Miss Maxse, perhaps none of this would have happened. Perhaps... She clenched her hands into fists, her gaze on the way the bones were gleaming white beneath their thin covering of skin. She'd lost weight. More weight than she'd thought. More than she could afford.

The sound of a drawer closing had her looking up, a sudden lump blocking her throat. The knitted green scarf that she'd last seen knotted around Harry's neck in Paris.

'We were saddened to hear about the loss of Harry Dennison. A fine chap with a great future ahead of him.' The major ran the scarf between his fingers, a muscle flicking in his jaw. 'This is yours, I believe?'

'Thank you.' Lenny placed the scarf on her lap, her hand resting on top, her fingers clutching onto the wool for dear life, her heart slamming against her ribs.

At least Harry was getting the recognition he deserved.

'You're a remarkable young woman. In fact, quite brilliant. To use your knitting as a way to share secrets. When I first heard what you were doing with your Morse code, I couldn't get my head around it.' She watched as he leant back in his chair. 'It's been added to our training schedules, you know, and not just for our SOEs. For all soldiers, whether air, ground or sea, in case of capture. What better way for our men to share what's happening than through their handiwork. While their letters are censured, their socks aren't.' He laughed at his little joke, only to stop abruptly at her continued silence. 'Yes, well, I'm hoping that this project is something that you'll lead on? Based in London, of course.'

Harry's project, not mine, she thought, sadly. *All I was doing was trying to learn Morse code.*

'I'm afraid that won't be possible, Major.' She lifted the scarf and looped it around her neck, remembering with a jolt that the last neck to hold it had been Harry's. She'd tried to knit when she'd arrived back in London. Nothing much. A cardigan. Something to do with her hands, but it seemed that she couldn't. The fine dance needed to coordinate wool and needles seemed suddenly impossible to manage.

Each stitch brought a memory. The knitting group in Guernsey. Darling Ellen, Finlay and Betty. Teaching Bill, Georges and even Johnny. The evenings she'd spent in France not truly realising that Marianne, Claudine and Maeva had been her friends. And, finally Harry, but she wasn't brave enough to think about him, and the reason she'd decided to hang up her knitting needles. She'd boxed up the grey scarf, along with her ID papers for Georgette Tournier, and shoved them in the back of her wardrobe.

'I haven't been able to knit since my return, sir. Seems I've lost the knack.'

'That is a shame.'

Lenny nodded, knowing he meant it.

'Are you staying in London?' The major thumbed through her file. 'We'll need an up-to-date address for you in case of developments.'

Lenny wasn't sure what to say. Everyone was being so nice to her. Miss Maxse had offered her the use of one of their apartments and had even put Forbes at her disposal for when she went to visit James in hospital. But she couldn't stay in London, not now she'd decided to resign from her post. James needed to get on with his life without having to worry about what she was up to.

She glanced down at her bag, remembering the letter from Angus that had been waiting for her when they'd arrived back in the capital. A chatty missive mostly about Betty, but with an open invitation to visit for as long as she liked. When she'd shown James, he'd demanded that she reply there and then. The upshot was that Angus was coming to London for a few days. She didn't know how to feel about that. Mostly ambivalent, as she was about most things these days.

'For the moment, sir. I'll let your office know if there are any changes.'

She'd arranged to meet Angus at the same Lyon's teashop. It was probably the same waitress hurrying across the room, laden down with an overfilled tray. The room certainly looked the same, she thought.

It was everything else that had changed.

Angus pushed to standing when she walked in, but even without this little courtesy she'd have recognised him. He was wearing the same jacket with the frayed cuffs, his trilby set on the chair beside him. She didn't notice his searching look or the way his expression changed from one of pleasure to shock, before masking it by pulling out her chair. She didn't notice, but she wouldn't have been surprised. A part of her had died in Paris. Her ability to care about anything and anyone, certainly not herself. James was harping on about getting back to work while Betty was thriving in the Scottish air. They didn't need her and she didn't know what she needed... now.

'It's good to see you, lass,' he said, his gaze resting on her face as he settled opposite. 'I've ordered tea and cakes. Alright?'

'Perfect. How's Betty?' Lenny had decided on a safe topic on the journey over and nothing was safer than Betty. They could fill hours talking about her, which meant they wouldn't have room to talk about anything else.

'Hot and bothered in this weather,' he said, as the waitress arranged crockery and a cake stand between them.

'If you wouldn't mind pouring?' Lenny spread her hand out, a little tremor running across the back. 'I wouldn't want to spill any.'

'Of course!' He slid her cup over and selected a cake before sliding that over too. 'There. All sorted.' Then, after a slight pause, 'I did think there was something.' He smiled briefly before turning his attention back to the cakes, as if they held the answer to the universe. 'I know you probably won't want to talk about it, but I've been told I'm a good listener.'

Lenny was disarmed by his words and his kindness. She dabbed at her eyes with her handkerchief before managing a watery smile.

'Thank you, but I don't think I can. Maybe later...' She shrugged, pushing the cake plate away and picking up her cup, her gaze finally meeting his.

'I didn't mean to pry.' He coughed briefly, a faint flush creeping up under his collar, his expression wary as if he was suddenly at a loss for words. 'I'd just like you to know that I'll always be there if you need to talk, or if you're in need of a friend. After what you did for Ellen, Finlay, Betty and me. Well, I owe you everything.'

'You don't owe me a thing, Angus. I only did what anyone else would have done.' Lenny uttered the platitude automatically, the words finding their way through a mind bankrupt of emotion. The past wasn't something she was able to talk about yet. She had to accept that she might never be able to deal with it.

She heaved in a breath then another, trying to gain some sort of equilibrium. Angus was a kind man, but he hadn't come to try and sort out her life for her. That was something she'd have to puzzle out for herself.

'My dear?'

He placed his hand over hers, the gesture causing her throat to tighten.

'I'm fine, really.' She withdrew her hand, instead tapping the edge of the cake plate. 'I haven't regained my appetite yet but, we mustn't let this good food go to waste and, in the meantime, you can tell me everything about Betty.'

Angus placed his hand back on his lap, his face blanched pale, his expression unreadable. 'Only if you promise to think about visiting us to see for yourself. A holiday away from this place would do you the world of good.'

FORTY-SEVEN

Tuesday 22 July, 1941 – Arisaig 3 pm

Lenny huddled in her chair, unable to get warm. The cold had sunk through her skin, straight to her bones. Further still. Straight to her soul. She was a block of ice instead of a living, breathing woman and the thaw was a long way off, if ever.

She'd been in Scotland a month but, despite Angus's entreaties, she didn't notice any difference, except maybe for a slight thaw in Betty's presence. It wasn't much. She didn't have that much left to give. The damage had started in Guernsey and been compounded in both London and Paris. Too many losses. The barrier was as thick as it was tall. An impervious wall that only Ellen and Finlay's child could breach.

A beautiful face. A gappy smile. A sweet-smelling hug. The cracks in her walled-up emotions were starting to show, but only to those who bothered to look. Only to those who persisted in trying.

Betty, who was sitting on a rug by her feet, Gary watching her. By all accounts her constant companion since they'd both arrived in Arisaig ten months ago.

'Hello there. This is where you're hiding.'

Lenny managed a smile, her gaze resting on Betty instead of Angus's face. She missed his concerned expression.

She hadn't been looking.

He was a man she didn't see. He wasn't either James or Harry.

'I have tea, bannocks, and treacle scones too. Mrs Campbell has outdone herself.'

'Thank you and thank her.' Lenny finally found her manners from where they'd been hiding.

Angus. The man who had arrived in her bleakest moment and carted her off to Scotland. Mrs Campbell had prepared a welcome feast, and aired the second-best bedroom, situated at the opposite end of the manse to Angus and Betty.

'Dada.' Betty beamed as she welcomed Angus, her hands held high to be picked up.

'Hello, how's my favourite girl?' Angus's smile was as wide as Betty's. 'Come on up, poppet, but only for a moment. Dada has the tea to attend to. There's cake. Your favourite.' He dropped a kiss on her head before placing her back on the rug, his attention on the tea tray and the two letters propped on the side. 'There's post. A letter for you and one for me. Your brother if I'm not mistaken. Mine, however, looks to be a bill.'

Lenny picked up the envelope, turning it over in her hands as she thought of other letters from him, other times. She hadn't heard from him in a couple of weeks. Nothing unusual in that. She knew he would be busy with his new job in the War Office. *All very hush hush. Wasn't it always.*

Running her finger under the flap, she withdrew the single sheet of Whitehall notepaper.

My dearest Lenny,

I hope all is well in sunny Scotland. Angus has been in touch. Says you're holding your own, whatever that means. If you need rescuing from his dour clutches – I hope he doesn't get to read your mail – then I'm your man. Only returning the favour.

The reason for my letter. I met someone on my first day back. Works for Miss Maxse. Her name is Gloria. Says you might remember her. She's clever and nice, which is just as well because I proposed last night and she said yes. It looks like I'm getting married! You'll meet her soon. We're not going to wait, but a honeymoon in the wilds of Scotland sounds ideal.

With love always,

James

Lenny folded the sheet of paper, replacing it in the envelope and, for the first time since arriving back from France, missed her knitting bag. Not that she wanted to knit something, but it was a useful hiding place for a letter that Angus mustn't see.

Gloria.

She hadn't thought of her in ages, and then only in relation to what had happened to Johnny. She hadn't thought about him either. It was all too much effort.

'My brother is getting married. Only just met her. Someone at work. Good for him.'

Angus handed her a cup and saucer. 'You're happy about that?'

Was she?

In a funny sort of a way, yes. Someone bright and vivacious like Gloria might be just what he needed. And a hard worker. She'd quickly replaced her as Miss Maxse's right-hand woman.

'I think so. James deserves all the happiness that's going.' She placed her cup and saucer on the edge of the table, sinking back in her chair, fatigue hitting her like a steam train.

'And you don't, Leonora?' he asked, arranging a beaker and a plate with a bannock, cut into fingers, under Betty's watchful gaze.

'What do you mean?'

'What I said, my dear. Life isn't a trial run or a game, you know. We only get to travel this way once. You could say it's a one-way trip. No return journey. No refund.'

'You're speaking in riddles, Angus.' She cradled her cup for something to do, lifting her face to the weak sunlight streaming in from the window opposite.

'Perhaps I am. Now, what about you, young lady?' He turned his attention back to Betty. 'Want to eat there or on my lap?'

'Mama.'

The word was rough, unhewn. Like soil in need of a good rake. A word that brought a tear to Lenny's eye, thoughts of Ellen flooding in.

It was an easy mistake for Betty to make. After all, Lenny had been a constant presence since her return to Arisaig. It was all very well her calling Angus Dada. Lenny was a stranger, a stranger who, at some point would have to pick up the reins of her broken life.

Unbearable.

'I think she means you, lass.'

'But...' Lenny looked between the two of them. Angus was concentrating on choosing a cake but Betty. Betty was sitting with her arms aloft, her face starting to crumple.

'Come on then, sweet pea.' It was the easy path, but one with many potholes up ahead. Too many to explain to a baby.

Impossible.

She held Betty's cup for her, her hand curved around her soft body, contentment warring with guilt.

'Why not eat something? Mrs Campbell is a wonderful cook.'

'All this pestering. It's not as if I'm fading away.' But Lenny did as he asked, choosing a bannock with care before taking a cautious bite, the rest ending in Betty's chubby fist. She'd lost weight since Paris, but her appetite had vanished along with her will. 'I don't know why you put up with me, Angus. The women of the parish think I'm after your virtue and Mrs Campbell, for all her fancy cooking, doesn't trust me as far as she could throw me. Probably thinks I'm after it too. You can't say it's common for the vicar to put up an unmarried woman.'

'There's nothing common about war, Lenny.' He picked up his

cup and saucer and rested it on his knee, before adding quietly. 'Actually, that's not a bad idea.'

'Pardon?' Lenny watched as Betty chomped her way through the rest of the cake, idly wondering if she'd heard him correctly and deciding that she needed her ears washed out.

Ridiculous.

'In the legal sense, of course, Leonora.' He took a small sip from his tea and returned the cup and saucer to the table. 'Betty needs a mother and, it would help keep my female parishioners from trying to fling their daughters in my direction.'

'Angus! I'm not sure I understand,' she replied, gaping at him.

'Oh, you understand perfectly well. You're just choosing not to interpret my words in the way they're meant.' He smiled briefly. 'You'd make me very happy if you agreed to marry me?'

There was no talk of love, which helped. It helped quite a lot. There was only room in her life for two men. One was about to get married, and the other was dead.

Lenny couldn't bear to think about that.

She knew the days, hours and minutes since she'd last seen him. Since she'd heard the shot.

When they'd finally dared to remove the board, all they'd found was a thin trail of blood. All that was left.

She squeezed her eyes tight, her heart tripping at the memory. A couple of deep breaths and she felt able to reply.

'Thank you, Angus. You really are the sweetest of men, but I don't think that's a good idea.' She kissed Betty's cheek before placing her back on the floor where Gary was waiting. A small respite in which to get her head around the idea that the vicar was still a man under his dog collar. Up to then, she'd never thought of him in terms of anything other than Finlay's brother and Betty's guardian. 'I...' She felt wretched about what she needed to say, but he deserved the truth. 'I don't love you.'

'There are many reasons for marriage, Lenny. I always view love as a precious flower. Adding water and sunlight to the soil allows it to flourish. It's the same with marriage.' His voice was even, but he didn't meet her gaze as he bent his head to smooth away the stray crumbs on his black trousers. 'With effort on both our parts, I think we could have a very happy marriage, full of love and laughter.'

She picked up her cup and, lifting her head, took her courage in both hands.

Angus was a good man. The very best of men who'd make a wonderful husband and father if given the chance. It gave her no pleasure to turn him down in such a final, irrevocable way, but life wasn't about being fair. He'd been good enough to rescue her from Whitehall, after a debrief that had nearly broken her. Marrying him would only bring unhappiness to both of them. He didn't love her.

Her thoughts stuttered to a stop as she glanced at him over the rim of her cup. That wasn't something she could know for sure but, whatever his feelings, it would still be wrong to marry him.

'I'm sorry, Angus. I know what you're trying to do, and I truly appreciate it. It's an honour for you to ask me, but the answer is no.'

'Can I ask why?' he said, selecting a treacle scone and adding it to his plate, but Lenny wasn't fooled. His hand had clenched, turning the cake into crumbs.

Her heart stumbled before picking up rhythm. If she answered honestly, she'd end up hurting the kindest, most gentle of men. So like Finlay that it was a physical pain.

'I don't think that's a fair question. Let's just leave it that the answer is no.' She gestured to the teapot. 'Would you like a top-up?'

FORTY-EIGHT

Monday 28, July, 1941 – Arisaig 7.50 am

The gunshot rang out, reverberating around the narrow confines of the tunnel.

Harry!

Lenny awoke, her heart pounding in her chest, her feet tangled in the sheets. She lay there waiting for her body to settle, her gaze on the ceiling, a different ceiling to the curved dome of the metro she'd been expecting.

It wasn't the first time she'd had the dream, but the first since arriving in Scotland.

Pushing her heavy hair out of her eyes, her forehead slick with sweat, she continued staring at the ceiling.

It had been an average Sunday. She'd taken Betty to church, Mrs Campbell accompanying her. Then, after lunch she'd taken her for a walk while Angus had parish work to attend to. There'd been nothing out of the ordinary, even down to their roast chicken for lunch and cheese on toast for tea.

All very strange. Over the last few days she'd been feeling a little better. Eating more. Tentatively able to view the future and what she might want to do with the rest of it.

The sound of feet on the staircase pulled her out of her reverie. Angus and Betty, if their chatter was anything to go by, which meant that she only had a few minutes until breakfast or Mrs Campbell would burst in, wondering what she was doing lazing about in bed.

Good old Mrs Campbell, with her starched hair and starched apron, her swollen feet squeezed into too tight slippers. She wasn't a friend yet, but there were signs that the thaw was underway.

Lenny didn't want to get out of bed suddenly, in spite of the dream. It was warm and safe. A strange thought as she sat on the edge of the bed, rummaging around on the wooden floorboards for her slippers, her hand patting around for where she'd draped her dressing gown across the end of her bed. Arisaig and Angus were safe. A safe haven, but not anymore as a sudden wave of nausea crept up her neck, vomit burning the back of her mouth, her eyes widening in panic.

No!

She knew in an instant. In less time than the tick of a clock or the thump of her heart.

Lenny didn't get sick. Outside of seasickness and the odd headache, she could never remember a time when she was laid up with anything more debilitating than a cold. There must have been childhood diseases like measles to navigate but, if there had, she'd been far too young to remember.

With a spurt of speed, she jumped off the bed and ran to the door, wrenching it back on its hinges so hard that it caused a dent in the pale lemon wallpaper. The landing was empty as she hurled along the passage, the sound of muted voices coming up the stairs telling her that everyone was in the kitchen.

The manse was an old Victorian building, with only one bathroom on the first floor, a separate toilet off to the side. A toilet she only reached in time before a spray of liquid gushed from her mouth, her stomach rolling like a ship in a gale.

After, she knelt on the cold linoleum. Her fingers clenched

around the wooden toilet seat, her eyes scrunched closed against the sight of the splattered bowl as she worked out her dates.

Only moments before she'd been hopeful about starting again. The possibility of being able to build a life without Harry.

She struggled to her feet, reaching for the flush, her eyes glistening with tears.

You might be gone, my love, but you've left a little part of you behind.

Count that as your favour repaid in full.

They took breakfast in the kitchen to save Mrs Campbell more work. Always at eight o'clock on the dot. It was five past by the time Lenny slid into her seat, wishing everyone a soft good morning. Betty was already in her highchair, banging her hand against the table, Angus spooning porridge into her tiny, bird-like mouth.

'No porridge for me today, Mrs Campbell.' She didn't know what she could stomach, but the traditional Scottish breakfast sprinkled with salt wasn't it. Even the sight of it had her heaving in a deep, sighing breath.

Mrs Campbell sent her a swift look before placing a slice of dry toast, cut in two triangles in front of her. 'Just what you need, my girl.'

'Everything alright?' Angus looked between them with a deep frown, his gaze lingering on Lenny briefly.

'Absolutely. Slept like a log for the first time in ages.' She took a small sip of her tea before returning it to the saucer, careful not to let it rattle against the china. 'What are you up to today?'

'I have to pop into the village for half-ten.' He glanced at his watch briefly. 'Fancy a walk? We could take this little pickle with us. She needs some new things.'

Lenny glanced at where Betty's arms were sticking out of the sleeves of her cardigan. She hadn't knit since the grey scarf. It reminded her of everything she was trying to forget, but clothes were hard to come by and Angus had been so kind.

She grimaced at what he was going to say when she told him about the baby. If she told him. She could always leave. No, she couldn't do that. But she also couldn't stay. There was enough scandalous talk about him having an unmarried woman at the manse, even if Mrs Campbell lived in and rarely left them alone.

Mrs Campbell. Lenny closed her eyes briefly at the thought. Angus's housekeeper had only taken the job at the manse after the death of her husband and, as a mother to seven, she was bound to know a thing or two about pregnancies.

She played with her teaspoon, careful to avoid looking in the woman's direction.

Her days at the manse were numbered, probably to the fingers on one hand. *Which will leave you enough time to make a thing or two for Betty before you leave,* she thought determinedly.

'How about I see what the wool situation is like in the general store. I seem to remember they had a good stock when I was here last time. It will be cheaper than buying clothes and better quality too.'

Angus reached across and patted her hand briefly. 'What a wonderful idea. Thank you.'

'No need to thank me. It will be my pleasure.'

The very least I can do for you before I leave, after all you've done for me.

It wasn't a long walk to the small village. Only five minutes. Angus headed off to his meeting, making a promise to join them outside the general store, which sold everything from food, baby clothes, wool, material and everything in between. With Betty secure in her stroller, her favourite cuddly bear in her chubby hands, Lenny concentrated on the array of wools stacked high. Arans, mohair and the softest baby wools in a kaleidoscope of pastels.

She hadn't been in the village since she'd arrived, apart from attending church. Instead, she favoured the seclusion of the high-walled back garden that the manse provided, but she recognised the woman behind the counter. She'd even bought wool from her to knit Betty the mauve cardigan she was currently bursting out of, on the pretext of buying training wools for the men back at Arisaig House. She blinked, remembering that Harry had accompanied her on that first visit to the shop. Eight months ago.

Seemed both longer, and only yesterday.

'Hello there, stranger. Thought we'd see you here before now. We have some beautiful wools just in.' The woman's soft burr of an accent was difficult to understand and it took Lenny a moment.

'Hello. Yes, I can see that.' Lenny ignored the first part of the sentence simply because she had no answer that she wanted to give. Arisaig reminded her very much of Guernsey and the way everyone knew everyone else's business. Difficult when she had so much to hide.

'Will it be something for yourself or Betty?' The woman came out from behind the counter, a broad smile on her face as she chucked Betty under the chin. 'The minister has his hands full, that's for sure, and poor Mrs Campbell isn't getting any younger. Time he got himself wed.'

'For Betty. I thought something in pink and a soft blue.' This time she ignored the second part of her sentence, but for the exact same reason.

Hurry up, Angus!

Lenny didn't choose the first wools offered, but she did rush when usually she'd be happy browsing for ages. Angus found her pushing Betty down the street, a little way from the shop, just far enough away in case the woman fancied looking out of her window.

'You didn't take long?' He stooped and planted a kiss on Betty's cheek before doing the same to Lenny, much to her annoyance. It was only a brotherly peck but still. By evening the villagers would have blown it out of proportion, she thought, remembering the woman's comment.

Time he got himself wed, indeed!

She held up the wool. 'What do you think?'

Angus laughed, taking the push chair and threading her arm through his. 'I'm not sure why you're asking me, lass. As long as you and Betty are happy, I'm happy. Now, what about taking the long way home. It's such a beautiful day. I have a fancy to show Betty the sea.'

FORTY-NINE

Lenny remembered the beaches that skirted Arisaig from the previous times she'd visited. The sugary white sand, framed by wild grasses to the backdrop of the small islands of Eigg, Rum and Muck embedded in the deep, cerulean sea. On her last visit, she'd stood and stared out over the waves, the wind wrapping her hair around her face like a silken scarf, regretting the inclement weather.

There was no trace of wind in the warm July air. With the sun high overhead and the heatwave continuing, she lifted Betty from her stroller and carefully removed her socks, shoes and cardigan, before securing a droopy cotton hat over her head to protect her from the sun.

'I asked Mrs Campbell to prepare a picnic.' Angus lifted a bag off his shoulder and quickly arranged a tartan blanket before plonking Betty in the middle, along with a bucket and spade. 'There's only sandwiches and lemonade,' he added, with a look of contrition.

'A feast fit for a king, Angus. Thank you.'

She watched him slip off his dog collar, before pulling off his shirt and stretching out on the rug beside her, a straw hat tipped over his face. 'If you don't mind looking after Betty for a bit. I was up half the night with one of my parishioners. In need of forty winks.'

'Of course.'

Lenny grabbed Betty, along with the bucket and spade and headed for the shore and the wet sand. With her hair dragged back in a ponytail, and her skirt hitched up to above her knees, she was soon crouched beside her.

'Time I taught you how to make the best sandcastle in Arisaig, Betty. It's a little like making a cake. The right ingredients and the knack for getting it out of the tin without breaking.' Betty gurgled beside her, happy to slap the sand with her hands.

Lenny felt happiness crowd in, shoving sadness and uncertainty into the background, and it was all Angus's doing. Not that she deserved it.

She'd often noticed the pallor in his skin, and the droop of his shoulders, but she'd done nothing to try and offset his burden. Instead, she'd accepted his time as if it was her right. Time he often made up late into the night. While the parish was a small one, many of Angus's parishioners were old and failing, while others were grieving lost sons and husbands.

She knew all about that.

That he'd offered her the perfect life with a ready-made family. Her hand dropped to her flat stomach. It wouldn't be easy raising a child on her own, but she'd manage. In the meantime, she'd make sure to do better and that started now by allowing him to sleep.

She left him for an hour, the lemonade cool in Betty's bucket.

'Time to wake up, Angus. Lunch is ready.'

He tipped his hat back, his bright eyes at war with the dark shadows underneath and the tiny crow's feet starting to radiate from the corners. She knew he was only twenty-nine. Some days, like today, he looked twice that.

'You don't mind if I keep my shirt off?'

'You'd be mad not to.' She smiled, gesturing to her bare legs stretched out in front of her. 'It's the beach, not church, although I do think some of your parishioners might have a thing to say.'

He joined her in a laugh, and they were soon delving into Mrs Campbell's cheese and home-made pickle sandwiches. Even Betty, although without the pickle. An adult taste she'd yet to acquire despite wanting to stick her finger into Lenny's sandwich.

'Yuck.'

'Yuck indeed, my sweet. How about a jam tart instead?' She turned to Angus, trying not to feel or act embarrassed at the sight of his bare chest. 'Mrs Campbell included a flask of tea and some cakes down the bottom of the bag.'

'I knew there was a reason I employed her when she came knocking. Bossy to a fault but with a heart of gold.' As she handed him his tea, he looked straight into her eyes and changed the subject with a suddenness that nearly made her drop the cup. 'I think I made a mistake last week, lass.'

'A mistake?'

'I didn't tell you how I felt.'

'Angus, I—'

'No, hold off a minute and let me say what I have to.' He smiled briefly, glancing at where Betty was cramming in the rest of her cake, her cheeks bulging. 'I think I fell in love with the sound of your voice first, even though the news broke my heart.' He gave up all pretence of his tea, abandoning his cup on the sand. 'Seeing you for the first time cuddling Betty in your lap. After, the way you didn't berate me for holding her all wrong when clearly I was useless. I knew then.' He wiped the back of his hand across his brow before plonking his hat on top, his expression bleak. 'I love you so very dearly and nothing would give me more pleasure than giving you the life you deserve.'

Lenny didn't know what to say. He looked distraught and she was only going to make it worse.

She blinked away a tear, her voice taking on a husky note, her gaze cast out to sea as she started to tell him the truth in a way that wouldn't break his heart any more than she had already.

'I'm so very sorry, Angus. You see, I fell in love too. In Paris. Not in the way it happened to you. I didn't like him at first, but he sort of crept up on me. He was called Harry. The bravest of men.' She shot him a quick glance, remembering that he'd met him that day outside the church. It all seemed so long ago now. 'He was a little like your brother, in fact,' she continued. 'He gave up his life for me and James. That's why I can never marry. Not you. Not anyone. It wouldn't be fair. My heart and my love belong to someone else.'

She saw him swallow, a flicker setting up in his jaw. He was hurting just as she was. But he deserved the truth.

'I can't compete with a dead hero, Lenny,' he replied softly.

'And no one would expect you to.' She paused a second to hand Betty another cake, before turning back. 'I can't change the past or what happened, but I can ensure that it doesn't affect anyone's future apart from my own.' She reached across, taking his hand in hers. 'You're a good man, Angus. Kind, charming and good looking. Somewhere there's a girl out there that—'

'Stop!' He withdrew his hand and sprang to his feet, glaring down at her. 'Whatever you say to me today, please don't belittle the feelings I have. Finlay always said he knew when he met Ellen that she was the one, and I'm the same.' He plunged his hands into his pockets, a slash of red across each cheek. 'I love you and you're in love with another man, someone I can't compete with, but that doesn't mean we can't be happy,' he pleaded. 'All you need to do is give us a chance.'

Lenny glanced across at Betty briefly, before turning back, trying to take her courage in both hands as she took the conversation into a place she'd hoped to avoid.

'You have to understand that things get out of kilter in war time. Things happen that would never happen otherwise.' She rested a hand on her belly, noting the way his eyes followed, his colour changing from healthy pink to pale grey as understanding surfaced. 'I can't expect anyone to bring up another man's child,' she continued, starting to pack up the flask with quick efficiency. 'It wouldn't be right.'

He knelt in front of her, replacing the flask with his hand, his gaze intense. 'Not even if they promise to make it their life's mission to love and care for the bairn as their own, if only to bring their mother some degree of the happiness she deserves? What then, lass?'

Lenny stared at Angus, unsure of what she'd done to merit a man like him. She knew she didn't deserve even an ounce of what he was offering. The truth was, she couldn't rewrite the past, and she didn't want to. Not if it was at the expense of what she'd had with Harry, albeit fleeting. But this wasn't about her. This was about Angus, his face ravished by emotion. She'd meant it when she'd told him there was a better woman for him. Her answer had to be no, no matter how much it hurt.

'I don't think...'

'Please, lass. I have enough love for all of us,' he begged, removing the last of her objections.

Lenny blinked back sudden tears. She'd made a mess of things in France, which she couldn't change. She could only be responsible for the present and the future. Their future. To reject him... She wasn't strong enough for that, she thought, a sigh escaping. Angus had lost just as much as she had in the war. Together, they might be able to build something new from the wreckage.

She finally smiled at him, a small, tentative pull of her lips.

'Then I think we need to go back to the shop. I got the wrong colour wool for Betty.' They glanced in unison at where Betty had added a layer of sand to her jammy hands, her wide grin infectious. 'She should wear white for the wedding, even if it won't stay white for long.'

FIFTY

Saturday 28 February, 1942 – Arisaig

'I'll let the vicar know the good news. He'll be chuffed it's a boy,' Mrs Campbell cooed, placing the sleeping baby in the tiny crib beside the bed. 'Be back in a moment. You get some well-deserved rest, dearie.'

Lenny sank back against the pillows, her hair sticking to her forehead, her bones turning to water as the energy drained away, the room blurring in and out of focus.

It had been a difficult pregnancy, which had led to her being stuck in this room for the last two months. Concerns over her blood pressure. Her swollen ankles and legs. Towards the end, she'd looked like a Buddha even though her appetite had tailed off to virtually nil. Mrs Campbell, Ada, had become a staunch ally after their difficult early relationship. Nothing was too much trouble after she recognised that Lenny had chosen to put her beloved vicar and Betty before everything else, as it should be.

She felt a featherlight touch on the back of her hand, before the subtle scent of Angus's aftershave reached her.

'Hello, my dear. How are you feeling?'

Lenny stared up at him, trying to read something from his expression, but it was like studying a foreign language with no dictionary in sight.

Theirs was an awkward relationship, full of things that could never be said interspersed by long, difficult silences. They acted well enough in front of company but that's all it was. An act. She could tell he'd been suffering from sleepless nights. The shadows pressed under his eyes were the giveaway, but she'd also heard him tossing and turning in the small room next door, the single bed squeezed up against the wall. Mrs Campbell had raised her eyebrows at their sleeping arrangements but had thankfully kept her thoughts to herself. Lenny wouldn't have known what to tell her.

'Like as if I've been run over by a tractor.'

He managed a laugh, which didn't meet the crinkles around his eyes. 'I always thought childbirth was meant to be this amazing, wonderful experience,' he finally said, picking up her hand and holding it between his. 'Over the last four days I've wanted to barge in and...' he shrugged. 'And I don't know what. I've felt completely helpless.'

There was a commotion outside, accompanied by the sound of little feet and a whoop of laughter before the door burst open and Betty arrived on the scene.

Darling Betty who was the heart of their home. The one thing that bound them together. The only thing. Lenny was sorry about that. She knew he'd expected more, but she didn't have more to give.

'Mama. Papa. My baby. A little brother and he's all mine.'

The tears came in a rush, an unexpected gush that had her sitting forward, gulping for air.

'Lenny, my love, what is it? You're worrying me.'

'Don't you upset yourself, vicar,' Ada interrupted, picking up the wrapped bundle and placing it in her lap. 'It's her hormones. Always got me that way, even with the seventh. She'll be alright in a minute. Come on, missy. I have some chocolate cake in the kitchen with your name on it. Leave your parents to get to know your little brother.'

In the quiet that followed, she felt rather than saw Angus leave her side and walk to the window, his hands dug deep in his pockets.

With a sweep of her hand, she brushed her hair off her forehead before doing the same with her tears, wishing she had a handkerchief, but feeling too awkward to ask. The bundle was light but then the baby had arrived a whole five weeks early. A honeymoon baby when their honeymoon had been spent in a hotel on the other side of Scotland where no one knew them, and no one questioned their separate bedrooms.

Her heart swelled to bursting as she looked down at their perfect little boy. Five fingers on both his left and his right hand. His eyes closed until, almost as if he recognised her, he flipped them open. There was no smile. It was far too early for that. Instead, there was a perfect set of blue eyes staring back. Eyes the same colour as Harry's. Lenny blinked down at them. She knew that all babies were born that way, but some mother's instinct told her that they wouldn't change.

A living reminder of Harry.

Lenny's thoughts shifted, along with her gaze.

There was another person in the room. A man who'd given his life to her in the presence of a church full of witnesses.

'Angus?'

'What is it, my dear?'

He still had his back to her, staring out into the garden, which was all bare branches and bare soil, waiting for the spring to arrive.

'You called me my love before.'

He turned at that, his hands still in his pockets, his expression unreadable.

'A mistake with the stress of the moment. It won't happen again.'

'Ah, that's a shame. Well, come and meet our son then.' She ran a finger gently down his plump cheek. 'He's beautiful. The perfect addition to our little family.'

He came over at her words, staring down at her, a little smile quirking at the corner of his mouth. 'Perfect.'

'Here, stoop down and take him. After all the lessons you had with Betty, you should be a dab hand by now.'

'What are you going to call him?'

Lenny rearranged the sheet, tugging it a little higher over her chest where her nightdress was gaping. It also gave her time to mull over his words. She'd planned on calling him Harold if it was a boy and Ellen if it was a girl but, suddenly that felt like the wrong thing to do. And Harry wouldn't mind. He'd have wanted her happiness.

There was also Angus's happiness to consider.

She watched the way he stared down at Harry's son, his face softening into a gentle smile. The last few months had been both challenging and confusing. Becoming his wife when her feelings had been trapped deep inside. Now it felt as if a door was opening wide, allowing a surge of emotion to escape. She'd never been quite sure what she'd felt for Harry, but she suddenly knew she'd been wrong to think that she couldn't love again.

All she had to do was to find a way to tell him.

'I'm not sure.' She glanced up only to find his eyes on her, his expression retaining a lingering softness.

'What do you think of Finlay Angus James, or is that too much of a mouthful?'

'Oh, my dear.'

Lenny had never seen a man cry before. There'd never been that many male role models in her life for that. And to be truthful, she didn't want to see Angus cry now. Her own eyes filled to capacity and overflowed at the sight of his tears.

With his head bent, the tears slid down his cheeks to land on Finlay's blanket. She reached out her hand and stroked his hair, the first time she'd touched him since their wedding that wasn't for show. It felt nice.

No. It felt wonderful.

'Is that a yes or a no, dearest?'

'It's a yes, my love.' He lifted his head, his eyes glowing. 'I'd like to kiss you, if I may?'

She smiled. 'I thought you'd never ask.'

FIFTY-ONE

Friday 14 September, 1945 – Guernsey

Dearest James,

Hope all's well. How's the War Office, not that you can tell me?

Arrived back last Tuesday. The boat was crowded. Sick as a dog but then when am I ever not!

Met so many people I hadn't seen in years. I hadn't thought of them either, but I didn't tell them that. Angus's good teachings rubbing off on me, finally. His new parish is a bit of a handful but we're getting there. I still can't believe that he was offered a place here.

I'm sure you will be pleased to hear that dear Mrs Gardiner is still going strong. We still meet up at the knitting group – it's a nice change to be knitting something other than socks! Betty and Fin are certainly keeping my needles busy.

I must dash. The vicarage is a mess, which I really must do something about in preparation for tomorrow. We've invited Fin's grand-

parents around for afternoon tea. It's about time they got to meet Harry's son. I thought they might want his flask back too. It's time. Angus's idea, of course. Dear Angus. Always getting it right, when I'm still usually getting it wrong.

So much to do.

Love to Gloria, Amy and Tommy

Lenny

Lenny sealed the letter and added a stamp before placing it beside her bag on the hall table, her second-best hat on top. It was getting on for two thirty, time to leave for the short walk to pick Betty up from her school and Fin from nursery. Nowhere was far in Guernsey, but that meant a good fifteen-minute walk from the manse to the reservoir. St Saviour's School lay nearly exactly opposite.

She knocked on the door to the study, the only room in the house that she did and then only on occasion. It was a hard learnt lesson. Bursting in on Angus when he was in the middle of one of his parish meetings or, even worse, speaking to the bishop had, to some extent, moderated her behaviour. She was still Lenny but, had learnt, on occasion that Leonora was a better fit.

Leonora was the well-behaved vicar's wife who'd learnt the art of holding sedate tea parties and wore her role with a decorum that fitted her position. Lenny was still there, an enduring presence, which only tended to show itself when she was alone with her family.

'Come in.'

'Oh, good. You're alone. How's the sermon going?'

He leant back and stretched, his reading glasses slipping down his nose. 'It's going, slowly.'

'Well, what about a walk to see if it gives you some inspiration.' Lenny checked her hair in the mirror above the Victorian fireplace, poking a stray curl back in place. 'Betty and Fin will be over-joyed. They get bored with only Mum picking them up.' She stepped back, frowning at the state of the room, which was still under furnished and with boxes of books everywhere. The German soldiers had taken over the building early in the war and everything that wasn't attached was burned for firewood, and even a few things that were. The walls had once been lined with mahogany bookshelves. They had a builder booked to try and replicate them, but getting hold of wood was akin to getting hold of gold.

Impossible.

'I think that's a fabulous idea. Let me get my jacket.'

'I'll be in the hall. Have a letter to post.'

She was pinning her hat into place when he joined her, leaning his head into her neck and planting a kiss where her collar met her shoulder. 'You smell good.'

She lifted her hand and cradled his head briefly. 'That will be the bannocks I've been trying to make. Ada would be ashamed of me if she saw them.'

'As long as they taste good that's all that matters.'

They walked in companionable silence, happy with their own thoughts until they reached the school gates.

Finlay trundled out first. A small, serious child of three. So very different to what she'd expected. His eyes had remained the same, but the rest of him was all her, even down to his nose and his smile. He'd skinned his knees in the playground, and it had taken the next five minutes, while they waited for Betty, for him to explain what had happened. Lenny glanced up at Angus, not believing a word.

Something was going on with him that he wasn't telling them.

It took a 'bouncing Betty-the bomb' to let them in on what was happening in their children's little world. A world so very different to the manse that Lenny could have screamed.

'They wanted to know why we have different parents.'

'Ah.' Lenny and Angus had decided early on to be completely

honest with their children about their parentage. That way they could avoid that awkward conversation when they were older.

'Jimmy was beastly. Pushed me over in the playground, told me my real parents mustn't have loved me.' Betty sniffed, her tough exterior only that. Inside she was as soft as butter. 'Fin came to my rescue, so he turned on him.'

'What happened next?' Angus said, looking grim.

Betty was examining her knees, and the hole in her white tights with interest. 'Nothing. I told them that we were lucky Mummy and Daddy got to choose us. Much better than imposing yourself.' She bit her lip. 'I wasn't quite sure what imposed meant?'

Lenny struggled not to laugh. Betty, the mirror image of her mother, coming out with a word like that.

'I think it fits perfectly, darling.' She took her hand while Angus walked ahead with Fin, his head bent as he listened carefully to his conversation.

My family.

Back at the manse, she sent the children to change and wash their hands. Angus joined her in the kitchen as she was sorting out drinks and a snack for the children.

'I was just on my way to bring you yours. Tea and burned bannocks do?'

'Absolutely, but I think I'll have mine in here for a change.'

Lenny grinned. 'Perfect. The children will love that. They don't get to see enough of you as it is.'

'And what about you, lass? Will you love that?'

She walked up to him and took his hands in hers.

This dear man who'd taken on a burden only to turn it into a blessing.

'If you weren't so tall I'd show you.'

'Hah.' He picked her up as if she weighed nothing and swung her around before kissing her soundly.

'What about the children, and the dratted sermon?' she finally said, the sound of feet pounding the staircase an interruption she suddenly didn't want.

'Exactly.' He set her down and pulled out a chair, balancing his elbows on the table, just like he'd done in that Lyon's teashop all those years ago. 'And, as for my sermon. I've come up with a topic, at last.'

Oh, yes.' Lenny was filling the kettle, ready to set it on the Rayburn stove.

'Not imposed but chosen, has a certain ring to it, don't you think? Imposed is too good a word not to waste.'

She kept her back turned, just for a moment, her eyes closed against sudden tears, her hand pressed to her mouth.

She'd been broken when she'd arrived in Arisaig, broken and pregnant with another man's child. Angus was what she'd needed then. He was what she needed still.

When she finally turned, there was a bright smile pinned in place. 'You'll have to warn Betty or there'll be ructions.'

'Warn me what,' Betty said, launching herself into the room before running over to her father, her knitting bag dangling from her fingers, Gary at her heels. 'And what do ructions mean?'

FIFTY-TWO

Saturday 11 April, 1981 – Guernsey 7.45 am

'Bonjour, ma petite...'

Lenny tutted at the French but simply switched to English instead of commenting. She'd decided at the start of her marriage that France, and everything associated with that time, would be relegated to the past. Angus had said he didn't mind. In fact, he'd encouraged her to teach the children in the early days, but it had never felt right. He couldn't speak a word and there had been too many barriers between them already for her to add another.

'Morning, James. You're up early.'

'I'm only back for the weekend... don't want to miss a moment.' James wandered over to the table, his bare feet making no sound on the quarry tiles. 'Any tea?' he asked, nodding in the direction of the brown teapot in the centre.

'Freshly made.' Lenny went to the dresser and fetched another cup before joining him. 'Gloria still asleep?'

'Absolutely! What about Angus?' he asked, picking up his cup and taking a cautious sip.

'Same.' They shared a conspiratorial smile, their bond still strong, despite the passage of time and the distance between them.

'It's his age catching up with him.'

'Seventy isn't old,' she snapped, but with a smile to soften her words. 'Not these days.'

'Any sign of him retiring? I thought Betty was keen to take him travelling to all those places you refuse to go?'

Lenny toyed with the handle of her cup, refusing to meet his gaze. When put like that it made her sound like a right tartar when that was far from the case. Her travelling days had started and ended with her mission to Paris. If Betty and Fin had decided to move off the island it would have been different, but everything that mattered to her was right here.

Why would she want to leave?

'Hopefully at the end of the year, and don't let Liz hear you call her Betty, or I'll never hear the end of it.'

James rolled his eyes. 'Bloody ridiculous. How am I meant to remember, after calling her that ever since I've known her.'

'But she's a serious artist now and, as she keeps telling me, who's ever heard of an artist called Betty! At least she saw sense and called her daughter Anna. Not a name you can really shorten to anything.' Lenny tucked a wayward curl in place, grey streaked and in need of a cut. 'I've taken to calling her love, or sweet pea, if that helps?'

James gave her a thumbs up as he reached for the pot and refilled their cups. 'What about Fin? I thought I'd see him yesterday. He's cut it fine even if he is only in Jersey. How's he doing?'

Fin. Six foot tall and forty next year. Where did that time go, she mused, but then she was soon going to be sixty, something she didn't want to think about too carefully. While she loved Betty – James was right, Liz didn't suit her at all – Fin would always have that little extra chunk of her heart.

'His flight was delayed. You'll see him later at the church. He's not going to miss his son's christening for anyone, least of all work.'

'And he named him Harry?'

Lenny abandoned her drink, instead propping her elbows on

the table and cupping her chin. Their conversation was always going to veer into dangerous waters. She couldn't remember the last time she'd spent any time with her brother without the presence of one or other of their partners or children present.

'We've always been completely honest with the children about their parentage, James. You know that. Not the easiest of decisions, but the right one in the long run.'

'I suppose it helps that Angus is a vicar.'

'It helps because we love each other very much, James.'

'And it shows.' He reached across and took her hand briefly in way of an apology, but he had nothing to apologise for. After Angus, he was her best friend and best friends were allowed to poke the tiger, but only if they were prepared to be on the receiving end on occasion. She always gave as good as she got.

'I was in two minds about this but...' He slipped his hand in his pocket and pulled out a couple of items.

'You still have Granddad's old cigarette case?' Lenny pounced on the case in amazement and, it must be said, a certain degree of horror. 'I thought you'd given up smoking years ago. What does Gloria say?'

'As if I'd do anything to upset her. I'm far too much of a coward for that.'

Lenny laughed. There was nothing cowardly about her brother. She didn't know what he did at the War Office but by all accounts, it was important.

Fiddling with the lid, she flipped it open to find a few ten-pound notes and, when she removed them, the engraving of her grandfather's name as fresh as the day when her grandmother had commissioned it.

'It's my lucky talisman! Even took it on that trip to Paris after the war. I had a few debts to pay and a very nice bottle of merlot to share with a certain barman.'

'Oh, yes.' Lenny had been in the throes of learning parish life at the time and could barely remember her name let alone where her brother had disappeared off to with Gloria. She also couldn't concentrate on the conversation with the second item in front of her.

A faded to yellow card with Harry's face on the cover.

'I thought I'd give Fin his father's ID book, if you think he'll like it? Not sure why I didn't think of it before. Only gathering dust with the rest of my papers. A good sort was Harry and the bravest of men.'

'He was that.'

The words came easily.

It was a long time since she'd thought of Harry in that way. Her love for Angus was different but all-encompassing. There was room for memories. Grief over the death of a young man, along with thoughts about the futility of war, but that was all.

That they'd made Finlay in that brief moment of stolen happiness was enough.

'Unlike us,' she finally said. 'We made a fine mess of things, didn't we?'

'Oh, I wouldn't say that exactly. We did more than most, sitting at home counting their coupons.'

'But what did we achieve? What was it all for?' Lenny pushed the ID card back, the sound of the gurgling pipe above the Rayburn telling her that the rest of the household would be descending shortly for the full English breakfast she'd promised.

'You could say that about everything, Lenny We did what we had to and what we could. That has to be enough.'

They turned in unison at the sound of the kitchen door opening.

Their time for confessions was over.

'What is it with you Galliennes and the need to be up with the lark?' Angus ambled towards his wife, a little stooped and a little greyer than the first time she met him, but with the same twinkling eyes and calming presence.

'Darling.' Lenny pressed a kiss against his cheek before

nodding in the direction of her empty seat. 'I really must be getting on with breakfast.'

'Just catching up on old times, Angus. Still trying to persuade that wife of yours that travelling isn't so bad, what with retirement looming on the horizon.'

'I gave up trying years ago, James. Learnt to accept that she's happier at home than anywhere else. Any tea left in that pot?'

FIFTY-THREE

Friday, 19 March, 2010 – Guernsey 5.10 pm

'How's Gran?'

'Very tired but managing to eat a little more. She's in her lounge snoozing in front of *The Chase*. Gives us time for a quick catchup.'

Anna dropped her bag onto the chair in the hall and followed her mother into the kitchen.

Gran had been home from hospital since Monday. A little vague, which was to be expected after the stroke, but well enough to be discharged with some additional help. That her home for the last two years was a specially built extension at the side of her daughter and son-in-law's house, made that process easier.

'That sounds good and, remember, it's early days. How's her speech?'

'She's not really speaking at all now she knows we can't understand her,' her mother said, flicking on the kettle and arranging mugs on a tray, before slumping into the nearest chair. 'I don't know, Anna. I hate to see her like this. Even your dad is at a loss, and his French is far better than mine.'

Anna pressed her hand against her mother's shoulder briefly, before finishing making the tea and joining her, the mugs set out between them. To see her lovely mum looking pale and drawn, was a shock. She was doing what she could to help, but work was busy. It was difficult to leave early, and weekends were just as bad. She used that time to catch up with everything she'd ignored during the week like food shopping, housework and her husband.

'Remember how the doctor said to give her time. A spontaneous return of her speech is what he's hoping for, even though he's never come across bilingual aphasia before.'

'It's certainly a new one on us too,' Liz replied, her voice dry. 'The issue is what on earth possessed her to hide that she could speak French. Never a word all these years...'

'Betty. Betty.'

She pushed away from the table with a heartfelt sigh, her tea barely touched. 'That's her now. Still determined to call me that despite being Liz for years.'

Anna suppressed a smile, her hand on her mother's arm. 'Stay and finish your drink. I'll see what she wants.'

The television in her grandmother's lounge was on mute, the subtitles playing out over the screen. The only modern item in the room.

'Hello. Bonjour.'

'Anna!' Her grandmother's face broke into a wide smile, her skin a myriad of wrinkles.

'Hello,' she repeated. 'Mum says you've lost your voice, but obviously not your wits if you're following *The Chase*.' She watched as her gran's smile broke into a chuckle, a deep throaty cackle that had her joining in.

Anna had always had a special relationship with her grandmother, one that seemed to defy the age gap that nearly spanned half a century. She liked to think that it was because they were kindred spirits but, as she caught sight of the knitting on her lap, she remembered that she couldn't knit or sew, and cooking was a challenge she'd yet to conquer.

'What are you knitting, and with these old needles too?' She touched the discoloured sticks with the tip of her finger, noting the slight bend in the metal and the reason she'd bought her a new set for Christmas. A glance at the built-in bookshelves, which housed many of her gran's books and precious trinkets, revealed the brand new knitting bag she'd bought to accompany them.

'I... I...'

'Yes, I... I...?' she said, her eyes filling with tears at the struggle in her gran's face. 'You're doing fabulously, darling. All my fault. I know my French isn't a patch on yours. The doctor did say it would come back all on its own and look at you.'

'These... needles... are like old friends. They... took... me to France and back. I won't be parted from them.'

Anna leant in, planting a kiss on her paper-thin cheek. 'You old fraud. And we never even knew you could speak French let alone visited. I remember struggling with my homework when you could have done it for me.'

'Probably the reason I decided not to tell you,' she replied, her voice starting to speed up along with her attitude. She picked up her needles briefly before rolling up the knitting and placing it on the table beside her, her face taking on the stubborn expression that Anna knew only too well.

A decision had been made. She wondered what it was.

'My box please.'

Obviously something important by the tone of her voice.

'The one on the second shelf?' Anna slid her gaze back to the bookshelves and the old-fashioned hat box tied with a faded pink ribbon.

'Oui. Yes,' she amended quickly, managing a little shrug at her slip back into French.

Anna placed the box on her grandmother's lap, before sitting on the stool by her feet.

She remembered the box from when she was a child. One of the few things her grandmother had never explained, but there'd been so many other things to talk about that it hadn't really registered.

Everyone was allowed their secrets, she remembered, thinking of the special trip to Paris that she was planning to surprise her husband with for his birthday.

Her gran removed a pile of yellowed documents first, an ID card in the name of Georgette Tournier on top.

Anna picked up the card, recognising the image of the curly haired woman straight away. 'She looks like you. How come?' she asked, watching her grandmother's mouth curving slightly, her hand intent on pulling a grey scarf out from underneath.

While Anna didn't knit, she knew the rudiments and the scarf looked special. The musty smell told her that it was old, very old indeed.

'It's time I told you a story, Anna. My story. It's about a girl who could knit.'

She ran her fingers over the weave, her eyes closed, almost as if she was reading the loops with her fingers instead of her eyes. She turned her head, smiling briefly.

'It all started with your Uncle James and the arrival of a telegram...'

FIFTY-FOUR

Tuesday 5 April 2011 – Paris 1 pm

Cherry blossom lined the boulevards while the Tuileries Gardens were ablaze with spring bulbs, but they'd flowered during the war, Lenny remembered. Even the Germans couldn't stop the trees from growing or the buds from opening.

It was everything else that was different. The noise. The cars. Everything!

Her only regret was that Angus wasn't here to share it with her.

Stupid old woman, so stuck in your ways until it was too late to do anything about it.

Ten years too late.

She blinked, picking up her cup, trying not to grimace at the bitter taste, but she'd learnt to her horror that the French didn't do tea very well. Green tea. Yes, fine, and herbal teas in all the flavours imaginable, but when it came to a nice strong English breakfast tea...

Hopeless.

Sitting in one of the many street cafés had become a habit over the last five days while Anna and her husband had zoomed around taking in the sites at a pace that Lenny found both exhilarating and exhausting. Instead, she wiled away the time people watching, a barely touched cup in front of her, her latest knitting project on her lap.

The smallest of matinee jackets in pale lemon.

A white-haired woman, whose face bore her own personal roadmap with a dignity that far outweighed her years, an old, faded pale blue sweater draped around her thin shoulders.

There had been no plan to accompany Anna when she'd burst in explaining that she'd booked her on a surprise trip to Paris and that she wouldn't accept no for an answer.

You'll come, won't you, please? I'd really like you to be there. To see Paris through your eyes.'

Lenny had looked up in surprise from where she'd been watching the news.

What do you think, Angus, my darling? Am I brave enough?

Lenny had started talking to him after her stroke. Only in her head – she hoped it wasn't out loud. It was a comfort. She always knew how he'd reply.

'Yes. You should. You're getting stuck in your ways, lass. Best go and enjoy yourself.'

I'm not sure I should after my little episode last year, Angus.

'If the doctor says yes then there's only yourself stopping you.'

So here she was sitting in a café by herself, waiting.

'Ah there you are, Gran.' Anna arrived in a flurry, her arms full of high-end paper carrier bags while her husband tried to catch the eye of the waiter. 'What have you been up to?'

A delicious afternoon, spent in the arms of my lover. We've been up to all sorts.

Lenny clamped down on the wicked response, although a little smile remained.

'Sitting quietly with my knitting, sweet pea. I can't believe Harry's wife is expecting. Last time I looked, I was changing his nappies.' She held up the lacy garment. 'Only the sleeves left to do.'

And the secret message hidden in the collar, but you don't need to know about that. That's between me and Harry's great-grandchild.

'Beautiful.' Anna turned to her husband, the waiter behind him carrying a tray with a couple of tall glasses. 'You angel. Just what I needed.' It took one sip to re-energise her.

'Right then, we're giving the rest of the day over to you. There must be places you want to see. We've hired a driver so that you can travel in comfort and, if you want to do it alone, that's fine by us.'

She looks worried, but not as worried as I'm feeling, Angus.

'*She will be, my dearest. Take her with you. It will help you both.*'

The pension was the first shock. It had been turned into an upmarket restaurant with the French version of a beer garden out back, although there wasn't a beer glass in sight. Lenny decided on a little pick-me-up. She needed it for what was probably her last chance at wandering through memory lane.

They settled in the sleek garden chairs with their drinks, but Lenny barely noticed the surroundings. In her mind, she was back in the pension's cramped parlour, watching Marianne with suspicious eyes. The irony still burned: the woman she'd feared most had become their guardian angel, instrumental in arranging the escape route that had brought them home alive.

She'd written to her after the war, and all she'd got back was the envelope with 'unknown at this address' stamped across the centre in French.

'Why don't we ask, Gran. Surely it won't hurt.'

And before she could object, she watched as Anna approached the middle-aged man behind the cash register.

'Bonjour, madame. Your granddaughter sent me over.'

Of course she did. Never any good at French.

Lenny allowed a sliver of guilt to take hold. Anna, Betty and

Fin could have easily been fluent. But that wasn't something she could reverse now and, at the time it had felt right.

'I was here during the war.' She paused a second, staring down the garden at where a new summerhouse filled the space of the old. Painted black with a white trellis. 'This used to be a pension run by a woman called Marianne Levain.' She swung back to him, capturing his look of surprise.

'The war was a very long time ago, madame.'

'Friendships don't come with a warranty or an expiry date, monsieur,' she retorted. 'If you know where she is, or what happened to her then...?'

He looked down at her before turning back inside without a word.

'Well, really. How rude.' Anna stared after him before retaking her seat.

'Oh, I'm not sure about that. The war still has the power to upset many people,' Lenny said, shifting her attention back to the drink she didn't want, her mind returning to the past. 'Who knows what kind of a war his parents went through.'

'A much better one, thanks to Marianne.'

Lenny looked up at the grey-haired woman approaching in an electric wheelchair, her features wizened, her hands gnarled with arthritis. But there was something about the blue of her eyes and the delicate shape of her nose that rang a bell.

'Claudine!'

'And you're Léonore. I'd recognise that curly hair anywhere.'

Lenny laughed as Anna moved a chair to make room. 'A little whiter than the last time we met. It's so good to see you. And here.' She spread her hands, encompassing the garden.

'When it came up for sale after the war we decided to buy it, for old times' sake.' She tilted her head towards the next table and where the man had settled. Acting watchdog no doubt. 'You've met my son, Gilles. He was happy to take it over when my bones got the better of me.'

'And Marianne?' Lenny said softly, the threads of the conversation weaving together at the sight of Claudine's sad expression.

'Disappeared in 1945, ma chérie. We still don't know exactly what happened, but we can guess.' Lenny watched as she pressed a laced edged handkerchief to her eyes, and her son's uneasy expression at the sight. 'She was working for the resistance by then. One day she was here and the next the Germans came and threw Maeva and me out on the street. Gilles's father saw what happened and came to our rescue.' Her expression softened briefly. 'I'm sorry it's not better news.'

'I'm sorry too.' Lenny closed her eyes, the distress as raw and new as if it had happened yesterday, and not over sixty years before.

'And Maeva?'

'Happily married with two sons, as well as grandchildren and great-grandchildren. I'm hoping to meet up with her at Christmas, God willing.'

After the wine bar, she shouldn't have been disappointed with the bookshop, but no warning could have been big enough.

The hairdresser was nice enough. They even did manicures, not that Lenny was interested in her nails.

'There, look.' Anna pointed in the direction of the plaque screwed into the façade, proclaiming Pierre Brossolette to be a hero of the resistance. 'What a lovely touch.'

Pierre and Gilberte had been more than that. *They were my friends.*

'Yes, dear. I think I'd like to go back now, if you don't mind.'

'Are you sure there's nowhere else you want to go before we leave?'

Lenny could see the sign for the underground station in the distance, albeit a little blurred. A trip to the optician was long overdue.

'No, dear.' She tucked the finished baby jacket in the top of her bag, her slightly crooked French knitting needles sticking out the top. The wind lifted her hair, dislodging a curl, the same blessed curl. She had a mind to cut it when she could get hold of some scissors.

I think we should leave, don't you, Angus? Don't want to miss the plane.

'No, *my darling. It's time for you to come home.*'

A LETTER FROM THE AUTHOR

Thank you for picking up a copy of *The Resistance Knitting Club*.

If you'd like to join other readers in being the first to know about all future books I write, just click the link below for my email newsletter. I'd be delighted if you choose to sign up.

www.stormpublishing.co/jenny-obrien

I hope that you have enjoyed *The Resistance Knitting Club* and if so, I would appreciate a review.

When I was thinking about what next to write after *The Book of Lost Children*, I was drawn to the history of the Guernsey jumper, which spans centuries.

The Guernsey, or Gansey jumper, is iconic. A word that has slipped into the English language and become synonymous with rugged craftsmanship. I've even knitted one, although it's not something I should brag about. It's a very poor example of the worsted wool garment. For more on locally made Guernseys, I recommend the Le Tricoteur website.

Knitting isn't exclusively for women but there is evidence of women knitting throughout wars and using this skill in devious ways.

I was hooked!

The Commando Who Came Home to Spy is a fascinating account of the life of Guernsey man Hubert Nicolle, by William M Bell. It details how another local man, Captain John Parker, MBE, was instrumental in spreading a secret M16 code for use between prisoners. This was via letters the prisoners sent home, but it sent me off on a tangent of knitting and coding and how to incorporate the two. YouTube came next and, yes, there are many videos on this to amuse. Too many to list here.

In Leo Marks' Book, *Between Silk and Cyanide*, Marks refers to a Colonel GD Ozanne. I had never heard of the colonel, but his name struck me as possibly having originated in Guernsey. Although Irish, I have lived in Guernsey for many years, and I knew that Ozanne was a relatively common local name. A little search into Guernsey's Elizabeth College school records proved that local man, Guy Durand Ozanne, held the senior position in the Signals Directorate, a department in the SIS, during WW2.

This, combined with knitting is how the book *The Resistance Knitting Club* evolved.

What's true and what's not?

Writing a historical novel isn't a lesson in history. There are many eminent historians who have proved expert in delivering factual accounts. Nevertheless, as a writer I like to ensure that when delving into history, my story is based on fact, even if the plot is mostly fictitious. Any mistakes in this book are mine alone.

In June 1940 there was a meeting between Neville Chamberlain, the former prime minister, Winston Churchill, the current one, and Hugh Dalton, Minister of Economic Warfare. It was here that the Special Operations Executive (SOE) was born, the formal contract signed a week later.

Marjorie Maxse was Chief of Staff for Section D, and the reason for including her in my book. While I think it would have been unlikely for someone in her position to interview a typist, I also think that a man like Hugh Dalton might have asked her to do exactly that. Miss Maxse's name is usually associated with Kim Philby, but not here.

Training of the SOE started in 1941. It is this early part, and how the SOE built into a force to be reckoned that interested me, and not the very well catalogued life of the individual SOE operatives after. Both Major de Wesselow and Major Young were key figures in this. I found Peter Churchill's book, *Of Their Own Choice*, invaluable in trying to get this part factually correct.

Wanborough Manor and Arisaig House were used as training camps for the SOE. Arisaig House has been recently sold so there are relatively recent photographs available for those of you who want to delve deeper.

Lenny starts her working life as a general factotum for the newly formed SOE, a role that was adopted by the indomitable Vera Atkins in 1941, and the reason for my timeline. I needed Lenny to be in training before Vera took up her post.

Peldon Avenue was a calm, residential road in Richmond. An oasis in the middle of London. On the night of the 20th September, 1940, a mine was dropped in the middle of the night, annihilating all forty-nine homes.

The worst single act of the Blitz.

There were survivors, those that were in their Anderson shelters, but not everyone survived. The avenue was never rebuilt. I was able to find two photographs to work from. One on a postcard before the bombing and one taken just after.

Georges Bégué was the first of the 470, SOE agents to land in France. A French national, he attended SOE training in the winter of 1940, before being parachuted into France on 6th May, 1941. He is the Georges mentioned in the book.

I decided to slot Lenny (Léonore, Nora) into the book, mirroring Georges Bégué's training and dropping her into France on the same day.

Pierre and Gilberte Brossolette are heroes of the resistance. They ran the Librairie Universelle bookshop along the Rue de la Pompe in the 16th Arrondissement. Their story has also been well catalogued. I first came across them when reading the autobiography of Agnès Humbert, entitled *Resistance*. Pierre's brother wrote a book about his brother. Sadly, it has yet to be translated into English, but I muddled my way through with my poor schoolgirl French to try and get a handle on this hero. The bookshop is indeed now a hair salon. Pierre was one of the key French resistance heroes and has over 600 schools, roads and plaques dedicated to him. It's an honour to share a little of his story with you.

Albert Camus was the author of one of the books mentioned in the bookshop. He was part of the French Resistance. The quote at the start comes from *The Fall* (*La Chute*).

Charles Coward, a Sergeant Major during WW2, was also known as The Man who Broke into Auschwitz. He experienced a case of mistaken identity, as recorded in his biography, *Passport to Courage*, by John Castle. This inspired part of James's storyline.

There are ghost stations in the French metro. The Champ de Mars is one of them. It felt like a gift when I came across this fact.

James's and Lenny's escape over the Pyrenees did cause me some initial concerns. I have camped in the Pyrenees with the kids, but it was a very long time ago. All I remember was the outstanding beauty, and the silence. Reading around the subject of allied escapes into Spain I happened upon *Hugh Dormer's Diaries*. Hugh was an SOE operative whose story of bravery captured my imagination. His subsequent death at the hands of the enemy broke my heart. The book was published posthumously and, to my knowledge, is currently out of print. This needs to change. A book anyone with an interest in WW2 must read.

Bannocks. Bannocks are a thick disk-shaped flatbread made from oat or barley flour. They are popular in Scotland and northern England.

Treacle Scones. These scones are a teatime treat in Scotland. The traditional scone recipe is combined with black treacle to make a hearty flavour. Traditionally served warm with butter, straight from the griddle.

Bilingual Aphasia is a rare language impairment following a brain injury, such as a stroke. Presentation differs but sometimes one language is favoured over another. So, in Lenny's case, her mother tongue of French returned before her secondary one of English.

Finally, knitting. Most of the knitting in the book revolves around socks. Knitting socks in the 1940s was done on four needles, which prevented the sock from having a seam. This traditional way is still used, although some knitters prefer to knit socks on a circular needle.

Lenny's needles are size eight, which translates to the modern four millimetre. In the USA, that's a size six.

For more on knitting and *The Resistance Knitting Club*, I have set up a Facebook Page with the same name. It's a place to share your own craft projects. You might even see one or two of mine.

That's everything, I think.

Jenny x

ACKNOWLEDGEMENTS

Thank you for choosing to read my Knitting Book, as it has been known ever since I dreamt up the idea. As a lifelong crafter, as well as a reader and subsequent writer, it was probably in the stars somewhere that I'd end up combining the two.

As always, the dedication first. Steve and Jac. Dear friends, who make the summers brighter and the winters less winterish!

A book like this doesn't write itself. It started with a discussion with my agent, Nicola Barr and my editor, Claire Bord. I couldn't have done it without you both, so thank you. The team at Storm Publishing is magnificent, from Oliver Rhodes and Alexandra Begley to Elke Desanghere, Anna McKerrow, Chris Lucraft, Naomi Knox and Maheen Mehmood. Thanks also to copyeditor Dushi and proofreader Shirley Khan. If you're listening to the audio version, you'll know already what a great narrator Shelley Atkinson is. And as for the cover designer Eileen Carey. Thank you both!

Last year, 2024, I was interviewed by the fabulous local historian, Nick Le Huray, for the Guernsey Literary Festival, during which there was a raffle. The following characters, based on real people, were chosen for inclusion in this book. Vivienne Gardiner, Mary Veron and Brenda Munro.

Valerie Keogh is my writing buddy. We talk every day. Thank you, Val, for everything, including Sark!

Books like this take a lot of research. I have already included a brief reading list of some of the books I accessed at the time. The staff at the Guille Alles Library, featured in the book, and the Priaulx Library, were quite frankly amazing.

Thanks too to fellow 'keyboard writing friends' Luisa Jones, Pam Lecky, Jane Mosse, Theresa Le Flem, S E Lynes and Sam Tonge. Also thanks to Kelvin Whelan. Island expert, writer extraordinaire and owner of the Writer's Block book shop on the Island.

Thank you, CHOG. If you know, you know. No Kari again!

Also thank you to my very special Dream Team. In no particular order, thanks to Beverley, Michele, Diane, Elaine, Susan, Lesley, Tracy, Amanda, Sarah, Sharon, Pauline, Jo, Daniela, Carol, Madeleine, Tracey, Terri, Maggie, Lynda, Hayley, Donna and finally Maureen.

A final mention as always to my family. Buns for tea!